Hell's Paradise

Holly Copella

ISBN:
ISBN-13: 978-1-947694-38-5

To

Jean & Carolyn Kriegh

& Zuko

Thank you for so many enjoyable conversations!

ACKNOWLEDGMENTS

Copella Books: First Paperback Edition 2026
Cover Artist: Unable to confirm d/t account issues w/SelfPub
Printed by CreateSpace, An Amazon.com Company

PUBLISHER'S NOTE

Chapter 1

Ocean. Night. The Italian yacht, Magnus Rattner, one hundred and forty feet of floating privilege, cut through the dark, still water. Below deck, eight luxurious staterooms waited with every comfort money could buy. As waves broke against the hull, the vessel glided forward, sleek and self-assured, like something that had never once considered it could sink. A young woman dressed in a simple black evening dress leaned on the ship's railing, letting the cool salt spray mist her face while others laughed inside the lounge. Twenty-two-year-old Harley McBride was more down-to-earth than the average 'rich daddy's girl'. She was possibly the only heiress who hated the country club scene and the snobby parties, only 'playing the part' when necessary. Harley preferred the quiet dark water to another round of small talk and forced smiles.

Attractive in her own right, Harley wore her long dark hair down, nearly reaching the cleavage of her slightly revealing dress. She wore makeup when she was out in public, but despised it otherwise. Ironically, it was her father who pushed her on her social appearance rather than her mother. She stared out into the night sea and the cloud-covered moon that left the horizon almost visible. The water was dark with little choppiness except where the yacht cut through. She loved the peaceful darkness, although she wished she could see the moon. Of course, that would make the evening a little too ***romantic***, and she certainly didn't need romantic overtones looming. Despite the sounds of the small party happening in the lounge just behind her, she remained distracted while alone on deck, wanting the time alone.

"Don't jump," a man announced, sounding almost cheerful.

Harley instinctively looked, despite recognizing the voice. An older, neatly dressed man in his early fifties, Conrad Davenport, approached with his usual quiet grace and stood alongside her. Despite spending most of his life as the family butler, Conrad had an almost regal appeal and quiet reserve. He was incredibly refined, impeccably dressed, and quite possibly the smartest person Harley had ever known. Although a bit shorter than average, being only five-foot-eight, and not considered excessively handsome by most standards, Conrad's charisma and refinement earned him a well-deserved 'silver fox' award. He had a full head of gray, slicked-back hair, an immaculately clean-shaven face, and piercing blue eyes that caught the attention of most women over forty. His 'Queen's English' refined British accent made him almost irresistible.

Several years ago, Conrad stepped out of the shadows of his former butler's life and into the sunlight as Harley's trusted aide, confidant, and often protector. He wasn't the biggest or fiercest man, but his loyalty to her went beyond that of any servant. He was more of a knight guarding his queen, and he took his job very seriously.

Harley sighed and looked back over the railing. "I'm not that desperate--***yet***," she insisted.

Conrad leaned on the railing alongside her. "I'm glad to hear."

"Is it bedtime?" she asked.

Conrad chuckled warmly. "You're well within your rights to turn in at any time," he reminded her. "But I'm guessing it would be frowned upon."

"Why should tonight be any different?" she remarked. "My father's going to be disappointed in me no matter what I say or do anyway."

"I thought we weren't talking about your father anymore this week," Conrad reminded her.

"We're in international waters," Harley announced. "Different rules apply out on the open sea."

Conrad hid his smile and chuckled.

"My mother seemed happy at Aunt Blair's wedding, don't you think?" Harley asked, happily changing the subject. "She's so much happier since she left my father."

"She seemed--" Conrad hesitated. "--***contented***."

"And it only took my grandfather's death and his vast fortune to set her free finally," Harley scoffed, resentment rising again. "First, she was controlled financially by her father and then by her husband. A tradition that's being passed down to me, I suppose." She groaned loudly, slamming her palm on the ship's railing. "I want to live my life now, Conrad, not twenty years from now."

"Yes, that is a problem. You can't access the trust fund your grandfather left you until you're twenty-five," Conrad reminded her. "And your father wants you to marry James. Loudly. Insistently." He hesitated a moment, then sneered. "***Annoyingly***."

"Please, don't remind me," she muttered.

"The situation won't simply go away on its own," Conrad reminded her.

"I just met the guy, and he's already naming our children," Harley scoffed, then looked at Conrad. "I don't like him. I mean, I don't like him ***at all***. My father was screwing around on my mother throughout their entire married life. I shouldn't have to marry his protégé."

"It doesn't ***quite*** work that way," Conrad reminded her. "You know your father. He's used to getting his way, and he'll make life miserable for you if he doesn't."

"I feel so trapped," she scoffed, again flopping on the railing. "Damn that James. If he were at least tolerable, maybe it wouldn't be so bad." She then straightened and turned to face Conrad almost commandingly. "And what's with that attack dog of his? Do you know how embarrassing it was for James to bring that cheap thug to Aunt Blair's wedding? Damon just stood there giving everyone that evil stare. Does he even have the power of speech?"

"His presence was a bit unsettling," Conrad muttered. "He was seated at my table at the reception. I don't recall him uttering a word."

"I did as my father asked. I agreed to meet James and spend time with him at Aunt Blair's wedding," Harley remarked. "The entire week, as a matter of fact, but I'm not going to marry him. I can't. There's no way I'm ever sharing a bed with that man." Harley grimaced as the image of sharing a bed with James flashed through her mind, turning her stomach.

"Ah, but do you tell James?"

"Absolutely not! He'll have Damon kill me for sure," she announced with wide, horror-filled eyes. Harley then groaned and sank against the railing. "I feel like I'm a prisoner in my own life. I can't make a move without my father knowing about it. I can't even get a job without him interfering and ruining any chance of supporting myself." Harley frowned and shook her head. "At least my mother's finally out from under him."

"And it took most of her inheritance to escape him," Conrad reminded her. "Between the prenup with your father, leaving her with nothing if she divorced him, and the team of lawyers she needed to fend off his ravenous attorneys, she's lucky she salvaged your grandfather's beach cottage on the island."

"Which is precisely why I can't live with her," Harley muttered. "If I tried to move in with her, my father would find a way to make her life miserable all over again. She's suffered enough." She considered her options, then sighed. "I'll have to get some money together somehow, without my father's knowledge, and run away where he can't find me until I'm old enough to access my trust fund."

Conrad stared out at the ocean for a long, silent moment. "Over the years, your mother managed to tuck some money away for you in a couple of investments," he informed her. "All I need is a few account numbers and some passwords, and we can transfer a large portion of that money into your personal account. Give me twenty-four hours after we're back home, and I can have you away from both James and your father--forever. Without them ever knowing."

Harley suddenly straightened and stared at Conrad with a surprised look. "But if you get caught--"

"I don't care for James," Conrad informed her. "I realize being the family butler for decades doesn't give me any sort of rights, but I didn't spend twenty-two years raising you just to hand you over to some playboy millionaire looking for a trophy wife."

"If dad heard you say that--" she remarked with a tiny, humored smirk.

"I don't care much for your father either," Conrad scoffed. "He and James are cast from the same mold."

Harley stared at Conrad's profile for a long, surprised moment. "I never heard you talk that way about my father before," she remarked. "I didn't think you'd ever be so, well, disloyal to him. You worked for him and his family your entire adult life."

Conrad straightened and met her gaze. "My loyalties lie with you," he announced. "Not your father."

"He signs your check," she reminded him, then frowned. "I don't know that I can afford to pay your salary until I get my hands on my trust fund." Harley choked on her emotions as she attempted a tiny smile. "I don't really want to be without you, Conrad."

"You wouldn't get rid of me that easily," he replied cheerfully. "Let's work on getting you out of your current situation first. I'll sort out my own employment problems later."

Harley placed her hand on his on the railing. "You're resourceful," she reminded him. "You'll come up with a plan where we both get what we want." Harley shivered slightly, although she wasn't sure it was from the cool evening air. She didn't want to think about a life without Conrad. He'd been the most stable thing in her world for as long as she could remember. "It's getting cold. I'd better make an appearance this evening, or it'll almost certainly get back to my father." She then shrugged, offering a tiny, amused smile. "Of course, I'll be tired from all the travel and turn in early."

"I assumed you would," Conrad announced with an equally humored smile.

Chapter 2

Harley stepped into the yacht's main lounge through the double glass doors with Conrad only a step behind her, joining the small, intimate party. Wall sconces illuminated an inviting arrangement of neutral sofas, plush armchairs, and low tables. The gathering space was designed for quiet conversation among those accustomed to luxury, but for Harley, it felt like a stage upon which performances were expected. Captain Shawn Rattner silently greeted them from where he stood by the bar that ran along the starboard side, its glass display case gleaming with rows of top-shelf bottles. The yacht's captain was quite possibly every woman's idea of a heartthrob. He looked like a movie star with his slightly longer, sandy brown hair, several days' worth of scruff on his chiseled jawline, and hazel eyes. The man in his mid-thirties stood over six feet tall with broad shoulders, bronzed skin, and an athletic build.

If Harley had to guess, she'd assume he was heavy into water sports. Probably swimming, surfing, and scuba diving. He wore the traditional captain's dress whites, minus the cap, leaving one too many buttons open on his pressed shirt. Although charismatic and confident, Harley was almost certain he had an ego to match. Shawn seemed the perfect fit to skipper a luxury yacht. She could imagine him fitting in very well with wealthy older women and young heiresses. Quite possibly charming his way into the pants of both. Despite his good looks and charm, Harley didn't find him attractive. She never did like 'pretty boys'. It was humorous that he was undoubtedly higher-maintenance than most of the women she knew. Although Conrad was high-maintenance too, he was far from a 'pretty boy'. Conrad's meticulous attire and appearance stemmed from decades of servitude, not arrogance.

By the captain's side was First Officer Brian, who maintained a more rigid posture. He was tall, ruggedly handsome, and athletically built. His athleticism came from hard work, preparing and running the ship, and doing everything that was beneath the captain. Brian's dark hair was cut short and neat, his face clean-shaven. He, too, wore his crisp white uniform, meticulously pressed, and a white undershirt beneath it, although it didn't matter, since he had his shirt buttoned almost to the collar. Brian seemed pleasant, although mysterious. He appeared to be busy from the moment they boarded that afternoon. The only thing that was abundantly clear was that Brian took his duties seriously.

Harley approached the bar with Conrad only a step behind her, always her shadow. Lester, the ship's steward and chef, was tending bar. The lowest-ranking crew member wore many caps. He was the steward, the chef, and even the bartender when he had the time. The deck hand, in his mid-forties, was of average height and build. He wasn't at all athletic, despite being the one in charge of providing activities for the passengers, and he wasn't the most handsome of men. He had short, dark, curly hair, a bronze complexion from spending most of his time on deck, and a clean-shaven face. He, too, wore his white uniform, but it wasn't as neatly pressed as Brian's. Since he tripled as the chef, he may have switched between aprons, making it harder to maintain his neat appearance. Although friendly and polite, he was almost a little too talkative. It was clear he liked socializing and enjoyed his job.

"Good evening, Miss McBride," Lester announced with a pleasant smile. "What's your pleasure?"

"Brandy, please."

Unfortunately, the man she had hoped to avoid most zeroed in on her the moment she entered the lounge. Wasting no time, James materialized at her side, inserting himself between her and Conrad, as if Conrad didn't even exist. There was no denying that James was a handsome man, but also an arrogant one. Standing six feet tall, the twenty-nine-year-old aristocrat was built 'country club athletic'. He was physically fit and lean from hours of playing racquetball, tennis, and golf. James kept his light-to-medium brown hair stylishly short with only the faintest of sideburns and the occasional five o'clock shadow. Rounding out his overall package, his pale blue eyes were swoon-worthy. Unfortunately, money and looks were all James had going for him. Vast wealth from old money had raised a spoiled playboy with a superior ego and zero tolerance for those he considered beneath him. Even his highly paid attack dog was 'beneath him', but even spoiled rich boys knew when to keep their mouths shut.

"Here you are," James announced. "I was wondering what'd happened to you after we boarded the ship. I was worried you turned in early without telling me, like you did every night at the island resort."

After having just barely met at the beginning of the week leading up to her aunt's wedding, James had been keeping tabs on her, as if she weren't allowed to make a move without him. When James's hand settled on her bare shoulder, his thumb tracing a slow circle as if marking his territory, Harley stiffened, fighting the urge to shrug him off.

She was suddenly in some bizarre world where a man she had only just met treated her as his possession.

"I needed some fresh air," Harley remarked, not sure why she even felt the need to explain herself to this man. "I'm feeling a little queasy."

"You can't possibly be seasick," James insisted and even added a throaty chuckle. "This yacht is one of the smoothest I've been on."

Harley never said it was seasickness making her queasy. It was the company, and just because he felt the ship was ***the smoothest***, that didn't mean someone couldn't get seasick on it. In many ways, James was worse than her father, if that were possible.

"I want to introduce you to my good friend, Randall," James announced.

"We've met twice already," she reminded James. "He was at the wedding reception."

"But he said the two of you never had a chance to actually talk at the reception," James insisted, barely acknowledging her comment. "I'll formally introduce you. You're going to love him."

James took her arm and led her away while Conrad waited at the bar for her drink. Harley internally protested rather than speaking out. Just like her mother, she let men in her life push her around. Harley believed she was being diplomatic, but she felt more like a doormat. The only man who didn't order her around was Conrad, but it was his job to take orders--not give them. James stopped Harley before another man, also dressed in fine, expensive clothing. Randall was of average height, about five-foot-ten, with a lean build. The man in his late twenties was reportedly into outdoor adventures, mostly hiking, kayaking, and skiing. For a rich guy, he wasn't nearly as stuck up as James. Randall's family had money, but they weren't exceedingly wealthy. He earned most of his wealth, so he wasn't technically one of the 'country club boys'. He had slightly longer, dark, curly hair, bushy dark brows, and a clean-shaven, baby face. Randall was average-looking, at best, but he was friendly and outgoing.

"Harley, this is Randall," James announced. "Randall, this is my intended, Harley."

"Nothing's official yet," Harley softly reminded James, although he didn't appear to be listening.

Randall politely shook Harley's hand. "It's a pleasure, Harley." He then looked at James. "She's lovely. Wouldn't know what she sees in you."

"A comfortable living," James replied almost smugly.

Both men laughed at the absurd joke as if Harley didn't have a dime to her name. She had millions in her trust fund! That she couldn't touch it until she turned twenty-five was irrelevant. Harley frowned and scanned the room, bored out of her mind, while they continued talking about her as if she wasn't there. Harley's eyes fell upon Damon, James's personal guard, who was only ten feet away. Of course, he was there. Damon was always close by. Although not as muscular as a bodybuilder, Damon was still built like a tank. The man in his early thirties stood at least six-foot-two, with broad shoulders and an intimidating stature, dressed in an expensive black suit. The fact that he was ruggedly handsome and filled out his pants rather nicely made his position as James's attack dog and his deplorable attitude even more tragic. He wore his short, nearly jet black hair slicked back like a 1940s gangster. His sparse beard was neatly trimmed, giving just enough facial hair to reinforce his intimidating appearance, while his dark eyes maintained a certain hawkish gaze.

Damon might have been incapable of smiling, but that's what James wanted. A barely housebroken guard dog at his side, prepared to beat the piss out of any man who looked at his boss the wrong way. Despite spending the last several days at the island resort in Damon's general proximity, Harley hadn't heard the man speak once. Damon leaned against the wall and lit the cigarette he held between his teeth like some common thug off the street. The flame on the lighter was over an inch high, drawing attention to him and his actions. The flame extinguished, and his eyes briefly met hers. He offered an unsettling smile as he blew out smoke from his cigarette. Harley felt as if he were sizing her up for his next meal.

"Damon--" James muttered, catching his hired goon's attention, then sharply eyed the cigarette. "Not in here."

Damon straightened and left the lounge without a word. He stopped just outside the door and casually leaned on the deck railing, smoking his cigarette without a care in the world. Harley stared at Damon through the window a moment longer. A brandy glass appeared before her. She looked at Conrad holding the glass and the charming smile on his face. Harley accepted the glass and attempted to hide her own smile. He knew she desperately needed that drink to make it through even an hour of this evening.

"Everyone has a price," James insisted as he talked to his friend, catching Harley's attention. "Some are higher. But in the end, money wins."

As both men again laughed, Harley mentally rolled her eyes and took a healthy swallow of her drink while looking away. Apart from being rich and handsome, James literally had nothing else going for him. He certainly didn't have any qualities she found attractive, and it wasn't as if she needed a man with money either. Harley then noticed the only other female passenger sitting on a nearby sofa. Ivy was a twenty-one-year-old, blonde bombshell with naturally wavy hair and a youthful, girl-next-door face. She was short, possibly only five-foot-two, and incredibly petite. Ivy was the only passenger out of the seven who hadn't been to Harley's aunt's wedding. She also appeared to be traveling alone, which put her on Tyler's radar the moment they set sail. As far as Harley could tell, Ivy was slightly timid but very polite and friendly. Despite her department store, off-the-rack dress, she made an impression on her fellow male passengers.

Ivy definitely didn't come from a wealthy family and obviously didn't have much wealth of her own either, which made her presence on the expensive yacht almost puzzling. Realizing her fellow passengers, who were not only strangers but also all wealthy, may have contributed to her shyness. Since they only set sail that afternoon, Harley didn't have time to properly introduce herself to Ivy. It had been a long, exhausting day, but she intended to get to know her better tomorrow, after a good night's sleep. Harley was just happy to see another woman on board to balance out all the testosterone. The shy young woman was attempting to elude Tyler, who was sitting on the coffee table before her, angled so she couldn't escape him if she wanted to. Harley was sure the poor girl wanted to escape by the way her eyes shifted for an exit.

Tyler was textbook 'old money'. Despite only being in his early thirties, he pretended to be everything Conrad was because he had wealth to back him up. To his credit, he ***was*** a moderately handsome man with short dark hair and blue eyes, standing about six feet tall. Despite being lean, he was far from athletic, spending more time at the country club bars than he did on the golf course. If Harley had to guess, his favorite pastime was probably trolling strip clubs for his latest conquest. Harley witnessed Tyler shamelessly working the room at her aunt's wedding. Any girl between the ages of eighteen and thirty was fair game. When he drank, he went from rich asshole to first-class pervert. Sober, he was cautious around girls from wealthy families; instead, he preyed upon those without connections to resist his ***charm***. Once he had a few drinks in him, even daddy's little girls were ripe for picking, as long as they were over eighteen. Societies' rules, certainly not his.

Harley had heard Tyler boasting his 'virgin' body count even more than his 'married women' count. The way he bragged about such things made her sick. Harley left Randall and James without a word and approached the sofa where Ivy sat.

"Hey, Ivy," Harley announced cheerfully. "Did you remember that book you'd promised to loan me?"

"I, uh, actually, I left it back in my room," Ivy replied and attempted to stand, but almost couldn't because of Tyler's legs blocking her. She finally managed to step over his legs, nearly falling into Harley to make the step. "If you walk with me to my cabin, I'll get it for you." She gently cleared her throat. "I was about to turn in anyway."

"Me too," Harley announced. "Thanks."

Tyler finally stood, looking stupid sitting on the coffee table facing an empty sofa, and walked away. Ivy and Harley dropped off their cocktail glasses at the bar on their way to the lounge door. Conrad remained only a step behind, without fail. As they left the lounge and headed onto the deck, they passed Damon by the rail, just finishing his cigarette. Harley could almost feel the weight of Damon's gaze as he watched them pass.

"Thanks," Ivy remarked while insecurely linking onto Harley's arm. "You saved me in there. And I thought that guy was a pervert ***before*** he started drinking! He didn't even care that I'm practically engaged."

"I heard you were traveling alone," Harley remarked. "Kind of a romantic trip to take without your fiancé."

"Well, Paul was called away while we were on vacation," Ivy replied with a dreary sigh. "I decided to remain the rest of the week, since we'd met another couple at the resort. I couldn't see wasting the entire trip when it was already paid for. You know, all-inclusive."

"Well, it sounds like you had a good time," Harley remarked.

"Would've been more fun with Paul," Ivy pouted. "I really miss him. Nearly a week since I've seen him."

Harley sighed while lost in a dream. "You're lucky to be in love."

"Yes, it's wonderful," Ivy replied, then eyed her almost suspiciously. "You came with that guy, James, didn't you? I thought I heard the two of you were engaged."

"Hardly," Harley scoffed. "Our fathers were good friends. They desperately want us to marry."

"Oh? I thought prearranged marriages went out with thumbscrews," Ivy remarked, then appeared curious. "Do you love him?"

"How can I love him?" Harley remarked, then chuckled. "I don't even know him."

"Your relationship is already off to a bad start," Ivy informed her. "You shouldn't go through with it. I could never sleep with a man I didn't love."

Harley groaned and rolled her eyes. "I don't even want to think about it."

Ivy laughed as they stopped by her cabin door. She turned to face Harley while Conrad paused, remaining several feet away.

"You really need to think long and hard about your future or what's going to be left of it if you saddle yourself to a man you don't love," Ivy informed her. "There's someone special out there for you, but you won't find Mr. Right if you're married to Mr. Wrong."

Ivy gave a tiny wave, then disappeared into her cabin. Conrad approached and walked with Harley the rest of the way to her cabin.

"Young but wise," Conrad announced. "I'd listen to her."

"I will," Harley remarked. "When we're safely back on land, so I don't have to worry about ***that one*** drowning me." She nodded back down the deck without even looking. Somehow, she knew Damon was still there.

Conrad turned and looked back. As predicted, Damon remained by the rail, despite having finished his cigarette, and seemed to be watching them. Conrad looked back at her and grinned.

"I wouldn't worry about him," Conrad teased. "He probably just has a little crush on you."

Harley groaned and rolled her eyes. "I'd prefer he drown me."

Chapter 3

Early the following morning, Harley slept peacefully within her small yet richly appointed cabin after a mostly restless night. The ship violently jolted with a thunderous bang, nearly knocking Harley from her bed. She clung to the mattress a moment, disoriented from being awoken so abruptly and violently, then looked around her dimly lit room. When she heard the sound of running feet on the deck outside her cabin, she realized she hadn't dreamt whatever it was that had woken her. Harley sprang from her bed and quickly dressed before hurrying out onto the deck that was engulfed in a thick fog. Harley could barely see the railing, only a few feet before her, through the dense fog. She couldn't remember the last time she'd witnessed anything quite so creepy. She heard voices not far from her. Harley placed her hand on the railing and cautiously walked along the slightly slippery deck in the fog.

Shawn, Brian, and Lester finally came into view up ahead near the bow of the ship, but she could barely make them out. All three peered over the railing while talking softly but harshly. As she made her way closer, Randall appeared from the bow at the opposite end and approached the ship's crew. Randall leaned over the railing to see what the crew had been looking at.

"You've got to be kidding me!" Randall cried out while straightening and facing the crew.

Harley paused only a few feet from them, keeping her distance from Randall.

Randall glared at the captain, appearing enraged. "Are you fucking drunk?"

"The computer system malfunctioned," Shawn insisted. "We couldn't see anything in the fog."

Harley peered over the railing. The starboard bow was wedged against a large reef. Because of the dense fog, she couldn't see much, or even if there had been any damage.

"Get some flashlights and check the damage," Shawn announced to his first officer.

When Harley straightened, she saw Damon standing only a foot from her, also staring over the railing. She gasped with surprise at his stealthy appearance. With limited visibility, there was no telling if he had been only a few feet from her the entire time. Damon moved past Harley and skillfully jumped over the railing, landing on the rock without releasing the rail. Brian grabbed an emergency flashlight from the wall and shone the light where Damon stood, although he wasn't able to see much from his position.

"That's a big, fucking hole," Damon announced, for the first time revealing his deep English accent.

Harley was a bit surprised by the accent. She hadn't even realized he was British.

"It's a big fucking rock," Shawn scoffed while staring over the railing, despite seeing very little through the fog. "Thanks for that professional observation." He looked back at Brian. "Check the lower deck. Make sure we're not taking on water."

"I'll radio for help," Lester announced.

Both Lester and Brian hurried away, disappearing into the fog. Randall continued staring over the side at the rock Damon easily stood on.

"Don't know how you could miss a rock that size," Randall scoffed.

Shawn glared at Randall, disgusted, then walked away. James and Conrad emerged from the fog behind Harley.

"What the hell's going on out here?" James demanded as he tied his robe sash. "Why have we stopped?"

Damon casually leaned on the deck on chest level from the rock and lit a cigarette. The flame immediately caught James' attention.

"Damon?" James demanded. "What are you doing down there?"

Shawn returned with a large, handheld spotlight, leaned over the railing, and shone the light on the water alongside the rock.

"My God," Shawn gasped. "We've run aground!"

"I'm on a very tight schedule," James reminded the captain. "I have early morning appointments on Friday. I can't be late."

"I'm sorry," Shawn announced while glaring at James, then pointed toward the stern of the ship. "Hawaii is about three hundred miles that way. You'd better start swimming."

"Don't be ridiculous," James scoffed.

"We're grounded and hung up on a rather large rock," Shawn informed him. "This ship's not going anywhere except maybe down."

"That's a bit dramatic, considering we're grounded," Randall remarked. "Sinking is out of the question."

Conrad looked over the railing at the water and then beyond the bow before squinting and pointing. "What's that over there?"

Damon turned and looked through the fog where Conrad indicated. Shawn approached with his spotlight and shone it in the direction the men stared. Although it was difficult to see anything through the thick fog, there appeared to be the faint outline of a palm tree. Damon transferred his cigarettes and lighter to his shirt pocket. He then removed his shoes and jacket, placing them on deck near Harley's feet, cast his cigarette aside, and slid off the rock and into the water. Harley watched Damon wade through the water up to his waist, then disappear into the fog, like some mythical monster.

"Where the hell is he going?" Shawn demanded.

"Doesn't pay to ask," James muttered.

Lester approached the captain and pulled him aside to speak with him privately. Despite noticing the two talking, Harley and Conrad were more interested in where Damon had gone.

"Where is that blooming idiot?" Conrad demanded under his breath.

"Maybe he drowned," Harley muttered.

"Couldn't be that lucky," Conrad huffed.

There was a tiny flame thirty yards away. It was Damon lighting another cigarette.

"What's out there?" James called to him.

"Sand."

"Smart ass," James muttered, then yelled to Damon. "Get back here!"

Chapter 4

Day one--stranded in hell's paradise. Although it took almost an hour after daybreak, the fog had eventually burned off, and the sun was now shining. The white sandy beach of the island was just thirty yards away. Twenty yards beyond the beach was a tropical paradise filled with palm trees, coconut trees, and other foliage. It had to be a decent-sized island, indicated by the length of the beach in both directions before them. All seven passengers stood at the railing, staring at the scenic landscape. The lounge doors opened, interrupting their peace. Lester appeared in the doorway.

"The captain would like to see everyone in the lounge," Lester informed them. "He wants to brief you on what's happening."

A few who had been leaning on the railing straightened and looked back at Lester, but no one made any attempt to approach.

"We're all right here," Tyler insisted. "Why doesn't he just come out here and tell us what's what?"

It was a logical question.

Lester frowned and fidgeted. "Come on, guys," he announced. "I'm just doing my job. Humor me."

There were several moans, but all seven reluctantly returned to the lounge. Lester shut the door behind Damon, who entered last. Once they had all gathered, Shawn and Brian entered the lounge from the control room.

"Please, feel free to take a seat," Shawn announced, then waited.

Everyone remained standing, just wanting to get the bad news out of the way and over with. When he realized no one wanted to sit, the captain cleared his throat and began with his report.

"At four-thirty this morning, the Magnus Rattner ran aground and struck a rock," Shawn began.

Randall immediately groaned at the captain's lack of getting to the point. The captain frowned, possibly annoyed by the interruption, but he proceeded to the point a little faster after that.

"Considering the time of the system's malfunction during the night, we're severely off course," Shawn informed them. "It could be several days before we're rescued."

There were more groans this time. The captain held up his hands to keep anyone from interrupting.

"I know," Shawn announced. "It's an inconvenience for all of us, but we'll be fine as long as we all keep our heads." He hesitated a moment. "Because the engine flooded, we're operating off the emergency generator. Now, there's enough fuel to keep that running for a few days, and we have enough food and water for at least that long. That being said, out of an abundance of caution, we're going to limit our water usage. No showers."

There were several more groans.

"Flushing toilets only once per day."

It was Harley's turn to groan.

"And we're going to ration what food we have to last at least that long," Shawn informed them.

Conrad cocked his head, and his eyes narrowed at the comment, indicating he was immediately suspicious of the captain's words.

"The emergency generator provides lights here in the lounge and the bridge, but only one light per cabin and limited lighting on deck," Shawn informed them, then hesitated and drew a deep breath. "On a positive note, there's an entire ocean to bathe in, and the bar is fully stocked."

The open bar comment seemed to appease some of the guys, but Conrad's narrow eyes remained locked on the captain. Harley knew Conrad was suspicious of the entire situation.

"That's it," Shawn announced, attempting to sound cheerful. "As long as we work together and are mindful of waste, we'll be fine."

Shawn and Brian disappeared into the control room, unwilling to take any questions, while Lester paused near the bar.

"I've been instructed to serve plated meals rather than the usual buffet," Lester informed them. "We're having eggs and pancakes this morning. Breakfast will be ready in an hour."

As Lester was about to head into the attached dining room with access to the kitchen, Tyler approached the bar and immediately stopped when he saw the padlock on the cabinet containing the alcohol.

"What's up with the lock?" Tyler demanded, stopping Lester short of the dining room entrance.

Lester looked back at Tyler. "The bar will remain closed until noon," he informed him. "But you'll find fresh coffee in the dining room. Two cup limit, please."

It was Damon's turn to groan as he lit a cigarette in disgust while heading onto the deck, slamming the door behind him. Conrad and Harley exchanged concerned looks.

"Let's hope Damon doesn't run out of cigarettes before we're rescued," Conrad muttered to her.

Chapter 5

Since there was little to do for entertainment that afternoon, Conrad suggested a trip to the beach. Despite being stranded, it was still a beautiful, sunny day on a tropical island with a peaceful, white-sandy beach. Most tourists paid good money for the private beach they had for free. While the passengers changed into their beach attire, Brian attached a rope ladder to the railing alongside the gangway opening for ease of access. By the time the passengers returned to the deck in their swimwear with their blankets and towels, Lester had packed a cooler with bottled water, a couple of bottles of wine, and seven individual plates of picnic food for a light lunch, one for each of the passengers. Lester even launched the small rowboat to take their towels, blankets, several smaller beach chairs, and coolers to the beach so they could keep everything dry. The only passengers missing from their little beach party were Conrad and Damon. No one bothered asking what trouble Damon was getting into.

James, Randall, and Tyler were already wading through the water behind Lester, who was pulling the small rowboat like a cart with their provisions. Harley and Ivy remained on deck, waiting for Conrad. Although Harley packed a conservative bikini on their tropical trip, she chose to wear her one-piece. She didn't need to give James any more ideas than he already had. Ivy wore her own conservative bikini with a removable swim skirt over it. Conrad still hadn't arrived on deck, which made sense. He had expensive taste in suits, and he always hung them up properly so they wouldn't wrinkle. He was worse about clothing than most women. While they waited for Conrad, both women seemed to focus on the same image. Damon swam in the water a short distance from the ship. When he emerged from the clear blue water, they could see his broad, toned shoulders.

Both women were mesmerized when he brushed his wet hair back with both hands, exposing his moderately muscular arms with tattoos on each bicep. Even in his casual suits, Harley knew Damon was built athletic to muscular, but she didn't realize he was ***that*** built. She heard Ivy whimper softly, causing her to look at the young woman alongside her. Ivy's eyes were wide and glued on Damon.

"Holy shit," Ivy gasped.

"Just keep reminding yourself that it's Damon," Harley muttered to her.

Damon hoisted himself from the water like Zeus rising from Atlantis and climbed onto a large boulder twenty yards from the ship. He paused a moment, looking out to the ocean in an unintended sexy, masculine pose. He wore only a pair of black, cotton boxer briefs that clung to him like a second skin. Ivy softly groaned while Harley couldn't tear her eyes away from the specimen of manliness with water glistening off the perfect amount of hair covering his chest.

"I guess the water's pretty warm," Ivy remarked, only loud enough for Harley to hear.

Harley glanced at Ivy, somewhat puzzled by the comment.

Ivy suddenly grinned. "No shrinkage there," she announced, then giggled.

Although surprised, Harley couldn't help but giggle and possibly even blush at the somewhat suggestive comment. Despite that Damon sat on the rock and unapologetically chewed the side of his finger in an unrefined manner, both women couldn't help but stare.

"God, I feel so dirty," Ivy groaned while keeping her eyes locked on Damon in the near distance.

"Yeah," Harley muttered, then sighed. "Yet, I can't seem to look away."

Conrad stood alongside Harley and followed her gaze to the man wearing only his underwear while sitting on the rock.

"You do realize that's Damon, right?" Conrad remarked, startling both women.

Harley jumped with surprise and placed her hand on her chest. "Don't do that," she gasped. "You nearly gave me a heart attack."

"I just remembered," Ivy announced while fidgeting. "I forgot my sunglasses." She hurried across the deck and back to her cabin.

"I can't believe you're actually gawking at James's attack dog," Conrad remarked, sounding almost ashamed.

"I wasn't gawking," Harley squawked, somewhat flustered, being caught staring at the man in his underwear. She collected her wits and attempted to hide her flushed cheeks. "We were just wondering about his tattoo."

"Sure you were," Conrad scoffed, then snorted a laugh. "And women say men are bad."

"I'm serious," Harley protested, defending herself. "Is that some sort of military tattoo? I don't recognize it."

Conrad frowned at her and shook his head before glancing across the water at the man on the rock. He stared a moment, then squinted.

"Yes, that is a military tattoo," Conrad informed her, his expression changing to something resembling surprise. "It's an SAS tattoo. Special Air Service. The British Army's premier Special Forces regiment."

"In English, please," Harley scoffed.

"It's the British version of U.S. Delta Forces or Green Berets," Conrad informed her.

Harley sharply eyed Conrad, somewhat surprised. "You mean that attack dog--?"

Conrad nodded, suddenly taking a greater interest in Damon, although not for the same reason as Harley had. "He's not an ordinary bodyguard," he remarked. "Damon is a highly trained combat soldier and possibly a very dangerous man. I suggest very strongly that you not provoke him."

Harley's eyes suddenly widened. "And I thought I was only kidding about James sending Damon to kill me," she gasped, then removed her sunglasses that were tucked into the cleavage of her swimsuit and placed them on her face. Ivy was right. If they were going to leer, they needed to make sure no one caught them.

Chapter 6

The afternoon sky was clear and blue with puffy clouds drifting lazily overhead. Although it was hot and humid, the sea breeze made it pleasant. Small waves rolled onto shore, breaking gently on the beach before rushing back out again. While relaxing on the beach for the first hour, Harley and Ivy sat on their low setting beach chairs, only partially reclined, sunglasses on, while secretly and silently gazing at Damon, who remained on his rock for the longest time, gazing out into the endless ocean. He seemed oddly fascinated watching the distant, four-foot swells, possibly mesmerized by their tranquil rhythm. Harley's gaze lingered on the water sliding down Damon's chest. Heat rose in her cheeks, and she quickly looked away, ashamed that she was fantasizing about the man she referred to as 'intimidating' and 'rude'. Yet, like a magnet, her eyes kept straying back to him.

Harley had to wonder if Ivy was feeling conflicted as well, considering she was 'practically engaged', a term with which she wasn't entirely sure of its meaning. Finally tearing her eyes away from Damon's distracting, toned body, Harley took in the rest of the view. Seeing the luxury yacht run aground on the large rock was almost surreal. She'd already taken several pictures of the scene with her cell phone, which was about all it was good for without a signal. That she'd taken a photo or two of Damon on his rock made her question her morals. His toned, bare chest was going to remain a distraction until he put his shirt back on. It would be best if he put on a pair of pants too. James, Randall, and Tyler kept themselves occupied by kicking around a volleyball on the beach, using it as a soccer ball. When they grew bored of the ball, they splashed around in the water, talking loudly and laughing. Out of everything he could take in, his book forgotten on his lap, Conrad's eyes were fixed on the two men talking on the yacht's deck.

Harley's gaze drifted back to the deck where Shawn and Brian stood talking, huddled close together, trying to read their expressions even though she couldn't hear a word. What did her friend find so interesting about the two men? Conrad was possibly the most observant person she'd known. He silently watched everything, gathering Intel on people, but he was rarely hyper-focused as he was now. It was a little unnerving. Since reading Conrad's mind would be next to impossible, Harley needed to take a more direct approach.

"What has you so interested?" Harley finally asked just loud enough that Ivy wouldn't hear.

"Nothing," Conrad replied without looking away from the deck. "And everything."

"Hmm. Mysteriously evasive," Harley remarked, mocking him. "Care to elaborate just a little?"

"Which would you like?" Conrad asked. "My lack of confidence in our captain as a leader, particularly in an emergency? Or the nagging suspicion that our crew is keeping something from us?"

"I'm afraid to ask," Harley muttered while studying her friend, then cringed. "What do you think they're keeping from us?"

"Well, I'm fairly confident the ship is pretty secure, lodged against that rock and in the ground," Conrad informed her. "So I don't think the ship is in danger of capsizing at the moment."

"You think they're not being entirely truthful about our rescue?" Harley asked, now concerned.

"It crossed my mind," Conrad replied, remaining deep in thought. "I'm worried that they lied about actually receiving responses to their distress calls, but if my concerns were valid, I'd think one of them would be on the bridge manning the radio at all times."

"While I agree something seems off with the crew, and I trust your instincts," Harley announced, then turned somewhat skeptical. "You have been known to overshoot the mark with your trust issues. We need to give Captain Rattner a little credit for intelligence. I mean, that's a prestigious position he holds. One isn't just handed the title of captain."

Conrad cast a befuddled look at her, then raised a skeptical brow. "Harley," he announced in a mildly lecturing tone. "You could buy a yacht tomorrow and become the ship's captain."

Harley stared at him a moment and raised her sunglasses, now confused. "Surely, you don't think--?" she began, then fell silent.

"Shawn owns the charter; he can be captain, if he wants," Conrad informed her. "James made our travel arrangements. I have no idea how credible the company is or who runs it."

Harley suddenly frowned and let her sunglasses fall back down. "That's not very reassuring," she muttered, now sharing Conrad's concern.

"You let James talk you into this five-day cruise from hell back to Hawaii," Conrad reminded her. "I wanted to fly home."

"It was five more days away from my father," Harley remarked with a groan. "It sounded like a good idea, at the time."

When Damon finally stood upon his rock twenty feet from shore, Harley's eyes instinctively followed. Despite being hidden behind her sunglasses, Conrad caught her gaze and gave her a disapproving glare.

Ivy groaned softly from behind her own sunglasses. "Wow," she muttered while discreetly holding up her cell phone and snapping a picture.

Harley shifted uncomfortably and leaned closer to Ivy. "Send that to me," she whispered.

"No internet," Ivy reminded her without taking her eyes off the manly specimen.

Harley cursed softly under her breath and secretly took a picture right before Damon casually dived into the clear water. Both women groaned softly, surprising Conrad, who stared at them, astonished by what he was witnessing. James had been approaching and seemed to notice the direction their heads were turned. He looked back and saw Damon swimming in the ocean, then cast his own disapproving look at Harley. Whatever his initial intention, James changed direction and returned to his friends.

§

An hour later, the six raided the cooler, enjoying the small picnic lunch Lester had provided. Damon finally emerged from the water after his extended swimming and floating follies and trudged through the surf onto the beach, raking his wet hair back with his fingers. This time, Harley and Ivy were a bit more discreet with their sweeping eyefuls of the well-built man. Harley blamed too much sunshine and vitamin B for her shameful arousal of James's attack dog, but she couldn't stop staring at the water glistening off the hair on his arms, chest, and legs. Conrad took note but barely looked up from his book, having given up on his quest to stop Harley from lusting after James's hired goon. As Damon trudged through the sand, making his way to the cooler, James approached him, cutting him off. Although James may have thought he was being discreet, the conversation was overheard by just about everyone.

"Could you show some decency and cover up?" James demanded of his attack dog.

Damon lacked emotion despite what must have felt like a personal attack. Out of everything Damon could have said, he chose to say nothing while maintaining his hardened stare and gave his boss a quick once-over. His boss wore shorter, form-fitting swim shorts that barely made it to his thighs, while Damon's cotton boxer briefs were several inches longer and covered more of his thighs. It was obvious James was insecure about his slim, hairless golfer's body compared with Damon's broad, lightly hairy chest, toned abs, and muscular arms. Despite being his boss, James flinched.

"I appreciate it," James announced, as if conveying he'd gotten his way, then rejoined his friends on the nearby blanket.

Damon resumed his course for the cooler and opened it. There was an uncomfortable moment as he peered inside, revealing that all seven plates of picnic lunch rations were gone. Harley and Ivy noted the look on his face and knew immediately that someone had taken his lunch. Since she ate with Conrad and Ivy, Harley knew for a fact it wasn't one of them, which meant it was James, Tyler, or Randall. Damon didn't even look in Harley's direction, immediately casting his hateful gaze upon the three men with four empty plates on their blanket. Rationing a growing boy's food was bad enough, but taking away his meager portion was akin to suicide. When the lid on the cooler slammed shut with a frightening bang, Harley was sure one of the three men would be turned into shark chum. Instead, Damon opened the drink cooler. Harley prayed they had left him some water. When she saw him remove a bottle of water, Harley let out the breath she had been holding. Ivy let out a relieved groan as well.

Damon then removed the last full bottle of wine, shut the cooler lid, and walked away with both the wine and water bottles. Perfect! Not only was Damon hungry and cranky, but he intended to drink his lunch, which would only make the situation worse. As he walked past, he snagged a vacant beach chair, carried it to the surf, and sat just within the water's edge.

Chapter 7

The dining room had eight tables of varying sizes that were bolted to the hardwood floor, in case they hit rough waters. A long sideboard usually contained the buffet spread, which now held pre-plated portions that seemed unusually small, considering how much food must have been left in the pantry. Either there was less food than there should have been for the remaining travel days on board, or the captain was rationing the food so it would last longer than a few days. Randall and Tyler were already giving Lester a hard time about the dinner portions while everyone else seemed to take it in stride.

"I thought the rescue would only be a couple of days," Tyler huffed. "If we were on course, we'd still be traveling to our destination. You're rationing as if it'll be two weeks rather than three days."

"I'm sorry," Lester insisted somewhat meekly. "I'm just following orders."

"The captain has some explaining to do," Randall scoffed while walking to the table with his plate.

Harley didn't complain, although it was obvious she and Ivy received less food than the guys did. She knew the average man required more calories than the average woman. She would, however, have complained if Conrad had gotten smaller rations due to his smaller stature. Harley, Ivy, and Conrad quietly carried their plates to a nearby table. Despite everything Harley had said and thought about Damon, he kept to his routine of a drink and a cigarette before dinner and waiting until last to get his meal. Even after having nothing but a bottle of wine for lunch, he still waited until last, even though he had to be extremely hungry. Harley hadn't even touched her food while watching Damon collect his plate from Lester.

"Did you notice the crew didn't take their meal with us?" Conrad asked in a soft voice so only Harley would hear him.

"Do you think they're not taking any rations?" Harley asked.

"That would be one way of thinking," Conrad informed her. "But I saw them eating in the galley. Maybe the rationing rules don't apply to them."

Harley considered what Conrad said but didn't comment. Instead, she watched Damon sit alone at a small table, distancing himself from his boss and his boss's friends. She didn't doubt he was still a little chaffed about his missing rations at lunch. It was bad business. Harley didn't care for the guy, but letting him go hungry was in no one's best interest. He was already volatile. If he challenged his handler's leash, it could get messy fast. Harley abruptly stood, much to Conrad's surprise, and approached James's table. When she paused at the table, James immediately smiled and pulled out a chair for her.

"Coming to join us?" James asked, enthusiastically.

Instead, Harley glared at the three men with a look of loathing. "What you guys did this afternoon was deplorable," she scoffed.

"What do you mean?" James asked, surprised by her hostility.

"You know what I mean," she snarled in response. "We're in a highly stressful situation already. We don't need the three of you making it worse."

"You mean with Damon?" James asked, then smiled. "We apologized, and he's already forgotten about it. There's no need to be dramatic or get hysterical over it. He can handle himself."

"I don't care if he's okay with it or if he's already forgotten about it," Harley scoffed. "I haven't. I realize I have no recourse right here and right now, but I run in the same circles as you mutts. You'd better know that I have a big mouth."

Harley spun on her heels, returned to her table, and snatched her dinner plate. She then turned, approached Damon, who was sitting alone at his table, and set her plate in front of him.

"I lost my appetite," Harley informed him, then left the dining room.

Conrad quickly gathered both their utensils, grabbed his plate, and hurried into the lounge after her. Harley sat at the bar and poured a glass of brandy to calm her nerves. Conrad set his plate down between them, sat in the chair alongside her, and handed her a set of utensils. Harley set them on the bar and held up her hand.

"I'm not hungry, Conrad," she insisted. "And I certainly don't want any of your food."

"You have to eat," he countered.

"I gained six pounds during the week leading up to the wedding," Harley reminded him. "I can afford to miss a meal, I assure you."

Conrad picked at his meal, lacking enthusiasm. "I'm proud of you for telling off James, but did it really have to be while defending Damon?"

"I wasn't actually defending Damon," Harley informed him.

"Certainly sounded that way."

"When I was a little girl," she announced. "I remember my father disrespecting you many times. He treated you like a non-person, and I never said anything."

Conrad groaned softly, then glanced at her. "You were a child," he reminded her. "And no one ever said the life of a servant was glamorous. We tend not to take things personally."

"Maybe you signed up for that, but that didn't make it right," Harley remarked. "And someone like Damon isn't going to put up with that sort of disrespect for very long. When he decides he's had enough, it could turn out bad for anyone in his path. Defusing the situation seemed like the best course of action."

"Whether the situation has been diffused remains to be seen," Conrad reminded her. "If we're being lied to about the timeframe surrounding our rescue, things could get a lot worse."

"I guess we'll just take it one day at a time," Harley replied.

§

Harley again turned in early that night, not wanting to spend more time than necessary in the same room with James. She changed for bed and found the book she was reading. Thankfully, the emergency overhead light provided more than enough light for her to read in bed until she felt tired enough to sleep. Harley's stomach rumbled lowly, reminding her how hungry she was. She wished she hadn't eaten the chocolates from the resort's turn-down service yesterday. They would taste so good right now. She was about to nestle in with her book when she heard a knock on the door. It was probably Conrad or maybe even Ivy. She approached the door and looked through the peek hole but didn't see anyone. Harley considered it for a moment, then opened the door. There was no one there. She then looked down and saw a chocolate power bar on the deck right outside her door. She picked up the power bar, stared at it a moment, and then smiled.

Chapter 8

Day Two. The sun rose over the horizon, spilling warm golden light across the calm, bluish-green water, which reflected the sky's rose, peach, and fading lavender before deepening to blue. Small waves lapped almost silently to shore before rushing back out again. High above, delicate mare's tail clouds streaked the sky. With the rising sun behind them, the clouds shimmered faintly with their radiant white strands drifting slowly across the blue sky. Harley stood on deck, enjoying her time alone before the others would rise and destroy her peace. She fell in love with the tranquil early-morning sunrise and, for a fleeting moment, forgot her problems entirely. As her gaze drifted to the beach, palm tree fronds barely stirred in the gentle, warm breeze, carrying the lingering scent of salty ocean air. Bliss! In an instant, her morning was suddenly ruined as loud, angry voices erupted around the corner. Harley looked toward the ship's stern and took a few steps closer while listening to the heated debate.

"I don't take orders, I give them!" James shouted.

"Not on my ship you don't," Shawn snarled back. "This vessel may not sail anymore, but I'm still in charge here."

Harley stepped around the corner and saw Shawn and James facing off like two aggressive dogs with their scruffs raised.

"That 'in charge' captain stuff is bullshit," James launched back.

"Your opinion doesn't matter," Shawn informed him. "We have to ration, and everyone has to follow the rules. The water supply is limited, and we can't risk people taking unauthorized showers."

"If I were you, I'd be a little more accommodating to your paying passengers, if you don't want to be sued over this," James shouted back at him.

"Don't threaten me," Shawn snarled. "All the money in the world means nothing if we run out of water before we're rescued." The captain straightened proudly. "Water to all staterooms has been turned off, and it won't be turned back on. The only functioning toilet is the one in the lounge, and the only running water is in the galley. Those are my orders."

Harley turned to leave before she was caught eavesdropping and collided with Damon, who was now standing behind her. She gasped with surprise, quickly removing her hands that had braced against his chest.

"Sorry," she muttered.

Damon barely acknowledged the incident, seeming more interested in the argument he'd also heard. Harley regained her composure and walked past him, returning to her cabin.

§

While in line behind James, Randall, and Tyler for their pre-plated, meager breakfast, Harley, Conrad, and Ivy overheard Tyler complaining about another decrease in their breakfast rations. Today was only two eggs, one strip of bacon, and a slice of toast. If that wasn't bad enough, he also informed them that they would be limited to one cup of coffee and one bottle of water. The sharp decrease in rations was moderately troubling. How long did they anticipate being shipwrecked? The three men groaned, cursed under their breath, and stormed away to their table.

"That's not good," Conrad muttered to Harley.

When Harley and Ivy received their rations, they were only given one egg, one strip of bacon, and a slice of toast. Again, Harley wasn't going to complain, and Ivy seemed fine with the decision. When Lester handed Harley a bottle of water, she pointed to the disposable, lidded cups containing coffee.

"I get a coffee too," Harley informed him, knowing she probably sounded a little snippy.

Lester looked at her as if she spoke a foreign language. "You don't drink coffee," he reminded her.

"I do," she replied. "On occasion."

"Is it for you?" Lester asked, almost accusingly.

Harley cocked her head and glared at the man, not much taller than her. Her stare must have unnerved him, possibly not expecting any trouble from her.

"What I do with my rations is none of your goddamned business," Harley scoffed, practically startling both Lester and Ivy.

Conrad had a difficult time hiding his smirk. It wasn't the first time he'd witnessed Harley's vengeful side. When Lester handed Harley one of the lidded disposable cups, Ivy couldn't seem to contain her giggle at the spectacle. All three chose their 'usual' table and sat down together to feast on the banquet before them. Harley tried to give Conrad her slice of bacon and her piece of toast, but he politely declined. When Damon entered, presumably after his morning smoke, Lester seemed anxious. The moment he approached the buffet table, the captain seemed to mysteriously appear from the galley, possibly anticipating trouble. Apparently, Shawn took the initiative to explain the new one-cup-of-coffee rule to Damon. Although he'd barely reacted to the restrictions placed upon them yesterday, the news of only one cup of coffee must have hit a nerve.

"Are you fucking kidding me?" Damon scoffed quite loudly.

Whatever the captain said, it was calm and quiet. Damon snatched his plate, bottled water, and one cup of coffee, looking like a raging bull on the way to his private table. While the passengers finished their meager breakfast, the captain explained the new water-conserving rule, though it seemed the rumor had already reached all seven passengers.

"Brian and I will head out onto the island today and do some exploring," Shawn informed them. "Lester will remain on the ship and assist you with anything you need. So enjoy the beach or cards here on the ship."

"Actually, exploring the island sounds like fun," Harley remarked.

The captain glanced at Harley and cocked his head in an almost patronizing manner. "Exploring the island is prohibited to the passengers," Shawn informed her. "We don't know what sort of dangers are lurking beyond the beach. Anything from poison to wild animals. For your own safety, we ask that you remain on the beach and stay within view of the ship."

"What makes it safe for you, if that's the case?" Harley immediately responded, not appreciating being treated like a helpless woman.

"We'll be taking the skeet shotgun," Shawn informed her, almost matter-of-factly. "Passengers remaining on the beach is not up for debate."

"Exactly when will we be expecting a rescue ship?" Conrad asked, speaking out for the first time.

"We don't have a specific time just yet," Shawn informed him, which was met by several groans.

"But there is a rescue on its way?" Conrad just about demanded, refusing to let it go.

"Of course," Shawn replied, seeming ready to bolt. "Enjoy your afternoon, and we'll reconvene later this afternoon."

Without waiting for further questions or conversation, Shawn left the dining room with Brian only a couple of steps behind him. Conrad finished eating and left the dining room right after James, Randall, and Tyler. It was odd that Conrad left Harley alone without even announcing his departure. Ivy and Harley remained sitting at the table, talking quietly between themselves while Damon finished his breakfast.

"I'm going to change into my swimsuit," Ivy informed her. "Are you hanging out on the beach with me today?"

"What choice do I have?" Harley remarked. "I need to save what's left of my book for the evenings."

"I'll meet you on deck," Ivy announced and hurried from the dining room.

Harley stood, collected her untouched cup of coffee, and approached Damon, where he unapologetically smoked a cigarette at his table. He briefly eyed her, blew out smoke away from her, but didn't speak, acting as if he hadn't been the one who'd left the power bar at her door last night. Harley placed the cup of coffee on the table and casually shrugged.

"I don't drink coffee," she informed him.

Damon briefly eyed the cup of coffee before practically lunging for it. Harley turned to leave, knowing there wouldn't be any conversation between them, and she wasn't sure she really wanted that sort of relationship with him anyway.

"Wear long pants and hiking boots," Damon announced, almost surprising her that he spoke. "And bring water."

Harley glanced back at him while lightly cocking her head. He sipped his second cup of coffee without looking at her.

"The island tour starts in half an hour," Damon remarked. "With or without you. I'll provide the bug spray."

Harley stared at the man who seemed more interested in his coffee and cigarette, clinging to both like a lifeline. She hid her smile, turned, and hurried from the dining room. Harley crossed through the lounge, looking for Conrad. She found him behind the bar, which was a bit odd. The booze was locked up until noon, and Conrad wasn't much of a drinker.

"What are you doing?" Harley asked, legitimately curious.

Conrad straightened, shook his head, and joined her on the other side of the bar. "I thought something looked off this morning when we passed through here," he remarked while guiding her from the lounge onto the deck. "There are four bottles of alcohol missing. They were there last night when I went to bed, and they're not in the trash."

"I guess someone is spending their evenings getting trashed," Harley remarked.

"Perhaps," Conrad remarked as they walked along the deck back to their cabins. "But as of last night, we weren't allowed to help ourselves."

"So someone swiped four bottles?" Harley asked.

"Maybe," Conrad replied. "But the lock wasn't tampered with."

"Who has keys to the liquor cabinet?" she asked, somehow knowing Conrad would have that information.

"Lester and the captain, for certain," Conrad replied. "Maybe Brian."

"Do you think they're purposely hiding bottles?" Harley asked, wondering what that could mean, not even sure what it mattered.

"I don't know," Conrad replied. "I feel like something more is going on around here."

"Well, you continue sleuthing," Harley insisted, then grinned while suggestively raising her brows. "In the meantime, put on your best hiking shoes. We're exploring the island."

Before Conrad could even question her, she hurried ahead of him toward her cabin.

Chapter 9

Shawn and Brian were already off exploring the island by the time Lester tugged the small rowboat to shore with provisions for the afternoon, which included everyone's backpacks, beach bags, and shoes. Once Lester placed everything on the beach, he abandoned the rowboat and waded back to the ship. Before he even reached the ship, Damon removed his picnic lunch, his two allotted bottles of water, and stuffed them in his bag, catching his boss's attention. When Harley and Conrad did the same, James became curious and approached. Ivy was also curious but immediately followed Harley and Conrad's lead without question. While all three removed long pants from their bags and slipped them on over their swim attire, James paused before them.

"What's going on?" James asked.

"We're exploring the island," Harley announced, possibly a little too cheerfully.

"There has to be a fresh water source on the island somewhere," Conrad insisted. "We're going to have a look around."

"Not alone, you're not," James informed them, as if he had any authority over them.

"We're not alone," Harley replied, then pointed to Damon. "We're following him."

Damon didn't even bother looking at them as he slipped into a leather shoulder holster that contained a nine-millimeter semiautomatic. She knew it! Harley suspected he carried a gun in a shoulder holster, but she couldn't confirm it until now.

"Can I come?" Ivy asked, eager and enthusiastic. "I brought shoes."

"Sure," Harley replied, although she wished Ivy had been wearing long pants.

"Are you serious about exploring?" James demanded. "You heard what the captain said."

"Yes, I heard," Harley replied. "We're going. ***Without*** the captain's permission."

James groaned and then motioned for his friends to join them. "We're going for a little walk," he informed them. "Put your shoes on and grab some water."

Randall seemed intrigued, although Tyler was less than enthusiastic. Since the captain and Brian went to the right, Damon led his group to the left. As they began their hike, Lester was heard yelling at them from the boat deck, attempting to stop them, but they easily ignored him. It wasn't as if he'd be calling the captain and telling on them.

§

Randall, Tyler, and James walked together on the beach while following Damon, forcing Harley, Ivy, and Conrad to bring up the rear. Randall and James were discussing the captain's strict rationing campaign while tossing around the word 'lawsuit'. Damon walked closer to the woods and paused, considering his options. Randall,

Tyler, and James stopped as well, remaining twenty feet away.

"What is it, Damon?" James asked.

"A path."

"You got me to go on this trek, but I'm not exploring the jungle," James informed him. "No telling what's lurking in there."

"We're looking for a fresh water source," Conrad reminded him. "We won't find that on the beach."

James glared at Harley. "What kind of servant do you have to speak out like that?" he demanded.

"An intelligent one," Harley scoffed. "And he's not my servant, he's my ***personal assistant***, if you don't mind. He hasn't been my father's butler for over four years."

James rolled his eyes, as if bored with the way she defended Conrad, a servant, every chance she got. Harley knew everyone had an opinion about Conrad being her shadow for the last four years, and she didn't care what any of them thought.

"If we're stranded here for more than a few days, we're going to need drinking water," Harley reminded him, hoping he'd listen to common sense.

"There'll be a rescue coming in another day or two," James insisted. "I don't know why everyone's getting worked up over this."

"Are you so sure?" Harley demanded. Obviously, James lacked common sense.

"The captain said there will," James reminded her.

"And you believe him?" Harley scoffed, parroting Conrad's words, knowing her friend retained too much of his servant ways to speak his mind in front of others.

"I don't think I like your tone," James snapped, putting his sexism on full display.

"I guess it's a good thing your opinion matters very little to me," Harley snapped back, then walked past James and his friends toward Damon and the path in the woods.

Harley's words must have struck a nerve with James, particularly in front of his friends. His lips were curled in a sneer, and his face was beet red. Damon waited at the beginning of the path and seemed to be watching the entire exchange, although he showed little reaction to the conversation. James glared with contempt when he saw Conrad hiding his smirk as he and Ivy followed Harley without hesitation. Harley paused near Damon and checked out his idea of a path. She was surprised that the path sort of looked like an old, overgrown road.

"Damon--" James scoffed in a threatening tone.

Damon eyed James while lighting a cigarette and raised a dark, curious brow.

"You're not to encourage her," James insisted, glaring at his man. "We're staying on the beach."

Damon blew out smoke while staring at his boss. It was uncertain if he was contemplating disobeying a direct order or merely humoring Harley. Harley glared back at James, annoyed by his attempt at controlling her, then walked onto the slightly overgrown path, not giving a damn if she went alone. Conrad and Ivy again followed without hesitation.

"Harley--" James scolded, as if she'd listen to him. Harley didn't bother looking back until she heard James suddenly call out, "Damon!"

Harley, Ivy, and Conrad stopped and looked back, not sure what to expect. Damon was now on the path behind them, puffing on his cigarette without a care. He passed them and continued leading the way. All three fell in line, following him without question. They walked the hillside trail for several minutes before reaching a large clearing. When they saw an old army barracks, all four stared with varying levels of surprise. The Quonset hut was a sixteen-foot-wide by thirty-six-foot-long metal arch building. Metal shutters could be lowered over the four windows for added protection during storms or attacks. The clearing around the barracks had a large, stone fire pit, which appeared to be used for some cooking as well as evening bonfires. Damon was the first to recover after the surprising find and was the first to approach the building. Conrad, Harley, and Ivy hurried to catch up with him, still stunned by what they saw.

"Looks like it was abandoned maybe ten to twenty years ago," Conrad informed them. "Definitely not much longer than that."

Vines and other plant life had grown up along the sides of the barracks, but there appeared to be little damage to the structure itself. Damon approached the main door and entered the building. Twenty army cots lined up uniformly with one another, ten on each side, their mattresses neatly rolled up by the head of the bed. Most of the mattresses appeared intact, with minimal damage from woodland creatures. Between each set of cots were open closets, uniforms still hanging. Each generic cot had a footlocker at the bottom. Although some dirt had found its way into barracks, the place still looked tidy, just not clean. There was a small kitchen, which a backup generator must have operated, but it was probably outside. There appeared to be no running water, but five-gallon water cans were close to the kitchen area. Several crates, possibly containing supplies, were piled in the corner near the counter. There were also two closets. One for perishables, and the other for linen storage.

Conrad approached the first footlocker and brushed the dust off the top. "United States," he remarked.

Ivy approached the door in the back, opened it, and cringed. "This could be why they moved out."

Harley and Conrad approached and looked through the doorway. There was a large hole where the back half of the barracks used to be, with very little left beyond it. As Ivy shut the door, Damon opened one of the crates and removed an MRE pouch.

"These crates are filled with MREs," Damon informed them. "Not much past their expiration dates. Enough to last months."

Harley witnessed Damon removing two packs of cigarettes from the crate. He groaned, a smile crossing his face, and stuffed both packs in his backpack.

"Now, if we can only find water," Conrad remarked.

"There should be a water source near this base," Damon informed him while tossing his bag over his shoulder.

Chapter 10

The four walked several yards to the left of the barracks before finding an old, worn path that led uphill. They didn't have to walk far up the path before reaching a building marked 'latrine' and 'showers'. The building had some vegetation growing up the sides, but it seemed fully intact. It was possible that the shower and latrine building was built stronger than the barracks. Built on a concrete pad, it had a stone base, then thicker metal sides up to the metal roof. There appeared to be only one entrance. On the outside of the building was an old-fashioned hand pump, indicating a nearby water source. All four checked out the building. Once inside the shower building, it was abundantly clear this was a military latrine.

The bathroom section featured a painted concrete floor and four old, grimy-looking urinals against one wall. On the other side were four toilets, out in the open, side by side, with no privacy partitions between them. Basically, the latrine was one step above an outhouse but with less privacy. Harley and Ivy immediately grimaced at the thought of sitting side-by-side while using the toilet. By the opening leading into the shower area, there was a bench and hooks on the wall to keep clothes and shoes dry while showering. Although not holding up much hope for the shower area beyond a door-free opening, it wasn't nearly as bad as either had feared.

The same painted concrete floor in the shower had several drains. The large, open area had two pipes from floor to ceiling, four shower heads surrounding it, and even a little shelf to hold a bar of soap or shampoo. There was a bench just inside the doorway, also with hooks on the wall for towels and clothes. Ivy turned on the shower lever, but nothing happened.

Conrad chuckled, mocking her. "Did you really think that would--?"

There was a metallic banging sound followed by loud groaning before brown water spurted from the showerhead, nearly spraying Ivy. It finally ran full strength, pushing out the dark water and becoming clear. Damon approached and eyed the water a moment. The longer it ran, the clearer it became. Ivy gasped, then clapped her hands together.

"It's water," Ivy cried out. "I never thought I'd be so happy to see running water!"

"There's no electricity or a generator," Damon remarked, now curious. "That must mean it is gravity-fed. The water source has to be further uphill."

Damon left the latrine and headed outside on a mission. Harley and Conrad were about to follow when they realized Ivy didn't seem interested in leaving.

"Are you coming?" Harley asked.

Ivy turned to face her while grinning. "Actually, I think I'd like to hang out here for a little. Can you pick me up on your way back?"

Harley managed a tiny laugh. "Enjoy your shower," she announced.

Ivy tossed her bag onto the bench and removed a bar of soap and her towel, then grinned. "I will," she announced, then gave Conrad a stern look. "No peeking."

Conrad groaned and shook his head while heading for the doorway. "I wouldn't dream of it," he muttered, then left the shower area.

"Watch out for snakes," Harley warned Ivy, then left with Conrad.

Once they appeared outside the latrine, they saw Damon waiting for them by a path on the hill, patiently smoking his cigarette.

"Where's Barbie?" Damon asked, sounding almost disinterested.

"Showering," Conrad replied, matter-of-factly. "You weren't invited."

Damon rolled his eyes, muttered something under his breath, and headed up the hill. Conrad and Harley followed him. A short walk up the path led them to a large, fresh water pond. Gravity provided water to the showers, just as Damon had surmised. The path continued uphill, further intriguing him. When Damon continued up the path, Harley and Conrad felt compelled to follow him. The short hike took them to the top of the hill and a massive clearing. When they spotted the enormous hangar, all three were relatively surprised, although maybe they shouldn't have been. The sixty-by-eighty-foot, sloped steel Quonset hangar, painted in jungle camouflage, was nestled close to the woods, keeping it partially hidden from anyone flying overhead. The double, rolling steel doors slid on a track to open the entire interior. There was a smaller door for access without opening the large bay doors.

Beyond the hangar was a long, slightly overgrown runway that led to a cliff. Because Damon seemed more interested in the runway, Harley and Conrad followed him across the long, grassy stretch. Harley was fascinated by the amazing view and wanted a closer look, which may have piqued Conrad's interest as well. Harley had never seen a sky that blue before, and without any trees or hills to obstruct it, it was almost mesmerizing. Damon paused at the edge of the cliff and took in the view as well. The high, wispy clouds flanked the horizon. It was truly incredible. While Harley took a few pictures with her cell phone, Damon eyed the steep fifty to sixty-foot drop to the deep ocean below.

"Now this is a view," Conrad announced while smiling. "I could build a house right here."

"Check out that sky," Harley remarked. "Have you ever seen clouds like that before?"

"Mare's tails," Damon casually replied.

Harley and Conrad looked at him, not exactly sure what he said.

"What's that?" Conrad asked.

Damon continued to stare across the horizon. "***Mackerel skies and mare's tails make lofty ships carry low sails***."

Both stared at him, not certain if he was even speaking English. Damon finally glanced at them.

"It's an old sailor's proverb, of sorts," Damon replied, then nodded to the horizon. "There's a storm brewing out at sea."

"As long as it stays out there," Conrad remarked.

"Only time will tell," Damon informed him, then looked back over the horizon. "Might be a good idea to hole up in the barracks tonight, out of caution."

"Maybe you should suggest that to our illustrious captain," Conrad muttered.

Damon cast a look at Conrad while lighting another cigarette and casually blew out smoke before snorting a laugh. "No one's telling Captain Queeg anything," he remarked.

"Captain Queeg?" Conrad asked, raising a brow. "You read "The Caine Mutiny"?"

Damon ignored the question. "The captain is micromanaging cups of coffee while his alcoholic ship's steward is pilfering bottles of booze from the lounge liquor cabinet."

"I knew it!" Conrad exclaimed.

Damon turned and headed back across the massive clearing toward the hangar in the near distance. Conrad motioned for Harley to follow him, and they hurried to catch up.

"What else have you noticed?" Conrad eagerly asked, wanting his suspicions confirmed.

Damon briefly eyed Conrad. "You've spent too much time in the company of gossiping housemaids," he remarked. "Stick to what you're good at. Mouth shut; eyes and ears open."

Conrad suddenly lagged behind while staring at Damon, who continued onward. Harley remained by Conrad's side and sneered at the man ahead of them, finding reason to hate him all over again.

"What a dick," Harley scoffed, feeling the sting of Damon's insult hurled at her friend.

"I don't think that was meant as an insult," Conrad remarked, stranded in his own thoughts. "Being a good butler is like being invisible. People forget you're there, yet you see and hear everything."

"I think you're giving Damon too much credit for being mysterious, deep, and cryptic," Harley scoffed. "Offensive and crude are more his style."

Conrad and Harley approached the hangar only a few steps behind Damon. There were a couple of overturned jeeps and one that remained upright. Conrad and Harley approached the smaller hangar door alongside the closed bay doors, seemingly losing Damon as they stepped inside. The hangar interior was almost entirely open. There was a fighter jet proudly displayed in the middle with the engine compartment open and the engine partially torn apart. The white Douglas TA-4 Skyhawk, with the U.S. Navy logo on the tail, was a two-seat trainer jet with tandem seating under a single elongated canopy with dual controls. The single-engine fighter jet was over forty-two feet long with a wingspan of over twenty-seven feet and a height of just a little over fifteen feet. Possibly most impressive was the two twenty-millimeter cannons and missile launcher, although the missiles weren't anywhere to be found. By the slightly faded paint and a little bit of rust, the jet had also been abandoned only about ten years ago.

In addition to the fighter jet, there were a few rolling metal tool chests, several barrels possibly containing fuel, two older generators, and a large rolling ladder used for working on the jet. In the back corner was a small office that seemed promising, as it might contain some kind of radio equipment. Rather than join them at the smaller hangar door, Damon poked around the old jeep instead, catching Harley's attention as she looked back out the door. He climbed inside and turned the key, frowning when nothing happened.

"You didn't really think it would work, did you?" Harley remarked.

Damon gave her an icy look, but she easily ignored it, chuckling at his expense.

"I'll take a look around inside for some sort of radio equipment," Conrad announced.

Damon finally followed Harley and Conrad in the hangar like a well-trained dog. When Conrad entered the back room, Damon checked out the portable generator. Harley followed Conrad, hoping he'd make an interesting find. The hangar office was about as basic and bland as it could be. The crude walls were made from thick plywood and two-by-fours. There was a bunk against one wall, a portable field desk, and a small folding desk that contained radio equipment. Possibly the most comforting thing within the office was the small wood-burning stove against the outside wall. There was barely enough room for the basic foot locker and the folding chair. The entire room was covered in dust and plenty of cobwebs. Papers and books were scattered over the desk and table, along with various electronic parts that may or may not have belonged to the radio. Conrad immediately bolted for the old radio and eagerly checked it out. When he frowned, Harley knew the prognosis wasn't good.

"I doubt if I can repair this," Conrad remarked, sounding defeated.

They heard a loud bang, like an explosion, outside the hangar, startling them. Conrad and Harley bolted from the office and across the hangar to the outside world. The old portable generator rumbled as it sat not far from the jeep, with its hood up and jumper cables attached to the battery. Damon sat partially behind the wheel, trying to start the old military vehicle, which repeatedly backfired, sounding like bombs exploding. Harley was surprised the older generator even ran. Thinking he could start the jeep sounded a little far-fetched. The jeep engine sputtered several times as it tried to stay running. Damon pumped the gas, revving it, attempting to keep it alive like a patient on a respirator. It finally ran but continued sputtering, taking its last breaths. Damon jumped out, approached the engine, and fiddled under the hood.

"What does he intend to do?" Conrad demanded. "Drive to Hawaii?"

Whatever he did, the engine now ran more smoothly and sputtered less. Damon removed the jumper cables, let the hood slam shut, and climbed back inside. He grinned and motioned for them to join him.

"I call shotgun!" Harley cried out, then smiled while approaching and climbed into the front passenger seat.

Conrad frowned and shook his head. "No, thanks," he muttered, apparently valuing his life. "I'll catch the next one."

Damon slipped into a pair of aviator sunglasses that he found on the dashboard, looked at Harley, and raised a brow.

"You may want to fasten your seat belt and tighten your bra straps," he announced while grinning a little too proudly.

Before she could even comment or react, Damon stepped on the gas, and the jeep burned out. Harley screamed and fumbled with her seat belt as they headed for a wide path on the steep hillside. When they didn't slow, Harley panicked, clutching at anything she could grab onto. Did he even know where he was going?

"Do the brakes work?" she gasped, her eyes wide in horror.

Damon's expression dropped as he looked at her. "I don't know."

As the jeep flew down the steep, narrow slope, both screamed. Plant life slapped the sides of the jeep as they flew past. They bounced in the jeep down the path, which was now becoming increasingly rocky, possibly from years of washout. The backside of the latrine and shower building came into view directly before them. Damon hit the brakes and made a sharp turn to avoid the toilets. Harley screamed while Damon laughed.

"They work," Damon teased while briefly glancing at her. "I was just fucking with you."

They hit a large bump just before the woods' edge, and the jeep was airborne. Both screamed again as the jeep flew from the jungle and landed roughly on the beach. Damon hit the brakes, and they skidded in a half circle, sending sand flying out from under the tires. Harley just barely caught her breath when Damon planted his foot on the gas pedal and thrust the gear shifter. Sand flew behind the tires, burning out only a second before they rocketed across the beach. They flew past James, Tyler, and Randall, who instinctively turned when they heard a vehicle. Damon honked the horn, grinned, and gave them the middle finger while flying past them. The three men stared at them, mouths hanging open, as they flew past. Damon laughed, enjoying himself possibly for the first time that Harley had seen. Harley, on the other hand, clung to the bar before her as if her life depended upon it. When they reached the far side of the island, the jeep sputtered and slowed to a stop. Damon lifted his sunglasses and stared at the gas gauge with childlike disappointment.

"Awe--"

Harley was slightly dazed and a little shaken. "Thank God that's over with."

Damon frowned and glanced around the beach before eyeing Harley with a serious look. "Do you remember passing a gas station?"

Chapter 11

Late afternoon. As Harley returned to the yacht with the others, Damon's comment about an approaching storm drew her attention to the changing weather from that morning. The sun hung high and aggressive overhead, the glaring sunshine turning the white sand almost blindingly bright. Palm tree fronds rustled more noticeably in a steady, warm breeze that had picked up since that morning, feeling charged and carrying the faded scent of distant rain and a heavier humidity that Harley could feel weighing heavily on her skin. The ocean had lost some of its glassy calm, and the waves were larger now, breaking with a recurring crash. Farther out, swells built subtly on the horizon with a thin haze of moisture in the air. The sky was an intense cobalt blue, allowing the sun to shine unhindered, but high above, the mare's tails had multiplied and spread. Scattered, puffy white clouds had grown taller since morning, some developing flat tops, signs of increasing instability and updrafts.

Although Damon showed little reaction as they approached the stranded yacht, Harley noticed subtle changes in his body language every time he looked out at the horizon. It was the same thing he was doing yesterday afternoon, and now she knew why. When she glanced at Conrad, he was staring at the horizon with renewed interest as well.

§

After dinner, Harley felt the pangs of hunger for the first time. As she walked onto the deck with Ivy, she could tell the young woman wasn't herself; her usually bright smile was replaced with a defeated frown.

"I'm still hungry," Ivy groaned to Harley. "I think we only got half of what the guys got tonight. I get that we need fewer calories than men, but this is just plain ridiculous."

Harley drew a deep breath and held it a moment before sighing. "Conrad said he was going to talk to Brian this evening," she remarked. "He thinks they're purposely withholding something from us."

"About the rescue?" Ivy asked, now concerned. "Like, maybe there isn't one?"

"I hope that's not the case," Harley muttered. "But not being able to reach anyone by radio could be why they're rapidly cutting the rations. They need the food to last longer than anticipated."

"What about those pouches we found in the crates at the barracks?" Ivy asked. "Do you think they're still edible?"

"Conrad seems to think so," Harley replied.

"I say we take a little walk up there and have ourselves a high-carb buffet," Ivy announced.

As they walked the deck, they heard Conrad talking with the captain. Although Harley could be wrong, Conrad sounded a little annoyed. She stopped Ivy just before the bow so they could listen without being seen.

"The barracks are far enough from the beach, have everything we need, and are the perfect shelter in the event of a storm," Conrad remarked to the captain.

"It does sound pretty ideal," Brian added while studying Shawn, who stood before them.

"We're in the tropics, Conrad," Shawn reminded him. "There are storms out at sea all the time. I see weather conditions like this every other day."

"All I'm suggesting is that we hike up there for tonight," Conrad insisted. "What would it hurt?"

Shawn groaned and shook his head. "We're better off staying here onboard," he informed him. "The ship is secure, and we can batten down the hatches if it comes to that. This ship was designed to withstand minor tropical storms."

"Maybe," Conrad snapped back. "But not with a hole the size of a Volkswagen in its hull and hugging a boulder."

"This conversation is over, Conrad," Shawn announced. "We don't need your unfounded paranoia infecting the others. No one is leaving this ship tonight. That's a direct order. See if you can follow it better than you did my earlier one about staying on the beach."

"Exploring the island for water and other necessities?" Conrad asked with a slight snarl in his tone. "I understand your concern for our safety, but we took Damon along for protection. And, I'd like to remind you, we found plenty of food and water to last us months on our little ***unauthorized*** stroll, which is more than what you found."

"That's insubordination," Shawn scoffed. "You don't talk to your captain that way."

"Your ship is grounded," Conrad informed him. "We're on solid land. Your authority is only as good as your leadership now."

Harley walked around the corner at that moment with Ivy in tow. She needed to back up whatever Conrad said or did next. To her surprise, she saw Damon leaning on the bow railing, his back to them, watching the island, but Harley was almost positive he was listening to every word. Maybe, he already had Conrad's back. It was difficult to tell. Brian couldn't even look Harley and Ivy in the eyes, keeping his gaze down at the deck. It was possible he agreed with Conrad but minded his place. The captain seemed slightly tense, now that he had an audience. Shawn cleared his throat and straightened proudly.

"First thing tomorrow morning, we'll check out the barracks you found," Shawn informed Conrad. "I advise everyone to stick close to the ship tonight out of caution, in the event there is a storm approaching." He raised his brows, looking from Harley to Conrad. "Does that sound like a fair deal?"

Conrad didn't appear happy, but he reluctantly nodded. "I suppose it'll have to do," he replied, then turned, collected Harley and Ivy, and guided them further down the deck just out of earshot of the captain and Brian. "I want the two of you to pack a small bag, just in case. Will you do that for me?"

Both nodded.

Chapter 12

That evening, patches of blue sky still lingered but dissolved quickly as heavy, towering clouds advanced from the horizon, their anvil-shaped tops glowing white as sunlight struggled to pierce through, while their undersides were now dark, purple-gray, churning with turbulence. As the storm approached, a solid wall of darkness emerged, dense and drab at the base, while rain was visible in the distance. The once gentle turquoise shallows were now choppier, with waves four feet or more crashing onto the shore in powerful, foaming surges, striking the rock and the yacht. The rhythmic crash of breakers was louder, more insistent, as the white sand was now whipped by gusting winds that bent palm fronds sharply to the side. Trees leaned dramatically, their trunks groaning and fronds thrashing while scattered debris tumbled along the shore. The air was thick with humidity and charged with the promise of lightning as distant thunder rumbled.

Harley and Ivy leaned on the railing on the ship's bow and stared at the choppy waves crashing onto shore. The gusty wind whipping their hair. Damon's theory of an approaching storm was now a frightening reality. The thick and moist air weighed heavily against Harley's skin as she watched the last streaks of sunlight succumb to the increasing storm clouds. Neither woman spoke, seeming preoccupied with what they'd heard earlier on deck. After a long moment of silence, Ivy finally spoke, possibly attempting to take her mind off the approaching storm.

"I would kill for a lobster dinner," Ivy announced.

"There might be fishing poles on board," Harley remarked. "Not exactly lobster, but maybe we can do a little fishing tomorrow."

"Yeah, I wouldn't mind fish either," Ivy replied, then made a face. "And I hate fish." She groaned softly. "God, I'm so hungry. If I knew they intended to starve us tonight, I would have snagged one of those vintage MREs Damon found."

"Hang in there," Harley announced with a sigh. "You and I are hiking up there tomorrow and having a mini feast."

"Until then, I'm heading inside and having a couple of drinks," Ivy replied with a low groan. "At least they're not rationing those."

"Of course not," Harley muttered. "I'll catch up with you in a few."

As Ivy walked away, Conrad approached and leaned on the railing alongside Harley. He stared at the beach, remaining silent for a moment.

"Almost makes one forget their troubles, doesn't it?" Conrad finally announced.

"Unfortunately, mine's stranded here with me," Harley muttered, then indicated the approaching storm that was still a couple of hours away. "Think Damon is right? Will that storm reach us?"

"He probably knows more about the weather than I do," Conrad remarked, then managed a tiny chuckle. "I'm more of an 'indoors' kind of guy. As long as it doesn't get too rough, we'll be fine if we stay inside."

While they stood another moment on deck in silence, Harley noticed Randall slipping out of the lounge and almost out of view. When he removed what looked like a woman's compact mirror from his pocket, Harley squinted, attempting to see what he was up to. Conrad noticed her actions and looked as well.

"What is he doing?" Harley asked, bewildered by the bizarre behavior of some.

Conrad frowned and looked back over the railing, minding his own business. "Cocaine," he muttered.

"What?" Harley asked.

"He's snorting cocaine," Conrad informed her. "I thought there was something a little ***off*** about that guy. I wouldn't have guessed drugs."

Harley groaned softly and leaned on the railing, now minding her own business as well.

"We should have flown," Harley muttered, causing Conrad to chuckle. There was an unusual moment of silence. "Conrad--?"

Conrad appeared distracted for a moment, then came back to life. "Hmm?"

"What happens if we're stuck here for a long time?" she asked. "I mean, how long before Ivy and I become the objects of castaway lust?"

"I'm afraid I don't understand," Conrad remarked, giving her his full attention.

"What's the breaking point?" she asked. "When do nice men become sex starved animals?"

"For some, a few short hours will do," Conrad teased, then turned serious and sighed. "Most decent men could sustain years, if necessary."

"But what about men like Damon and Tyler?" Harley asked. "Tyler's a walking gland already, and Damon, well, we don't want to go there."

Conrad placed his hand on hers and smiled. "I think you're worrying over nothing," he insisted. "Your biggest concern is James. He already believes you're going to marry him, and he'll be after you day and night if you don't tell him it's not happening."

"I can't tell him now," she informed him. "He'll have Damon kill me. Disposing of a body around here would be very easy."

"James wouldn't dare have you killed," Conrad insisted. "I'd never allow that."

Harley smiled warmly and patted Conrad's face. "I love how you look out for me," she announced.

"Habit," Conrad replied. "I've been doing it since you were in diapers."

Chapter 13

The sky began rapidly darkening after Conrad and Harley had gone inside. By dusk, the last of the blue sky had vanished, and the horizon was engulfed with a massive wall of dark, towering clouds, turning from gray to black with unnatural greenish undersides. Lightning flashed frequently within the clouds hovering over the ocean, followed by cracks of thunder that shook the heavens. The sharp drop in pressure thickened the salty air, the overhead sky pressing down heavily just before the first squalls of rain swept in ahead of the main system. Waves surged higher, crashing to shore with explosive force. Palm tree fronds whipped violently, rain lashed horizontally, visibility dropped, and the beach became a wild place, raw power replacing serenity. The once turquoise sea turned gray and chaotic under Mother Nature's fury. It was a rapid, primeval shift from tropical utopia to nature's raw display, beautiful but commanding respect.

Inside the lounge, passengers and crew tried to block out the storm's roar, but whipping gusts and sporadic thunderclaps kept breaking through, reminding them that Mother Nature was in charge. At the center table, James, Tyler, and Randall played Bridge, slapping down cards in deliberate rhythm against the rising howl outside. Harley and Ivy occupied the sofa, making small talk in an attempt to block out the sounds of the storm. Conrad, who sat in a plush chair not far from them, held an open book that he hadn't even read a single sentence. He was quite possibly annoyed with himself for not pressing harder for an evacuation, and was silently cursing 'Captain Queeg' for being such an idiot. Damon, always watchful, sat in a chair near the window, staring out at the rapidly intensifying storm. Brian hung out at the bar, talking with Lester, who stood behind it, fixing another round of drinks. Shawn approached Brian and talked quietly with his men.

The faint creak of the ship was barely audible above the wind and rain. Damon eyed his glass of whiskey on the window ledge. The contents were now slanted. He aggressively picked up the glass, drained it, and then returned it to the ledge. He stood and left the lounge without a word. Several watched him out of curiosity. Shawn said something to his first officer. Brian immediately grabbed his raincoat, slipped into it, and headed outside as well. Harley glanced at Conrad, silently questioning what they had just witnessed. Conrad stared at the door for only a moment, then approached her.

"I need to return to my room for something," Conrad informed her. "Do you need anything from your cabin while I'm out?"

Although she was surprised that Conrad was about to venture out onto the deck to go to his room, she didn't question him. Harley knew Conrad was up to something, and it was best just to let him be.

"No, thanks."

Conrad gave a slight nod, then left the lounge. Every nerve in Harley's body seemed to twitch at once as an overwhelming feeling of dread swept through her. Perhaps it was Conrad's behavior that unnerved her. Was it his reaction to Damon's sudden departure? The conversation between the captain and his crew? Or maybe Brian's hasty retreat? Conrad returned after only ten minutes. He was completely soaked and enraged in a way Harley had never witnessed before.

"The ship is secure, is it?" Conrad shouted, catching everyone's attention as he practically lunged for the captain at the bar. "You knew what was going on out there. We need to leave the ship at once!"

Harley immediately sprang to her feet at his startling outburst.

"There's no immediate danger," Shawn assured him. "Brian's just packing some supplies in case we need to leave."

As Harley approached Conrad at the bar, Ivy leapt from the sofa and insecurely clung to Harley's arm, remaining close to her.

"What's going on?" Ivy asked. "What's Conrad talking about?"

"The ship's moving against the rock," Shawn replied, downplaying the issue. "The ocean undertow is pulling the sand away." He looked back at Conrad and adopted a commanding tone. "Stop upsetting the other passengers with your paranoia. The most likely outcome is that we'll become more deeply embedded in the sand. There's nothing to worry about."

The ship groaned and shifted, momentarily throwing everyone off balance. Conrad caught Harley, keeping her from falling. Ivy screamed, clinging to Conrad as well, after losing her balance. James, Tyler, and Randall grabbed onto the table as their drinks crashed to the floor.

James was the first of the men to spring up from the table. "I'd say you're mistaken," he scoffed.

"There's no reason to panic," Shawn insisted more loudly while standing, attempting to stop the fear before it began. "We're perfectly safe."

"Thanks for your professional opinion," Conrad announced. "But I think Harley and I will be collecting our bags and abandoning ship."

Harley attempted to leave with Conrad when James caught her arm, stopping her.

"Maybe you should stay here with me," James insisted, sounding concerned.

"Maybe you should be packing your own bags," Harley replied, then hurried for the door after Conrad, who was waiting for her.

"Wait for me!" Ivy called out and ran after her.

As Harley and Ivy followed Conrad onto the deck, both were alarmed by what they saw. The ocean appeared almost chaotic and dangerous, not more than an hour after they'd gone into the lounge. The waves had built steeply before breaking hard with white foam and explosive spray, striking the rock and the yacht's side. It wasn't just the angrily crashing waves, but the rain poured down on a slant and almost immediately soaked them. The ship moaned loudly, startling both women. Harley and Ivy attempted to block the fierce wind while struggling to walk along the increasingly slippery deck behind Conrad. All three clung to the railing for added support, trying not to fall.

"My God!" Ivy cried out, practically shocked by the storm's intensity.

Despite how bad it sounded from within the lounge, it was a thousand times worse when they saw it up close and personal. After an incredible struggle to walk along the slippery, slanting deck, they finally reached Ivy's cabin. Harley helped her with the door, keeping it from being ripped off its hinges.

"Grab your bag and meet us at the ladder," Conrad shouted to Ivy above the wind and the roar of the raging ocean.

Ivy nodded and pushed her door shut with some effort. Conrad ushered Harley along the deck to her cabin door and just about shoved her into the room. He grabbed her bag and practically threw it into her arms.

"Collect Ivy and wait for me by the ladder," Conrad instructed. "I'll only be a minute."

"Are you sure?" she asked. "Maybe I should wait for you."

"My room is right next door," Conrad replied. "I don't want you waiting here. Get to the ladder. Hurry."

Conrad hurried to the door and opened it for her. As soon as he shut the door behind her, he headed for his cabin just one door down. Harley clung to her bag while clutching the railing and returned to Ivy's cabin. She promptly pounded on her door. Ivy opened the door with her bag clutched in her arms.

"We need to go," Harley announced.

"I'm scared," Ivy practically sobbed. "We're never going to make it."

The ship again groaned, sending a deep vibration beneath their feet. Ivy gasped and darted onto the deck with Harley. They continued along the deck together, clinging to their bags, the railing, and each other. As they reached the opening, Damon ascended the rope ladder, seemingly appearing from the depths of the ocean. Despite being startled by his sudden appearance, they could do little more than stare at him.

"We need to get you to the beach now," Damon announced loudly over the nearly deafening sounds of the ocean and the storm. "The current's getting rough."

Both women looked over the railing at the already tall waves. Ivy started sobbing, clutching her bag with both arms.

"We're never going to make it," Ivy cried, no longer able to control her emotions and becoming hysterical. "We're going to drown!"

Damon grabbed two life jackets from the nearby bench compartment and tossed one to Harley. He didn't say a word to Ivy; instead, he pulled the bag from her arms and, without patience or compassion, physically stuffed her into the life preserver. Ivy didn't seem to know if she was coming or going at that point. Once he had her securely in the vest, he shoved her bag back into her arms. When he turned to Harley, she dropped her bag and quickly put on the life preserver, not wanting him to physically put it on her as he had Ivy. While she did that, Damon grabbed a rope and tied it around Ivy's waist as she stifled her sobs. He measured fifteen feet, then easily sliced through the rope with a Bowie knife Harley didn't even know he had. Damon replaced the knife in his boot and then approached Harley and tied the end around her waist, showing no mercy regarding personal space. He tied the ends of both ropes around his own mid-section and headed for the rope ladder, tugging them along like dogs on a leash.

"I have to wait for Conrad," Harley shouted above the nearly deafening storm, attempting to stop him from pulling her.

Damon paused on the rope ladder and glared at her through the pouring rain and sprays of waves that struck him.

"Get your ass on this ladder," Damon snarled. "You can either climb on your own or be dragged. Your choice."

Damon had to yank on Ivy's rope several times before she climbed onto the ladder with the strap of her bag over her neck and shoulder, leaving her hands free. Harley wanted to wait for Conrad, but she feared Damon would carry through with his threat and pull her in. The knot on the rope was so tight and well-tied that there was no way she was loosening it before he'd pull her into the water behind him. She reluctantly climbed onto the rope ladder behind Ivy with her bag over her neck and shoulder as well. The entire scene was frightening and chaotic. Harley wasn't even sure when she reached the water with the way the waves crashed against her, beating her against the side of the ship. Her knuckles struck the hull more than once while gripping the rope ladder. She barely felt the pain or the stinging of the salt water in the bleeding scrapes on her knuckles. When her feet touched the ocean floor, she knew she was finally in the water, but the waves picked her up and attempted to cast her forward and back against the side of the ship.

Harley almost struck the ship when she felt something tug harshly at her waist, pulling her away. Ivy was screaming over and over, "Oh, God!" Harley could barely see the young woman practically alongside her as the waves relentlessly crashed against her, attempting to push her off her feet. She clung to the rope in front of her as a barely visible Damon trudged through the heavy surf with the rope wrapped around each hand, keeping them from tearing into his abdomen, as he guided the women through the rough waters to shore. Neither woman was able to maintain their balance for long, fighting the waves attempting to claim them into the depths of the ocean. As they closed in on shore, Damon didn't stop, practically dragging them onto the sand as they fought to keep their legs under them. Each time they tried, the undertow attempted to pull them back out, knocking them down.

Both women were partially dragged and partially crawled onto shore far enough to avoid the deadly undertow. Damon immediately sank to his knees, exhausted, but not enough to stop him. He removed the knife from his boot, easily sliced both ropes, rather than wasting time untying the now incredibly tight knots. Damon no sooner replaced the knife in his boot before trudging back into the unruly surf. He only walked a few yards before diving into a large wave and disappearing from view. Harley stared after him a moment, then turned her attention to Ivy, who was coughing up ocean water. Ivy took several deep breaths before giving Harley a thumbs-up in the pouring rain. Harley moved to her feet and frantically attempted to untie the excessively tight knot while shifting her gaze back at the yacht. Where was Conrad? She had to find him!

Harley stared at the violent waves crashing to shore, striking the rock and the ship. She was so focused on the ship that she hadn't even realized Brian was pulling the rowboat, filled with provisions, onto shore. As soon as the boat was secure, he approached them and helped untie the rope around Ivy's waist. Harley already had hers off and waded a few feet into the surf, watching the ship for Conrad. Her heart was pounding as fears of the man, who'd been more of a father to her than her own father, might already be dead. The sinking feeling in her heart was so painful that Harley almost couldn't breathe. At that moment, she spotted Conrad with his duffel bag on the ship's deck near the rope ladder. Harley held her breath as Conrad descended the ladder into the crashing waves.

Conrad wasn't a big man, and she remembered how easily the waves tossed her around. What if he couldn't make the trek? He might be pulled out into the ocean and drown at sea. Conrad didn't have a life preserver either, so once he hit the water, she couldn't spot him amid the violent waves. Damon suddenly appeared on the large rock against the ship. He looked around the water only a moment, then dove back in. Harley held her breath as her eyes widened in fear. She didn't see Conrad anywhere! She should have been able to see him by now! Damon suddenly surfaced, only to be nearly taken back under. He managed to keep his balance and again trudged through the rough water with Conrad's duffel bag over his shoulder. Conrad clung to the rope tied around Damon's waist and trudged through the raging waves behind him.

Harley stifled tears of joy and waded through the rough surf, attempting to reach them. The undertow was too much, and she was left floundering, attempting to maintain her balance. Harley was practically thrown into Damon, who managed to keep her from being pulled under, his arm firmly around her waist. Unable to control her emotions in the highly emotional situation, Harley threw her arms around Damon's neck and kissed him quickly on the lips, then pulled away before even realizing what she'd done. Harley immediately grabbed Conrad's bag, freeing Damon from the weight, and trudged to shore with Conrad. Conrad collapsed to the sand while panting heavily. She'd have to wait until later to find out what exactly had happened to him, but for now, he was alive, and that was all that mattered.

The battered ship creaked loudly against the rock and the relentless, unforgiving waves. The terrifying sound rose above the raging storm. Harley and Conrad spun at the water's edge and looked back in time to see swells and wind drive the yacht free from the rock. Thunderous cracking echoed loudly as the haul was torn apart, scraping past the rock. By the time they had looked back, Damon was already gone, possibly making a return trip to the yacht. There was a flurry of activity on the deck as James and his friends, as well as the captain and Lester, rushed to the ladder in pure anarchy, pushing and shoving their way to climb down next. Cursing and yelling were heard above the roar of the ocean as the situation rapidly deteriorated.

The ship capsized with a long, loud creaking, sounding like a freight train, now on its side in the shallow water. Once it was freed from the rock and the sand, the rough current tossed the yacht forward and backward on its side as if it were a child's toy, scraping sand before being pulled further out, slowly disappearing with the undertow. The remaining five men appeared in the rough water and trudged through the waves, dragging themselves to shore where they eventually collapsed. By the time the men looked back, the ship was completely gone, claimed by the deep, dark sea. The ocean continued to roar as water surged further up the beach, now churning with debris.

"Nothing to worry about, huh?" Tyler scoffed while panting, exhausted, from his position on the sand.

Shawn frowned but didn't respond. Harley continued to scan the surf, the storm turning the tranquil island into a trap as it unleashed its fury.

"Where's Damon?" Harley asked, unable to take her eyes off the violently crashing waves.

"Get everyone to the barracks on top of the hill, Brian," Shawn ordered his man, who was helping Lester pull the small rowboat closer to the forest edge and safety. "I'll look for Damon."

Since the raging storm stopped for no man, James, Tyler, and Randall gathered their bags and followed Brian along the beach to the old jeep trail. Harley, Conrad, and Ivy refused to move even as strong gusts of wind attempted to knock them off their feet. They stared at the embattled rock where the ship was once secured. Despite what they had already witnessed, the storm was just warming up. The wind surged dramatically stronger, hurling rain sideways in stinging sheets that pelted the four on the beach. In addition to the harsh rain, they were being slapped by flying palm fronds that tore loose. Lightning exploded over the water in blinding white cracks, while thunder sounded like repetitive sonic booms, almost as loud as the deafening crash of waves pounding the shore. Despite nearly dying, Harley couldn't deny that nature's wrath was somehow majestic. Damon suddenly appeared on top of the large rock the ship had once occupied.

Ivy saw him and pointed. "Look," she cried out. "There he is!"

Damon sat hunched over on the rock, battered with waves, his arm over his knee as he panted and coughed several times. Shawn motioned for him to join them. Damon waved them onward, indicating he'd be along. It was possible he had nothing left for one last trip to shore, particularly in the strong surf he'd have to maneuver.

Harley wasn't sure how she felt about leaving the beach before Damon made it safely to shore, but it didn't appear as if he was moving anytime soon.

Chapter 14

As the storm raged, the small group trudged up the slightly muddy hillside through the woods. Frequent flashes of lightning illuminated the jungle in brilliant bursts, thunder cracking almost instantly, so violently that Harley felt it travel through her feet and into her chest. The wind had picked up significantly, whipping palm fronds, banana leaves, and thinner branches around her and her shipmates. Gusts of wind pushed against Harley like invisible hands, sudden blasts that forced her to lean forward or even brace, clutching Conrad's hand as he kept her moving. Rain was falling steadily, threatening to pry her fingers from Conrad's slick hand, leaving Harley soaked more than she thought humanly possible. The path was soft under her feet, firm dirt now spongy and slippery, but she could still maintain her brisk pace to keep up with Conrad, tugging her along. Harley grabbed onto anything for balance, not wanting to take Conrad down with her if she fell.

Around her, the jungle was alive with the storm's energy, leaves thrashed wildly, and smaller branches snapped and fell with cracks. Visibility was drastically reduced. Trees were blurred into dark shapes, but she could still make out Conrad and her fellow shipmates on the path ahead. More than once, Harley was consumed with concern for Ivy, since she couldn't see her, but then she'd remember Ivy was safely tucked between Shawn and Lester, trudging along the path behind her. Physically, the relatively short journey was demanding, but instinct pushed Harley and her shipmates onward. It was a frightening race against the worsening weather, reaching cover before Mother Nature unleashed the full force of her fury. They finally reached the clearing and the barracks, practically hidden in the darkness. Brian was the first to enter, followed by James and his friends. The wind blew the pouring rain into the barracks, pushing it several feet inward, drenching the floor. Brian attempted to gather his bearings with the small flashlight, which barely brightened the large interior.

Brian was still fumbling around in the dark with his flashlight when the captain entered with his group, consisting of Conrad, Harley, Ivy, and Lester. Conrad used the dim lighting from Brian's flashlight to find his way to the old lantern he remembered seeing earlier that day. Thankfully, there were matches next to it. He lit the kerosene lamp, brightening the room considerably. Everyone dropped their waterlogged bags as the room brightened and collapsed onto nearby chairs and cots.

"There are dry army fatigues in all the foot lockers," Conrad announced. "We can change into them until our clothes dry."

§

Almost half an hour later, the barracks were brightly lit by several kerosene lamps around the room. Everyone had dried off with the towels they'd found and changed into dry, camouflage fatigues or the solid green shorts and undershirts. The pouring rain on the metal roof echoed so loudly within the barracks that they could barely hold a conversation while only a few feet from each other. The non-stop thunder sounded like a war raging outside their door, and the wind was like a never-ending freight train rolling past, lightly rattling the building. Harley couldn't imagine Damon attempting to make the trek anymore tonight, but she didn't know where he'd seek shelter either. She wasn't sure why she was concerned about him, yet she couldn't understand why the others weren't. Conrad unrolled a mattress for Harley and Ivy, then found flat sheets and pillowcases for them to make their beds. The others followed Conrad's example and, soon after, collapsed into their bunks.

The barracks' door suddenly flew open along with a massive gust of wind that practically ripped it off its hinges. Everyone jumped with surprise and looked at the open door. A waterlogged, mud-covered, and exhausted Damon dragged himself inside and put some effort into shutting the door behind him. He sloshed across the barracks to one of the back, vacant bunks, dropped his soaked duffel bag on the floor, and collapsed on the empty cot, not caring if the mattress became soaked or muddy. Harley watched him for several minutes, but he didn't bother drying off or changing out of his wet clothes. He continued panting and coughing for several minutes before finally falling asleep.

§

Harley woke sometime in the middle of the night, disoriented, and looked around the barracks, only dimly lit by a single lamp turned low. It hadn't been some bad dream after all. She heard coughing, which may have been what woke her. Harley looked across the room to Damon's cot. He was now beneath the sheet on his bunk, and his wet, muddy clothing lay on the floor. Although he appeared to be asleep, he shivered beneath the covers. Harley turned on her side and watched him for a few minutes. His continuous shivering concerned her, fearing pneumonia. She got up, grabbed her blanket, and approached Damon on his cot. She paused near his bunk and gently placed the blanket over him. Damon jerked awake with a gasp and looked at her through the dim lighting. He exhaled, rolled his eyes, and allowed his head to fall back to the pillow.

"Jesus, you scared me," Damon muttered.

"I thought you could use another blanket," Harley whispered, then uncertainly backed up a step. "I didn't mean to startle you."

Damon shivered while huddling beneath the heavier blanket. "Thank you."

Harley knew she owed him more than a warm blanket. Damon risked his own life to save both her and Conrad. How did she even begin to thank him for that? Harley smiled meekly and returned to her bunk. As she slipped under the sheet on her cot, she felt cowardly for not expressing her gratitude properly. There was always tomorrow for heartfelt sentiments, but Damon would go back to being Damon, and she'd return to loathing him. Harley groaned, disgusted with herself.

Chapter 15

Day Three. When Harley stepped outside the barracks into the jungle early that morning, it felt like entering a freshly reborn world, calm and quiet after Mother Nature's wrath. The air was cooler than the previous day but still thick with humidity that carried the purest, cleanest scent imaginable. Thin remnants of storm clouds drifted high while rising steam hovered among the trees. Sunlight caught on millions of water droplets, clinging to every leaf, branch, and spider web, turning the jungle into a glittering cathedral. Harley breathed it in. Deeply. Peacefully. Fallen branches and debris from the storm remained scattered on the ground, reminding her of their harrowing survival. She shivered, remembering the ship's groaning hull and the waves trying to drag them under. She rubbed her chilled arms, trying to shake off the memory.

The sounds of the jungle were alive but peaceful, a sonata of renewal, the rustle of leaves shedding raindrops, and the occasional soft thud of fruit hitting the ground. The cool, moist air on Harley's skin after a night cooped up in the stale, damp barracks felt refreshing, almost sacramental.

It was one of those rare, perfect tropical mornings. She was able to enjoy the quiet morning for another fifteen to twenty minutes before the others stepped out of the barracks, ready to assess the damage and plan their next move. Brian and Lester strung a rope between two trees, creating a makeshift clothesline for everyone to hang their wet clothes and almost everything from their bags. Harley hesitated before hanging her bra on the line alongside the boxers and briefs of men she barely knew. Had it just been Conrad's undergarments, she would have found it somewhat amusing, but that wasn't the case. Ivy joined her and reluctantly hung her bra on the line as close to Harley's undergarments as possible.

"This feels weird, right?" Ivy muttered so only Harley would hear her.

"Thank God," Harley moaned softly. "I'm glad it's not just me."

Both women giggled at their odd insecurities. Conrad approached them wearing his camouflage army fatigues and lace-up military boots. Harley eyed him and attempted to keep from laughing. She rarely saw him without a suit and tie.

"Get it out of your system," Conrad announced, also hiding his smile. "Once all of our clothes are dry, it's back to business as usual."

When Damon approached the line with his bundle of wet, muddy clothing, all three noticed he was wearing his own clothes and not the borrowed army fatigues. They exchanged silent questions.

"I guess someone has a waterproof duffel bag," Conrad muttered. "Wish mine had been. It'll take weeks for my book to dry out."

"I didn't even pack my book," Harley remarked, now disappointed she wouldn't have anything to read, particularly since she didn't know how long they'd be stranded.

"I think I saw some books in one of the foot lockers," Ivy informed her. "Maybe we could look later." There was a moment of hesitation. "You know, after we shower."

"It'll be nice washing off in something other than salt water," Harley muttered.

"And, being the holding pond is rainwater," Conrad remarked. "It'll replenish itself naturally, especially after last night's storm. We certainly won't run out. No rationing necessary."

"And plenty of fucking coffee," Damon muttered, surprising them that he had been listening to their conversation.

They watched Damon light a cigarette as he walked toward the building and reclaimed his 'cup' of coffee that was literally coffee in a cookpot. Apparently, there wasn't a mug big enough for the amount of caffeine he required after last night. As everyone gravitated outside the barracks, some with coffee, the captain approached and called everyone together for a 'meeting'. Lester and Brian had left shortly after hanging the wash line to recover the supplies Brian had towed to shore during the storm.

"We're now in a desperate situation," Shawn announced. "Everyone will need to pitch in and do what they can for our survival while we wait for a rescue. Lester and Brian are bringing the food rations we were able to get off the ship before last night's disaster, and there are some MREs here in the barracks. In addition to that, we're going to need plenty of firewood for cooking, water brought to the camp from the shower house up the hill, fresh food, and whatever else we can find. Lester and Brian are alternating shifts in the small rowboat with some flares to facilitate our rescue."

"I'd be willing to collect firewood," Randall announced. "I'd like to explore the island anyway."

"I remember seeing some fruit further down the path," Ivy informed them. "Maybe if I had some help, I could collect enough."

"I could go with Ivy for the fruit," Tyler remarked, offering a sly sort of smirk.

Ivy rolled her eyes, not exactly crazy at the prospect of spending time alone with Tyler.

"Harley and I will clean the barracks and take inventory of the supplies," Conrad announced a little too enthusiastically.

Harley internally groaned at his volunteering her. He and his cleaning fetish!

Shawn nodded, then looked at James and Damon. "That leaves bringing fresh water down from the shower building and cutting firewood."

Damon eyed the axe sticking out of the old tree stump that had been brought out of the barracks earlier that morning.

Shawn seemed slightly tense at the image of Damon with an axe. "Perhaps I'll cut the firewood."

Damon removed the axe from the stump, slung it over his shoulder, and raised a twisted smile. "I can manage," he insisted.

Everyone exchanged looks after seeing Damon looking a little too ***at home*** with the axe.

"I'm ***not*** toting water," James scoffed.

"Relax, I'll carry the water," Shawn replied with a defeated groan. "You can help Randall collect firewood."

"Oh, joy," James muttered.

Chapter 16

Harley and Conrad pulled everything out of the kitchen cabinets, looking for supplies and taking inventory. In addition to enough cleaning supplies to last a year, there were plenty of other creature comforts. As for provisions, there were more than enough MREs to last them for two or three months, if necessary. In addition to the two cases of MREs, there were four bottles of whiskey, plenty of kerosene for the lamps, which would probably last two months, two cases of coffee, two tubs of powdered creamer, and several bags of rotted sugar. Thankfully, each MRE pouch would have sugar. Sadly, not one damned teabag. The cot linens were kept in a tall metal cabinet, with two sets of sheets for each bunk, several heavier blankets, and two cords of nylon rope. Next, they did an inventory of the foot lockers. Apart from five sets of fatigues in each foot locker, there was also a second pair of boots, five undershirts and briefs, and five pairs of socks.

Each locker had personal items as well, which Harley stacked on one of the cots and counted. Twenty toiletry kits, twenty-five girly magazines, six books, fifteen lighters, eight pocketknives, five Bowie knives in their sheaths, ten flashlights with dead batteries, ten decks of playing cards, two sets of poker chips, two packs of cigarettes, and ten cigars. Since Damon was the only smoker, Harley placed the cigarettes under his pillow. No one needed to know, and, honestly, who would really care? Harley and Conrad had a pleasant conversation while cleaning the barracks. Conrad enjoyed cleaning. More accurately, he enjoyed the feeling of accomplishment when something dirty became clean. While they worked, they could hear Damon chopping wood outside. The sound was continuous, indicating he was hard at work. As Harley returned the neatly folded, slightly musty-smelling linens to the cabinet, Conrad picked up one of the ropes.

"Perhaps we could fix a privacy curtain for you and Ivy," Conrad announced with a knowing smile. "Keep the perverts from sneaking a peek."

"Sounds good to me," Harley replied, happy with the suggestion. "Let me shake out my rag, then I'll help you tie the rope."

Harley stepped outside to the increased sound of wood being chopped. She looked across the clearing and saw Damon splitting logs with the axe. He had removed his shirt and hung it on a nearby branch, along with his shoulder holster. Harley eyed the gun only a moment, then returned her attention to the shirtless man, glistening with sweat, wearing dress pants and black combat boots. She admired him a moment longer, oddly fascinated by the entire scene, then resumed with her task of shaking out her dust rag. When she turned, she saw James sitting against the side of the building, taking a nap. They'd only been working for an hour. How could he possibly be so tired that he needed a nap? Harley returned inside, disgusted, and approached Conrad, who attempted to untangle the rope.

"That lazy bastard's just going to allow everyone else to do the work while he does nothing," she scoffed.

"Who?" Conrad asked.

"James," Harley replied. "Who else?"

Conrad frowned and shook his head, finally untangling the rope. "There's not much you or I can do about that right now," he insisted. "We'll have to let Shawn and Brian deal with him."

"That won't be easy," Harley remarked. "Not with Damon in his corner and Randall and Tyler by his side. How long before James declares himself king and turns the rest of us into his slaves?"

"You have a seriously overactive imagination," Conrad informed her.

"Maybe I have less faith in my fellow man than you do," Harley remarked.

They realized the sound of the axe splitting wood had stopped when they heard Damon shouting angrily. Harley and Conrad immediately bolted for the door and appeared outside in time to see Damon thrusting the axe into the chopping block while glaring at James, who stood only a couple of feet from him, looking a little outraged himself.

"Don't fuck with me," Damon snarled. "I'm not in the mood."

"How dare you talk like that to me?" James scoffed. "I'm still your boss, and you do what I say."

"I do, do I?" Damon demanded. "Well, maybe it's time we renegotiated the terms of my employment."

"Oh, so you want more money, huh?" James snarled, then raised a cocky brow while folding his arms across his chest. "A bonus of some kind, perhaps?"

Damon caught a glimpse of Harley and Conrad near the barracks door. He picked up the axe and held it firmly in both hands while his look remained harsh and unpredictable.

"We can discuss the terms of my employment another time," Damon informed him before sneering. "Will that be all, ***sir***?"

James stared at the axe, then nodded uncertainly. "Yeah, that'll be all."

Damon spun and swung the axe into the log with a little more vigor, easily splitting it in two. Randall suddenly appeared, hurrying into the opening with only a few pieces of firewood in his arms. He was gasping for air and looked behind him as if he were being chased. He dropped the firewood onto the ground and ran trembling fingers through his hair before realizing James, Harley, and Conrad were staring at him.

"Are you okay?" Harley asked.

Randall jerked his head in her direction and stared a moment as if uncertain how to respond. He caught his breath, attempted to relax, and then nodded.

"Uh, yeah," Randall finally announced. "I got a little turned around, that's all."

Without another word, Randall hurried past them for the path that led to the shower building. Only a moment after Randall vanished on the path, Lester and Brian appeared on the trail from the beach with just one duffel bag of the provisions they were supposed to retrieve from the beach. Shawn approached from the direction of the showers with two five-pound containers of water. Seeing his men looking slightly out of sorts, he set down the water and approached them. When he attempted to guide them away to speak privately, Conrad darted across the camp and cornered them.

"Sorry, Shawn," Conrad announced loud enough to catch everyone's attention, including Damon, who stopped chopping wood to hear what he had to say. "With the dramatic shift in our situation, I'm not comfortable with you and your men discussing things that involve the entire group without us hearing what's being said."

Shawn stared at Conrad a moment, possibly prepared to lecture him as he had on the ship, when he saw Damon resting the axe against his shoulder and lightly cocking his head, almost arrogantly, as if awaiting the captain's response.

"Fine," Shawn replied and indicated for his men to speak freely.

"When we arrived on the beach, all of the provisions in the rowboat were either destroyed or gone," Brian informed them. "It looks like a combination of storm damage and island critters."

There were several groans at the news.

Lester then indicated the duffel bag he carried. "We were only able to salvage a couple of bottles of booze, some fishing poles, and the first aid kit."

"What about the flare gun?" James demanded. "And the shotgun?"

"I had the flare gun and four boxes of flares in my bag," Brian informed him. "It was one of the few things I took while abandoning ship."

"I had both shotguns and shells in my bag," Shawn informed them before frowning. "My bag was lost at sea during the storm."

"The rowboat and ores are intact," Brian assured them. "We can still row away from the island with the flare gun and signal any passing ships for help."

"Why would you need to ***wait*** for passing ships?" Conrad asked, now skeptical. "I thought our SOS was received, and rescue parties were looking for us."

"Nothing has changed," Shawn assured them. "A rescue will be along."

"No," Brian finally spoke out, surprising Shawn. He looked back at Conrad. "There was no SOS. The radio malfunctioned along with the rest of the ship's instruments the night we ran aground."

Shawn glared his disapproval at Brian, but his first officer didn't seem to care.

"We have to watch for passing ships," Brian continued. "When we see one, we can signal for help."

Shawn immediately fumbled over himself, attempting to regain control. "There will be rescue ships out there looking for us," he insisted. "When we don't reach port in Hawaii, they'll come looking for us."

"Wait," James suddenly snapped while waving his hands around. "We weren't supposed to dock until sometime tomorrow. Are you telling us no one will even realize we're missing for another day or two?"

The captain nodded and was immediately met with nervous chuckles and disgusted moans.

"They'll find us," Shawn insisted. "It might take a week or so, but they will find us."

"We were off course," Conrad reminded him. "You can't be sure they'd ever find us."

"Don't be infecting the other passengers with your paranoia and worst-case scenarios," the captain snarled at Conrad. "We need to remain positive and continue working together for the good of the group." Shawn took a moment to collect himself. "Now, from what I've seen, there are at least enough MREs in there to last us a month or two. If we start rationing them now, we might be able to stretch that to three or four months. The water supply should last for months if we only use it for drinking and cooking. No showers. We can use the pond further uphill for bathing."

"Are you out of your fucking mind?" Damon bellowed, startling everyone, finally chiming in and slamming the axe into the stump. "That pond is your fucking drinking water. You contaminate that, and we're all fucked."

"I don't think--" Shawn began, but was immediately cut off by Conrad.

"You're right," Conrad scoffed. "You don't think. Your authority sank with your ship. Now, you're going to listen to those of us with an IQ over eighty."

Harley smirked, reveling in Conrad's newfound vocal disdain for stupid people in a survival situation.

"We're on a tropical island," Conrad informed the captain. "Fresh water is plentiful. That pond will renew itself just about every night. There's no reason to deprive anyone of daily showers and maintaining a standard of cleanliness. As far as rationing the MREs, there's enough there for two months. There's no reason to cut anyone's caloric intake beyond a normal daily limit. Again, we're on a tropical island. We've seen numerous fruit-bearing trees, and there's a ton of fish out in that ocean. We're not starving anytime soon." Conrad straightened proudly. "There you have it. My worst case scenario and paranoia, at its finest."

Damon smirked and snorted a laugh before returning to his chores. Harley 'slow clapped' Conrad's outburst. Shawn sneered before casting a look at his men. Brian and Lester remained silent and avoided his gaze. The captain silently fumed and stormed off. Harley approached Conrad and kissed him dramatically on the cheek, then patted his shoulder.

"That uniform brings out the beast in you," Harley informed him, unable to hide her grin.

When she caught a glimpse of Damon eyeing them between splitting logs, Harley tensed slightly before returning her attention to Conrad.

"Actually, the shorts are incredibly itchy, and the shirt feels like cardboard," Conrad announced. "Apparently, the U.S. Army never heard about fabric softener."

Harley couldn't help but laugh at Conrad's expense. The man was possibly more pampered than she ever was. Ivy stormed back to camp, nearly colliding with Lester and Brian, who were returning to the beach for the rescue ship patrol in the small rowboat. Both eyed the clearly annoyed young woman but didn't stop to question her. She immediately approached Harley and Conrad with her empty sack.

"Everything okay?" Harley asked while eyeing her empty bag. "Did you need some help reaching the fruit?"

"I had help," Ivy scoffed. "But he wasn't reaching for fruit."

Tyler returned to camp a moment after, eyed Ivy with Harley and Conrad, and then headed for the barracks past Damon, who seemed to be assessing the current situation.

"What did he do?" Harley asked, groaning.

"Would you like me to have a word with him?" Conrad asked. "My shorts are just itchy enough that I might be able to take him in a fair fight."

Ivy eyed Conrad, somewhat puzzled by the comment. She then frowned and shook her head. "No, I handled it," she huffed. "That man is a pig, and I hate that he doesn't take a hint." She considered her comment. "Or flat out 'no'. Next time, I'll flatten his boys."

"I never should have let you go alone with him," Harley scoffed. "He'd never pull that shit with you while I'm around."

"That's because your father is someone he either respects or fears," Ivy informed her. "I don't have a family name or money, so he sees me as less of a person. Low hanging fruit."

"That's unacceptable," Harley insisted, then glanced at Conrad. "Options?"

"Castration is the easiest, most effective solution," Conrad replied.

Both women eyed him with raised brows.

"Sorry," he replied. "That's the starched shorts talking." Conrad then considered it a moment longer. "I think the three of us need to get him alone and have a real conversation with him about his advances. Stand in solidarity against his behavior, and let him know it won't be tolerated." He hesitated a moment. "Then we threaten to castrate him."

"Maybe we start with the first part," Harley informed her friend, then looked back at Ivy. "Guys like Tyler have reputations to uphold. Maybe he doesn't feel threatened by you, but he'll think twice knowing I'd ruin his reputation when we get home if he doesn't play nice."

"Might just make him mad," Ivy muttered.

"We need to end his harassment before it escalates," Harley insisted.

Ivy finally nodded. "You're right."

§

Tyler remained in the barracks the rest of the morning, possibly taking a nap. When it was getting close to lunchtime, Conrad, Harley, and Ivy decided to have their 'intervention' with the man while he was alone. Tyler was sitting up in his bunk with his head resting against the wall, enjoying his nap.

"We'd like to have a word with you," Conrad announced as they approached his bunk.

Tyler briefly opened his eyes, groaned softly, and again shut them. "What do you want, Conrad?" he softly demanded.

"It's not what I want," Conrad informed him. "It's what *we* want."

Tyler opened his eyes, saw Harley and Ivy, and again groaned. Conrad sat on the bunk across from him while both women remained standing, attempting to look intimidating, their arms folded across their chests and their heads held high.

"We might be here for a while," Conrad continued in a firm but forceful tone. "And while we're stranded here, your harassment of Harley and Ivy will not be tolerated. You will be respectful toward them, or you will not speak to either of them. I know you think you're untouchable, but I'm telling you here and now that you're not. I don't think I have to explain the many ways a man in your position can be ruined. We'd appreciate it if you don't force our hand."

Tyler eyed Conrad but refused to look at Harley or Ivy. "I promise to keep my hands to myself," he muttered. "I promise to behave." His eyes again shut. "Now, will you leave me alone?"

Conrad eyed Harley and Ivy, who both were somewhat puzzled, more than relieved.

"As you wish," Conrad replied.

Chapter 17

Day Four. After a high-calorie, high-carb breakfast of army MREs, Harley and Ivy hiked to a pond they'd found a short walk from camp yesterday evening. Naturally, Conrad went along to look after the women. Both women wore their bikinis, since Conrad would be the only man at the pond with them, and he hoped to catch some fish for their lunch. Brian would undoubtedly bring some fish back closer to dinnertime when he returned from his shift in the rowboat, but that wouldn't do them any good for lunch. With only two fishing poles and ten people, they weren't sure how they'd ration the catch of the day. Yesterday's ocean catch was only two decent-sized fish, which didn't divide evenly among ten people.

Despite Conrad giving the captain a verbal lashing yesterday, Shawn was still attempting to rule the roost, now micromanaging the fresh fish his men caught. That's when Conrad decided to catch his own fish, and the pond would be a good starting point. The bathing pond they'd found was roughly the size of a hotel swimming pool, but much deeper near the middle, and surrounded by raw beauty. Large boulders formed a natural barrier around the light, turquoise water, while ferns, palms, and other foliage grew among the rocks, lending a tropical beauty rarely seen. The crowning glory was the twenty-foot-tall, ten-foot-wide waterfall, plummeting downward, hiding a small grotto. The clearing surrounding the pond was large enough that the sun glistened off the water throughout most of the day, leaving the area sunny without being too hot. The pond was accessible via the stream, past several large rocks, for zero-entry. Although the fastest, easiest way to enter the pond was to climb down from the rocks along the edge.

After swimming around for nearly twenty minutes, Harley and Ivy leaned against a ledge of rocks and hung out, gossiping. The lighthearted conversation turned more serious as Ivy sank into a darker world.

"Do you suppose Paul thinks I'm dead?" Ivy finally asked what was actually on her mind.

"No, of course not," Harley insisted. "We were supposed to be docking in Hawaii sometime today. At the moment, no one even suspects that we're missing."

"Okay," Ivy replied with a soft huff. "What about tomorrow? He's going to think I'm dead."

"Eventually, he might," Harley admitted. "But we have a better chance of being rescued starting tomorrow. When they finally realize we never made it to port." The captain's lie stung a little when she thought about it. "A few hours after we're overdue, they're going to start searching for us. By tomorrow, everyone will be scanning the ocean looking for our ship."

"But our ship's at the bottom of the ocean," Ivy reminded her while holding back her tears.

"Which is why Lester and Brian are taking shifts in the rowboat from sunup to sunset," Harley added. "They have the flare gun, and they'll flag down any passing ships. Ships looking for us." Harley offered a warm, sympathetic smile. "Paul will be waiting for you to come back home, and your romantic reunion will be on the news, in the papers, and all over the internet."

Ivy managed a tiny smile, but something seemed *off*. "Paul didn't propose," she finally admitted.

"Well, you did say you were ***practically*** engaged," Harley reminded her. "I assumed that meant ***not yet official***."

"No," Ivy replied with a heavy, defeated sigh. "I thought he was going to propose on our trip, but he didn't. When he invited the other couple we'd met to join us every day, the trip no longer felt romantic." She hesitated. "When I brought it up, he said we were there to have fun, and that we always spend time alone together at home. He spent the next two days doing guy stuff with his new friend and seemed to completely forget I existed."

Ivy's admission was heartbreaking for Harley to hear. She had no idea what Ivy had been dealing with before their shipwreck.

"Sometimes, men can be like that," Harley replied with a soft sigh. "My dad never had time for my mom, but he always had time for his pals at the country club."

"When he was surfing with his new friend," Ivy announced, a quiver in her voice. "I saw a text come through on his phone. It was from a woman. The part I saw, she said she ***missed*** him."

"That's not necessarily anything," Harley reminded her. "If you didn't see the whole message, it's easy to take it out of context."

"After he saw the message, he texted back and forth for nearly an hour," Ivy informed her. "On our way back to the room, he told me there was an emergency at work, and he had to return home right away."

"Oh," Harley replied somewhat timidly, not sure what to say to that.

"After he left, I called his boss with some lame excuse that he forgot something on his rush back to the office," Ivy announced. "His boss said he didn't call him back for any emergency."

"I'm sorry, Ivy," Harley replied softly. "But if he could do that to you, you're better off without him."

"I know," Ivy whispered. "But I thought he loved me. I thought we would be getting married in a year or two." She stared at Harley for a long moment. "What if he's happy I'm gone?"

"Then he's an asshole," Harley announced firmly. "And you shouldn't lose a moment of sleep over someone like that."

"What if no one else wants me?"

Harley was a bit surprised by the question. "What are you talking about?" she just about demanded. "You're a beautiful young woman. You can have your pick of just about any man. Why would you think you're not every man's fantasy?"

Ivy shrugged with little emotion. "I was never really popular in school," she replied. "I wasn't asked out a lot. Paul was my first real boyfriend."

"Sounds like Paul was putting you down because you were too good for him," Harley huffed.

Ivy considered the comment, then eyed Harley. "You know, he kind of did do that," she remarked. "We're about the same age, you and I. Why does it seem like you're so much wiser?"

"My father may have been an asshole," Harley remarked, then indicated Conrad across the pond. "But I was raised by a very intelligent man."

When Harley and Ivy looked at Conrad, he stared at the hook on his fishing pole and the worm in his hand as if he'd never seen either before.

"Harley," Conrad announced. "Can you show me again how to impale the worm with the hook?"

Harley glanced at Ivy and smiled. "This is his first real experience in nature," she announced. "Until now, he's actually only read about it."

Chapter 18

Although Conrad only caught two fish, he was proud of his first-ever catch. James joined Conrad, Harley, and Ivy at the official 'cleaning of the fish' ceremony. All four stood around the tree stump and stared at the two fish in the partially filled basin on the massive cutting board. Conrad held the boning knife from the kitchen in his hand and seemed to be considering his options.

"Any suggestions?" Conrad asked James and the women.

"Aren't you supposed to cut the heads off and gut them, or something?" James asked.

Conrad casually extended the knife to James. James refused to take it and held his hands in the air.

"We can ask Randall when he comes back," James insisted. "He's the outdoors man, not me."

All four continued to stare at the fish that seemed to be staring back. Damon walked past, hesitated, and then returned to the stump, also eyeing the fish. He finally removed the Bowie knife from his boot, flipped it in his hand, and removed the first fish from the basin, slapping it on the cutting board.

"Step one," Damon announced. "Descaling."

All four watched as Damon held the fish by the tail and used the serrated edge of his Bowie knife to swiftly remove its scales. He did the second side, then rinsed the fish before slapping it back on the cutting board.

"Step two," Damon continued. "Gutting. Light but precision slice from groin to throat."

As Damon swiftly created an incision along the fish's underbelly, Ivy grimaced and walked away. When he started scooping out the innards with his fingers, James groaned, held his stomach, and left. Harley remained, although making a face pretty similar to the one Conrad was making.

"Step three," Damon announced. "Decapitation."

Damon placed his knife just behind the fish's gill on the first side and put some weight behind the knife. It made a hideous crunching sound as he sliced the head halfway before flipping the fish and doing the same to the other side. As the head rolled from the cutting board to the ground, Harley groaned and walked away as well. Conrad looked slightly sickened, especially considering he had a tough time hooking the worm. Damon placed the cleaned, beheaded fish into the basin and removed the second one, slapping it onto the gut-covered cutting board. He extended his Bowie knife to Conrad and proudly indicated the second fish. Conrad appeared slightly sickened while slowly accepting the knife.

§

Despite the fact that Conrad looked like a serial killer with his messy hands and gooey fish guts smeared across his shirt, he had successfully cleaned his first fish. When Lester returned with two more fish of his own, it made for larger portions for everyone. Considering Brian was out in the boat, possibly catching his own fish, and Randall was still out gathering wood, a second seating for lunch worked perfectly. With the large bunch of bananas Damon had brought back, they had enough food for lunch without touching the MREs. When Damon took a second banana, Shawn gave him a shaming look.

"We should be rationing those," Shawn insisted. "One per meal per person."

Damon glared at the captain, cocked his head, and pointed the banana at him like a loaded weapon. "Tell me what to do again when it comes to food I bring to the table, and I'll shove this right up your ass."

Shawn stared after Damon with his mouth hanging open and watched him walk away. Harley removed one of the thirty remaining bananas and glared at the captain as well, but he didn't notice her dirty stare.

§

When it was time for dinner, Conrad approached the crates within the small kitchen with their supply of MREs. He had spent some time organizing the meals so there would be two entrée choices each meal, bringing about some normalcy to mealtime. He knew exactly how many meals they started with and exactly how long the pouches would last at three meals per day. By skipping lunch for a fresher option, they put themselves ahead by one meal. When he went to grab the ten pouches for dinner, something appeared off. As Conrad counted the pouches, Harley entered the barracks. It wasn't as if she were eager for her MRE that evening, but she preferred to stick close to her friend and assist where she could. Conrad abruptly straightened and eyed Harley, clearly concerned.

"Something wrong?" she asked.

"We're missing several pouches," Conrad announced, still somewhat stunned.

"Think someone got hungry and helped themselves?" Harley asked.

"There's at least fifteen missing," Conrad informed her while shaking his head, disgusted. "Fifteen since this morning."

"Who would take fifteen MREs?" Harley practically demanded.

"I don't know," Conrad remarked. "But it has me concerned. Obviously, it wasn't someone who was just hungry. No one needs fifteen MREs. They'd be blocked up for a week."

Harley grimaced. "Do we tell the captain?" she asked, not sure how she felt about that.

"I don't want to feed into Shawn's power trip," Conrad informed her. "He still thinks he's in charge after all his screw-ups and cover-ups. We should communicate our problems with one another openly and freely like ten grown-ups."

"But there aren't ten grown-ups," Harley reminded him. "A few grown-ups and a bunch of adolescents."

The barracks door flew open, startling Conrad and Harley. Damon stormed inside with James on his heels.

"Don't walk away when I'm talking to you," James shouted after him.

"I was finished talking with you," Damon snarled without even looking back at his boss, or perhaps that was now his former boss.

James grabbed Damon's arm, stopping him. "We had a deal!"

Damon spun to face him, pulled his arm free, and glared at James. "Touch me again, and you'll be scraping your ass off the floor."

It was then that James noticed Conrad and Harley at the other end of the room in the kitchen area. Although they were pretending they weren't listening, it was obvious they were. Damon glanced across the barracks as well, although his expression didn't change when he saw them. James glared at Damon.

"Stop looking at her like that," James snarled loudly enough for them to hear, catching Damon's attention.

Damon glared at James through squinted eyes and cocked his head. "What's wrong with you?"

"Just looking out for Harley's best interest," James retorted louder than necessary.

"You want to talk?" Damon snarled. "Fine, let's talk."

Damon turned and stomped across the barracks, then threw open the door and exited. James offered an apologetic smile to them, then hurried after Damon. Conrad and Harley exchanged bewildered looks.

"What the hell was that?" Harley asked.

"I have no idea."

Chapter 19

Day Five. Early that morning, before breakfast, Harley and Ivy headed up the path to the latrine and shower building with their towels and army toiletry bags. The men who chose showering over the pond seemed to prefer using the shower building after breakfast, which made pre-breakfast better for the two women.

"I can't get over how polite Tyler has been since our intervention," Ivy remarked, managing a tiny chuckle. "Honestly, I didn't think that was going to do anything, but it really worked."

"Well, I wouldn't put my guard down around him just yet," Harley reminded her. "It might only be a temporary fix."

"Trust me," Ivy announced with a tense sigh. "I'm not putting my guard down around any of them. Well, except maybe Conrad. He's a pretty good guy."

"He's like a father to me," Harley remarked. "I trust him with my life."

"I like First Officer Brian, too," Ivy informed her, then frowned. "I just wish the captain wouldn't ride him so hard.

Shawn needs to chill a little. On his orders, all Brian and Lester do is take shifts in the rowboat and sleep."

"Conrad suggested putting a third man in the rowboat patrol rotation," Harley remarked. "But Shawn shot it down."

"I think he's still a little butthurt from Conrad telling him off that first day at the barracks," Ivy announced with a giggle.

"Doubtful," Harley muttered. "He still acts like he's in charge, and he's been getting a little more assertive with his bullying."

"I think he's just trying to keep Damon in line," Ivy insisted. "Tensions seem to be pretty high between James and Damon. I mean, without James holding Damon's leash these days, there's no telling what he'll do if he's left unchecked."

"As long as he brings back bunches of bananas and sacks of coconuts every couple of days, I don't have a problem with him," Harley remarked.

They entered the clearing and approached the mostly peaceful shower building. Conrad and Damon were the only ones up and about that early in the morning, and Conrad was preparing the fire for coffee when they left. Damon was probably on another one of his great banana hunts, but would be back the moment he smelled coffee. That left the shower building all to themselves, though they still locked the door. Neither woman was that trusting. They entered the shower building through the latrine and paused in the changing portion, setting their towels and their toiletry kits on the single bench. Both women slipped out of their shoes and removed their shirts, revealing their bras. Just then, Damon emerged from the shower area with his towel loosely tied around his waist and immediately paused when he saw both women undressing.

Harley and Ivy gasped with surprise and jumped, clutching their shirts to their bra-clad bodies. It was much like coming across a wild animal in the woods. They just stared at Damon, frozen. Damon barely reacted and continued past them, his own toiletry kit in hand. It was at that point that they'd noticed his clothes hanging on a hook on the wall, which they hadn't seen when they entered. Neither woman moved and stared at him as he removed his towel, his back to them, and proceeded to dress without a care in the world. Ivy and Harley remained frozen while staring at his naked buttocks, stunned that he didn't even care that they were there. Once he finished dressing and tightened his combat boots, he unlocked the door and left the shower building without uttering a word. Ivy darted for the door and bolted it. She looked back at Harley with something resembling shock.

"That was freaky," Ivy remarked.

"And, ironically, we were the ones gawking at him," Harley muttered.

Ivy stared at Harley a moment as if suddenly realizing she had been right. Both women smiled, embarrassed, and laughed at themselves.

§

After breakfast, Harley helped Conrad straighten the barracks, which seemed to be his strange joy. He felt the need to make everyone's bed and even fold their clothes, whether they were dirty or clean. He needed the barracks orderly to maintain some level of normalcy in his new world. He never could quite let go of his former butler days. While he swept the floor, Harley placed the trash in their appropriate bins. One for burning, one for compost, and one that was solid trash.

"Are you okay?" Harley asked, eyeing Conrad as he aggressively swept the floor.

"Another ten pouches of MREs disappeared," Conrad informed her, shaking his head. "I don't understand how it happened. Someone must have taken them last night after dinner."

"But why?" Harley asked. "There are plenty of bananas, coconuts, and whatever that fruit is that Ivy and I brought back yesterday."

"Maybe our MRE thief likes a variety," Conrad remarked. "Maybe he prefers meat or bread. I just don't know."

Harley eyed him suspiciously. "You want to check their foot lockers, don't you?" she remarked.

"If you're willing to be my lookout," Conrad replied.

Harley groaned and nodded. "Fine," she scoffed. "Just make it quick."

"I will," Conrad informed her. "I have it narrowed down to three people."

"Please tell me one of them isn't Damon," Harley groaned softly.

"Actually, no," Conrad replied. "He's been eating his weight in bananas lately."

Harley propped open the barracks door and swept dirt outside while Conrad conducted his investigation. He went to Lester's footlocker first and opened it. Just beneath Lester's clothes were a few full bottles of whiskey and several empty ones. Conrad shook his head and then moved on to James's locker. Hidden beneath his clothes were several girly magazines that had disappeared from the general 'library' and into his personal collection. Harley heard someone moving around outside.

"A little faster, Sherlock," Harley muttered, alerting him to someone in the general vicinity.

Conrad went to Shawn's footlocker next and opened it. He removed several pouches of MREs and glanced across the barracks at Harley. She stared at his find, momentarily shocked.

"Are you kidding?" Harley gasped. "How many?"

"About ten," Conrad replied.

"What do we do?" she asked, surprised.

Conrad removed the pouches and returned them to the crate. "That's what we do," he announced while slamming the crate shut. "It's not as if he can say anything. Maybe he'll get the message."

Harley allowed the door to shut and approached Conrad. "I can't believe he'd steal provisions," she scoffed. "He's the one constantly harping about 'rationing'."

"I have this really bad feeling he fears losing power," Conrad informed her. "It's possible that he wants to cling to his power badly enough that he'd create scarcity to justify his food rationing."

"But there's plenty of food," Harley insisted. "Damon brought nearly fifty bananas late yesterday afternoon. We're hard pressed to eat them all before they rot as it is." Her eyes suddenly widened. "Please tell me he hasn't been tampering with the coffee supply. If Damon doesn't have his pot of coffee in the morning, he's going to be extremely cranky."

"I already hid the extra cans of coffee where no one would ever think to look," Conrad informed her.

Harley cocked her head in silent question.

Conrad grinned, pleased with himself. "In the bottom of ***your*** foot locker."

"I don't drink coffee," she reminded him.

"That's why no one would ever look there for it," he replied.

Chapter 20

As lunchtime drew near, Damon sat on the ground outside while cutting bamboo with his Bowie knife. There was no telling what he was doing, and it didn't pay to ask. He was always working on something, keeping himself entertained. As the captain entered the barracks, Conrad emerged with nine pouches of MREs on a large serving platter. Honestly, he looked exactly as Harley remembered him while growing up, when he would serve tea and pastries to her mother and her friends. Of course, his white dress shirt and black dress pants were thoroughly wrinkled from line drying, his dress shoes were traded in for combat boots, and he ditched the tie. It was still rather humorous. Brian appeared on the path, returning from his early morning to early afternoon rescue patrol while proudly toting four decent-sized fish.

"The fish are biting today," Brian announced cheerfully. "Hopefully, Lester has the same luck this afternoon."

Damon glanced at Brian's catch and gave a nod. "Save me the heads and guts," he remarked, catching the attention of those within earshot.

Brian eyed Damon almost suspiciously and nodded. "Sure," he replied. "Whatever turns you on."

Conrad cheerfully offered everyone their rations, allowing them to choose their own packet. Lester had already taken his lunch MRE with him for his shift on the afternoon rescue watch.

"This afternoon, our selections are beef stew or chili with beans," Conrad announced.

Just about everyone made faces while selecting a bag, most without even looking. So far, they all seemed to taste the same. Harley only really cared about the crackers, cornbread, and whatever dessert accompanied the meal. Only their seventh MRE pouch, and the castaways were trading rations like it was opening hour at the stock exchange. Some traded sugar for creamer, salt for pepper, and both salt and pepper for Tabasco sauce. That was Damon, the Tabasco sauce king. Instant drink mix swaps were fast and furious, certainly not for the faint of heart. Fruit punch was like gold. Then, of course, there was the rare and coveted chocolate bar. The most godawful, generic chocolate ever created, yet Ivy and Harley were practically willing to sell their soul for one.

Men were searching for chocolate bars like golden tickets. The captain found one in his pouch last night, and Ivy offered to kiss him for the coveted bar. Harley and Conrad were a little uncomfortable about the trade, but it seemed to be a light-hearted exchange and made for a humorous moment. It would seem as if none were found this afternoon, and some playful jokes were made about it. Randall arrived just in time to take his MRE pouch and go off on his own to eat, which he had been doing since yesterday afternoon. Everything seemed quiet. Only a moment later, Shawn stormed out of the barracks, looking half-crazed. Although he didn't say anything, he shifted looks at those around the fire pit.

"Everything okay?" Tyler asked the captain, curious about his actions.

"It's nothing," Shawn scoffed, then snatched the remaining pouch from the tray and flopped on a nearby bench.

Conrad and Harley exchanged looks, knowing exactly what had the captain in a foul mood. He realized his stolen MREs had been discovered and confiscated. After swapping her chili and beans for Conrad's peanut butter crackers, Harley decided to make her move and play "Let's Make A Deal" with Damon for his instant tea. She approached Damon while he continued working on whatever bamboo contraption he was building, as his beef stew heated on the provided heat unit. She sat on a rock near him and held up her packet of Tabasco and instant coffee.

"Trade you for your tea," she announced.

Damon nodded to the pouch on the ground near his feet so he could continue with his work uninterrupted.

"You know," Damon remarked as she helped herself to his tea packet. "I'm sure James would give you his tea if you asked."

"Asking him for anything comes with too steep a price," Harley remarked. She couldn't be sure, but she thought she saw him grin at the comment. "Thanks for the tea."

As she was about to get up, Damon caught her wrist, surprising her. He secretly passed off the coveted generic candy bar, placing it in her hand, then resumed working without acknowledging her. Harley hesitated, dropped the candy bar into her MRE pouch, then stood and returned to Conrad.

"Making new friends?" Conrad asked just loud enough for her to hear.

"Doubtful," Harley replied. "But I don't mind mutual tolerance."

Once they finished lunch, Randall disappeared to 'god knows where', Brian went into the barracks for a nap after his full morning of fishing and watching for rescue ships, and James and Tyler headed to the showers. Ivy and Harley stayed to offer Conrad moral support on his solo fish cleaning expedition before he accompanied them to the beach for a little afternoon sun. The pond was nice, but it wasn't 'sun, sand, and surf' nice. Damon continued working on his bamboo projects while having his after-lunch cigarette. If Harley was correct in her assumption, he was only smoking five cigarettes a day, and she was almost positive it had to do with rationing rather than an effort to actually quit.

"When you're finished with arts and crafts class," Shawn announced to Damon while standing. "Maybe you could help out and tote some water from the shower building to the barracks."

"Did that this morning," Damon remarked, his cigarette hanging from his mouth, without looking up from his work. "Gathered coconuts, chopped some wood, and refilled the kerosene lamps." He continued working on his bamboo creation and finally looked up at the captain, who stood only a few feet away. He removed the cigarette from his mouth, casually blowing out smoke. "There's a load of laundry that needs to be washed and hung up to dry. You should probably get on that."

"I don't like your attitude, Damon," Shawn scoffed.

"Right back at you, Captain Queeg," Damon replied, locking his eyes with Shawn's as he pinched the cigarette between his teeth.

Conrad heard the comment and immediately stiffened, casting a glance at the scene that was about to unfold at the massive insult.

"It's Captain Rattner," Shawn reminded him in a gruff tone.

Conrad groaned and shook his head. It seemed impossible that any ship's captain worth his salt wouldn't know the name of the famous captain from "The Caine

Mutiny". At least Shawn's limited intelligence kept him from exploding on Damon.

"Whatever," Damon muttered through his cigarette. "I believe I made my point."

"Actually, it's called insubordination," Shawn informed him.

Damon grinned with the cigarette still between his teeth and actually chuckled. "Perhaps," he replied. "If I were stupid enough to actually work for you." Damon took a puff from his cigarette, crushed it, and slowly rose to his feet, facing the captain and staring him down. "I've been pulling my weight around here. Maybe you need to start pulling yours." Damon cocked his head. "***Sir***."

Shawn looked from Damon to Conrad, Harley, and Ivy, who just stared, mostly shocked. He then looked back at Damon.

"In case you'd forgotten," Shawn announced. "I'm in charge."

"Maybe you didn't hear. I'm a free-lance agent," Damon casually remarked. "Honestly, you couldn't afford me, and I don't ***remember*** anyone putting you in charge."

"I'm the ship's captain," Shawn reminded him.

"We're not on your ship," Damon informed him. "Actually, I'd heard your ship is on the bottom of the ocean."

Conrad smirked and looked away, knowing Damon was quoting him.

"When someone I respect starts giving the orders, that's when I'll start taking them," Damon remarked. Without taking his eyes off the captain, he picked up the small bamboo cage he'd been working on, holding it up. "Conrad, what does this look like to you?"

Conrad looked back at Damon, then eyed the nearly finished cage. "Looks like a lobster trap," he replied. "Your request for fish guts and heads almost confirms that's what it is."

Damon still didn't take his eyes off the captain. "Conrad, lobsters are cold-water crustaceans," he scoffed, lacking emotion. "What possible purpose would a lobster trap serve in the tropics?"

"The spiny lobster lives in tropical oceans," Conrad replied.

"Look at that," Damon announced, raising his brows. "The ship's captain, bested by the butler. This conversation is officially over."

The captain sneered at Damon and stormed back to the barracks.

"No starch in the butler's boxers," Damon called after him, then smirked and chuckled to himself.

Despite keeping to himself and remaining mostly silent, Damon just announced to the camp that he'd heard every word they'd said. Harley couldn't help but wonder just how intelligent Damon was. People often underestimated Conrad's intelligence because he was a servant; perhaps the same was true of Damon.

Chapter 21

Half an hour later. As Harley and Ivy headed down the path that would take them to the beach, Conrad lagged several yards behind, carrying one of Damon's lobster traps. Ivy seemed a little preoccupied on their short walk to the beach.

"Damon's really starting to push the captain's buttons," Ivy remarked while shaking her head. "I don't like the storm that's brewing between those two."

"You have to admit, Shawn had it coming," Harley reminded her. "His long list of bad calls helped create our current situation, and ordering people around isn't going to make him any more popular."

"It's not the captain that worries me," Ivy insisted, her shoulders tightening as she glanced around the woods. "We've only been on the island for five days, and Damon is turning into a ticking time bomb."

"I wouldn't consider him a time bomb," Harley remarked. "I think he's venting his frustration with the situation, much like Conrad did the first day at the barracks."

"But Conrad isn't Damon," Ivy reminded her. "Damon is the size of a tank and carries a gun." She hesitated and looked back at Harley. "I think you should do something about him."

"Me?" Harley gasped, surprised. "What do you expect me to do about it? He's James's attack dog, not mine."

"I get the feeling he quit or was fired," Ivy muttered. "And that's not what I meant."

Ivy fidgeted and insecurely rubbed her shoulders as they stepped onto the beach and into the warm, bright sun. She stopped and turned to face Harley while Conrad continued past them to find a spot to drop and tie off his trap, but first, he needed a weight to hold it down.

"You seem to get along with Damon," Ivy insisted.

"You think I get along with Damon?" Harley asked, somewhat surprised to hear that. "I give him coffee and Tabasco for his tea. That hardly makes us BFFs."

Ivy groaned and threw her arms down. "You know what I mean," she announced, defeated. "He likes you more than he likes me."

"Correction," Harley remarked. "He tolerates me. I'm not sure he actually likes anyone."

"Whatever," Ivy scoffed, losing patience. "You need to take one for the team and get him under control."

Harley stared at Ivy for a long moment, grasping what she was actually trying to say. "Wait--" she practically gasped. "You want me to ***seduce*** Damon so I can ***control*** him?"

"The guy obviously needs to get laid," Ivy insisted. "One of us has to do it before things get out of control." She cocked her head, looking at her matter-of-factly. "I mean, you said you're not with James, right? So, it's not really that big of a deal."

"It is to me," Harley scoffed as she folded her arms across her chest. "And getting the guy laid isn't going to change anything. Shawn's just going to continue pushing him, and Damon's going to continue pushing back until one of them backs off and caves."

"Which is why you should ***talk*** to Damon," Ivy reminded her.

"That's not how it works, Ivy," Harley reminded her, then shook her head, almost stunned. "If you honestly think Damon will back off and take orders from Shawn just because he's getting laid, you're insane!"

"I don't understand why you won't even try," Ivy huffed, now irritated.

"I don't understand how you think it's in any way acceptable to ask me to do something like that," Harley shot back.

"It's for the good of the group," Ivy reminded her. "I've been kissing up to the captain all morning, and he's been more tolerable. The least you can do is try kissing up to Damon."

"You're playing a dangerous game, Ivy," Harley informed her. "If you lead Shawn on, he's liable to take it further than you're willing to go."

"We've been stuck here for five days, Harley," Ivy snarled. "Better to pick a side now than be forced on one later."

"This conversation is over," Harley snapped back. "Don't do anything stupid."

Ivy sneered at Harley, then spun and headed back for the path. Harley groaned while raking her fingers through her hair, uncertain whether she should follow Ivy, stop her, or just let her cool off. The latter sounded uncomfortably concerning.

Chapter 22

Day Six. The following morning, Ivy was still mad at Harley when it actually should have been the other way around. Harley had hoped that giving the girl some space might make the situation a little better between them, but Ivy didn't even make an effort to go to the shower building with her that morning. Given her general distrust of her fellow passengers, Harley opted to wait until Conrad had time to make the trip with her or, instead, possibly even swim in the pond later that afternoon while her friend fished. It wasn't just her safety she worried about, but Ivy's safety as well. Being the only women, they really needed to stick together. Breakfast that morning was very uncomfortable. More than just Ivy keeping to herself, everyone seemed a little off. Shawn was giving death glares at Damon, who was already on his third cup of coffee. James and Tyler appeared to be having a tense conversation, which may also have involved Damon.

And it wasn't just them. Conrad was grumpy about another ten MREs vanishing overnight, which meant they would be poking around in Shawn's footlocker again.

Honestly, the man would have to be incredibly stupid to hide them in there a second time. Randall took his MRE pouch and, this time, left camp without a word. Then, there was Lester, who looked hungover or possibly still drunk. The only lucky person was Brian, who had left early that morning for his shift on the rowboat. After breakfast, Harley changed into her two-piece swimsuit behind the curtain of her shared space with Ivy while Conrad finished his morning ritual of making everyone's beds.

"I'm uncomfortable leaving her alone," Harley remarked before slipping around the curtain and joining him in the main barracks. "I'm probably just being paranoid, right? I mean, the guys haven't really shown any signs of sexual aggression."

"Apart from Tyler that first day, no," Conrad replied. "I haven't noticed any concerning aggression. Well, not the sexual kind. Aggression between Damon and the captain, that's another story." He shook his head almost shamefully. "I can't believe Ivy is mad at you because you refused to 'service' Damon."

Harley groaned softly and rolled her eyes. "God, it sounds even more 'transactional' when you say it," she scoffed.

"Because that's what she wants you to do," Conrad remarked. "Trade your body for favors."

"Not even shipwrecked for a week," Harley huffed. "Have things really fallen apart this fast?"

"It's been a stressful week," Conrad reminded her. "Ivy went through a lot in her personal life even before being shipwrecked. She probably feels as if she no longer has any control. I think she's desperately looking for some sort of emotional support, and she thinks the captain will provide that stability. Unfortunately for her, Damon undermining the captain's authority threatens that delusion."

"Well, she's probably not wrong," Harley muttered, then sank into thought before finally looking at Conrad, her body stiffening. "What if Ivy's right? ***Would*** it be in everyone's best interest if I 'took one for the team' and kept Damon occupied?"

Conrad stared at her, his eyes wide and his mouth falling open. "Harley, don't let Ivy's insecurities infect your mental stability," he announced, sounding almost irritated by the mere suggestion. "No one expects you to sleep with the guy to keep the peace."

"But ***would*** it make things better for everyone?" Harley asked.

"It'd make things better for Damon," Conrad scoffed, raising a cocky brow.

"Come on, Conrad," she huffed. "You know what I mean. Would it ease tensions between Damon and Shawn? Am I being selfish?"

Conrad became flustered. "I can't believe we're even discussing this hypothetical question," he huffed, then raked his fingers through his hair while groaning in frustration. "Sex would be a short-lived distraction for someone like Damon. Long-term, it could make things worse. Possessiveness and jealousy can come out of nowhere." Conrad held his breath a moment before attempting to rationalize the situation with Harley. "Shawn is an incompetent leader, and, personally, I think it's in our best interest if Damon challenged his authority and dethroned him." He stared into her eyes with a stern, serious look. "You don't want your first time to be a peace-keeping mission."

"I also don't want to be stranded on an island where the only other woman hates me because she thinks I'm being selfish," Harley informed him.

"You're a little too old to be giving in to peer pressure," Conrad reminded her. "Obviously, you can do whatever you want, but I don't want you regretting that decision later. No one should be pressuring you into doing anything you don't want to do."

"Maybe I need to step back and think about it a little longer," Harley finally replied. "A rescue could be right around the corner."

"Yes, remember that," Conrad replied, then indicated the barracks door. "Let's get to the pond before rush hour. You know how much I despise crowds."

Harley left the barracks with Conrad, only a step behind her. As they stepped outside, they saw Damon and James in a stand-off near the fire pit. Both looked at them with stern expressions, as if they had interrupted something. Harley and Conrad exchanged looks, grimaced, and made a beeline for the pond path.

"You want to accuse me of something?" Damon snarled at James as Harley and Conrad attempted to make their escape. "Do it in front of an audience!"

"Stop embarrassing yourself," James scoffed.

"Sorry, I don't embarrass very easily," Damon remarked, then cocked his head. "What's the problem, James? Are you worried your ***girlfriend*** likes me more than she likes you?"

Harley immediately stopped on the path and looked back at James and Damon. Conrad attempted to keep her moving, but she was now invested in the conversation once they dragged her into it. She was briefly reminded of her kiss of gratitude when Damon saved Conrad, something she'd almost forgotten. That was a lie. She hadn't forgotten about that. Not at all. And perhaps Damon hadn't either. It was possible Damon intended to throw it into James's face to provoke him into a fight.

"Harley is way out of your league, Damon," James snarled, provoked by the comment. "She won't be slumming with you anytime soon."

"Dogging women is really more your thing," Damon scoffed.

James caught a glimpse of Harley on the path with Conrad, possibly listening to their entire conversation. He looked back at Damon, pointed a warning finger at him, and said something Harley couldn't hear. Damon smirked, amused. James then turned and walked away. Conrad managed to spin Harley back onto the path toward the pond.

"What the hell do you suppose that was all about?" Harley demanded as they continued along the path on the short walk to the pond.

"Just Damon pushing James's buttons," Conrad replied. "I guess we can assume Damon no longer works for James, and he's burning his bridges."

"Well, I wish they'd keep me out of it," Harley muttered.

They walked in silence for the next few minutes before reaching the pond. As they got closer, they heard something or someone in the water. Both hesitated and approached with caution, keeping out of view just to be safe. They hadn't run into many animals on the island, but that didn't mean they weren't out there. Both immediately tensed when they saw Ivy and Shawn, naked in the pond together, aggressively kissing and possibly doing a lot more. Conrad frowned and guided Harley away from the pond and back in the direction of camp.

"Seems a little crowded at the pond today," Conrad informed her. "I knew we should have gone ahead of rush hour."

"I can't say I understand the attraction," Harley remarked. "But if it helps her get over her ex-boyfriend and gain a sense of security, I'm happy for her."

By the time they reached camp, Brian had returned early from his shift in the rowboat, carrying a large sack over his shoulder. Although the bag seemed heavy, Brian was grinning. Damon appeared curious and approached along with Harley and Conrad.

"Damon's lobster traps worked," Brian announced and set the sack near the fire pit. "We're feasting on lobster for lunch. Lester said to save one for him."

"Well, this day is finally looking up," Conrad replied cheerfully. "Now, if we only had butter."

§

After the finest meal they'd had on the island, Ivy finally made the first move and approached Harley while attempting to conceal her glowing smile, looking a bit like a blushing bride.

"Hey," Ivy announced somewhat timidly.

"Hey," Harley replied, almost surprised the girl approached her at all.

"I'm sorry about yesterday," Ivy just about whispered while shifting uncomfortably. "I had some time to think about what I'd said, and I realized how awful it actually sounded. Can you forgive me?"

"Of course," Harley replied, overjoyed. "I'm sorry about the way I reacted to your concerns. You were obviously trying to convey your feelings, and I wasn't quite hearing you."

"Friends?" Ivy asked, grinning.

"Yeah, we're friends," Harley replied.

"How about that afternoon on the beach?" Ivy asked. "I already have my swimsuit on."

"Me too," Harley replied with renewed enthusiasm. "I'll grab some towels."

"I'll grab the beach blanket off the line," Ivy announced and hurried in the opposite direction.

Harley entered the barracks and nearly collided with the captain. He didn't even acknowledge her, nearly knocking her over as he stormed outside. She eyed him almost suspiciously while frowning, then headed across the barracks. He didn't act like a man who'd just gotten laid.

Weren't men supposed to be all mellow and relaxed after having sex? When she saw Damon wiping blood from the corner of his mouth onto his hand, she hesitated, putting together what must have happened right before she entered. Harley gently cleared her throat and continued on her way to get the two towels.

"Making friends?" Harley remarked, then immediately cursed herself for even speaking to Damon.

"More like 'coming to an understanding'," Damon swiftly replied.

Harley grabbed both towels, then turned toward him, almost surprised he responded.

"Looks to me like he hit you," Harley corrected while attempting to hide her smile.

"Small price to pay," Damon replied.

"For coming to an understanding?"

"For me to hit him back," Damon informed her. "The understanding comes later."

"I'm sorry I asked."

"No, you're not," Damon remarked, matter-of-factly, then snorted a laugh. "If you're heading to the beach, be mindful of the current. There's a storm approaching. You have maybe two hours before it'll start getting rough out there."

The word 'storm' sent an icy shiver racing down Harley's spine. Damon's suggestion that there would possibly be another storm frightened her more than she thought possible.

"As bad as the last one?" she asked.

She didn't want to think about another monsoon while still suffering trauma from the last one she'd witnessed, up close and personal. Damon smiled almost sympathetically, possibly feeling her pain.

"No, it won't be that bad, but you don't want to be caught outside in it," Damon informed her. "When you see

Lester hauling ass back to shore, it's time for you to head back."

"Good to know," she replied, then nodded. "I appreciate the heads up."

Chapter 23

Day Seven. Morning. The rain continued to pour down, as it had the entire night. There had been some wind along with plenty of thunder and lightning. Harley couldn't deny she had a tough time sleeping, reliving the night they evacuated the ship. The experience weighed on her more heavily than she realized. She felt like a dog in a thunderstorm, looking for something to hide under until it passed. Things weren't looking too cheerful within the barracks after she finally got up, either. It seemed as if they'd be stuck inside all day, which made everyone cranky or, in most cases, crankier. Since there'd be no patrol in the rowboat that morning, Brian suggested a friendly game of Texas Hold'em. It was quite possibly the first time the men all agreed on something. Even Damon seemed to put aside his differences for the sake of a good poker game.

Randall, Harley, Ivy, and Conrad were the only ones who didn't accept the offer to play. Conrad and the women didn't know how to play and didn't really feel like learning on the fly. Randall seemed restless while trapped inside, alternating between pacing the barracks and attempting to sleep, except he didn't actually get any sleep. By this point, everyone knew about his cocaine dependency and speculated he had run out of his supply. Withdrawal was hitting him hard. For now, it seemed best to give him some space. When the last of the cigars and the remaining bottle of whiskey came out, Harley knew it was going to be a long day. Conrad had snuck a peek in Lester's foot locker yesterday, and the ship's steward had taken his last pilferage bottle of whiskey with him on his late afternoon patrol. That meant he was officially out.

Between Lester running out of booze, Randall taking his last snort of cocaine, and Damon possibly having smoked his last cigarette yesterday afternoon, as evidenced by the way he clung to his cigar like a lifeline, things were about to get pretty wild around the barracks. They had to hope for a rescue soon, before tempers flared and anxieties spiked. Today, though, Harley enjoyed watching the guys play poker, grateful she hadn't joined them. The game was testosterone-filled, whiskey-fueled, and slathered heavily with crude banter. Even James and Tyler were having a difficult time keeping up with the raw masculinity displayed with each dealt hand, and it only got worse with each swallow of hard liquor.

Although intrigued, Conrad was even a bit intimidated by the direction the game swiftly turned. Brian displayed a little more grit than expected, possibly in his element, and showed little sign of backing down when the banter became almost insulting. Oddly enough, Damon dialed his crudeness back after getting a few drinks in him. Shawn, on the other hand, upped his rawness, turning into a sailor on shore leave. It was the first time Harley had seen the man drink, and buzzed Shawn was worse than sober Shawn. Though she kind of liked buzzed Damon. He talked, smiled, and laughed more than she'd seen since she'd met him almost two weeks ago.

Despite not playing in the poker tournament, Harley, Ivy, and Conrad each had a glass of whiskey. Considering it was the last of the alcohol for the foreseeable future, it seemed like a good idea at the time. Harley had drunk brandy before, but she had never had whiskey. She thought it was harsh, burning her throat, but she intended to finish it. The strong whiskey instantly relaxed her, and for that, she was grateful. She needed something to take the edge off the storm outside, which had left her a little tense. She particularly enjoyed the tingling sensation in her toes. That in itself was worth the burning in her throat. Unfortunately, there was another side effect of the strong drink. Harley enjoyed the overwhelming masculinity a little too much, like some awakening beast, filling the barracks. Most of her focus was on Damon and the strange, sudden urge she had to kiss him as she had on the beach.

No one had actually seen the kiss, and its rumor hadn't gotten around either. At least, Harley was relatively confident Damon hadn't told James. She hadn't even told Conrad, reasoning that it wasn't a big deal and a legitimate response to a highly intense situation. But as she watched Damon from across the barracks, Harley was finally able to admit to herself that it was a big deal. If it had been James who saved Conrad, her reaction would have been dramatically different. While lost in her own somewhat naughty thoughts, Harley wasn't quick enough with her reaction when Damon's gaze swept past her, and they briefly made eye contact. She was a bit like a deer in headlights, lagging any sort of reaction, especially looking away. Damon smiled and winked before returning his focus to the game.

Harley's heart just about stopped at the small, discreet action. She quickly minded her drink, although glancing at the others at the table. It didn't seem as if anyone had noticed Damon's playful reaction. When Harley looked beside her, Conrad stared at her with something resembling shock. Well, almost no one had noticed.

Chapter 24

After dinner, the thunder and lightning had finally ceased, and the rain was less of a downpour and more of a steady, light rain. The poker game was finally winding down, with Brian eventually beating Damon. Harley and Ivy decided to make the trek to the showers and wash up. They took a less-traveled path to the shower building to avoid the now-muddy main trail. Harley really just wanted to wash her hair. She didn't like the way her hair felt after spending time in the ocean, and they didn't have time to shower when they got back from the beach yesterday. Although Harley just took a quick shower to wash her hair, Ivy spent a little more time, despite the water being on the colder side. Harley tied back her wet hair and hung her towel on the rail while Ivy finally dried off.

"I'd love a hot shower," Ivy muttered.

"I'd settle for a lukewarm one myself."

"I know what you mean," Ivy sighed. "But I suppose we should be grateful for what we have. It could be a lot worse."

Harley sat on a bench within the shower area. "I saw you talking to Tyler last night. I guess he's mellowed a little."

"I'll admit, he's been a lot better," Ivy reported. "He's actually kind of tolerable now."

"Ironic that he improved, and the others have gotten worse," Harley remarked.

"Just a frame of mind, I suppose," Ivy replied. "Not being an addict helps. Randall's suffering some pretty heavy withdrawal. I guess he's trying to keep busy by collecting wood all day." She groaned softly. "I mean, we have enough firewood to last us weeks."

"Lester and Brian have kept themselves pretty much isolated on the rowboat," Harley informed her. "Both of them are starting to look like lobsters."

Ivy snickered softly at the comment, knowing it to be true. "And your guy, Conrad, has turned into a clean freak. He doesn't stop."

Harley snorted a laugh and waved her off. "That's just Conrad."

Ivy laughed as well before turning serious. "But something's definitely not right with Damon," she remarked. "He's been acting creepy."

"Creepy?" Harley questioned. "Strange and elusive perhaps, but I wouldn't say he's been acting creepy."

Ivy approached now dressed. "I'm serious," she insisted. "Shawn said Damon doesn't sleep at night. He just sits on his bunk and stares at the wall."

"That is a little odd," Harley remarked, now deep in thought. "I'm pretty sure he ran out of cigarettes yesterday. That could make him irritable and restless, I suppose." She then considered the day they'd had. "I'll admit, the poker game put all of them in a better mood. At least James left me alone most of the day."

"He's not so bad," Ivy insisted. "You should give him a chance."

"Not so bad?" Harley scoffed. "He's nice to you. Around me, it's the same thing. Nonstop talk about my new life as his slave and mother to his children."

"Surely you exaggerate."

"I wish I were exaggerating," Harley replied with a deep sigh.

They left the shower building and headed down the lesser-traveled path to avoid the mud again. As they approached the lit barracks in the darkening sky, they heard yelling from inside. Harley and Ivy barely exchanged looks before running for the building. As they reached the door, they heard more yelling followed by a crash. Damon charged through the door with his duffel bag in his hand and stormed past them. Both women stared after Damon, then entered the barracks in time to witness James and Shawn lifting themselves from the floor. Conrad entered a step behind them, having missed whatever had happened as well. Lester helped Shawn to his feet while James gingerly rubbed his abdomen.

"He's insane!" James shouted.

Shawn touched his bleeding lip and sneered. "We need to do something about him."

"We'd better form a plan in case he comes back," James insisted.

"I don't think he'll be coming back," Lester informed them.

"What happened?" Ivy asked.

"Damon was showing signs of psychotic behavior," James informed them. "He's been making sexual comments about the two of you, and we feared he might try something."

"In your best interest and ours, we attempted to disarm him," Shawn remarked.

"It's not a good idea to allow him to keep his gun," Lester announced, agreeing with the captain.

"He went insane at the suggestion," Shawn remarked.

Ivy and Harley stared at James and Shawn, stunned at what they were hearing.

Conrad seemed confused at how quickly things had escalated. "I don't understand what happened in here," he remarked. "I was only gone a couple of minutes."

Conrad's comment caught Harley's attention, putting the incident into perspective. It seemed strange that all of this occurred when Conrad left the barracks for only a few minutes. Probably out pissing behind a tree. Did they wait for Conrad to step out before approaching Damon and attempting to disarm him? She had to admit that the timing was very suspicious.

"What are we going to do?" Ivy asked, fidgeting after what happened.

"We have an hour before dark," James replied. "We'll think of a way to safely disarm him."

"But won't he become more agitated?" Ivy asked, her eyes wide with fear.

"We may have to tie him up for a few hours," Shawn insisted. "We're hoping he'll settle down once he's unarmed and restrained."

"Or piss him off more," Ivy muttered as she rubbed her chilled shoulders.

There was a strange silence among the men in the barracks. Conrad was giving Harley crossway glances, obviously not happy about what had happened and what he was hearing.

"We'll decide what to do when the time comes," Shawn assured her.

"I'm sure you have the best of intentions, but another assault on Damon will only result in another physical altercation," Conrad informed them. "I believe we all have the right to discuss our feelings on the current situation. I, personally, don't believe violence will help. I'd like the opportunity to speak to Damon first."

"Speak to him?" James gasped. "I wouldn't plan any tea parties if I were you. Just because you're both from the same country--"

"That has nothing to do with my feelings on the matter," Conrad insisted. "Apart from whatever happened here tonight, I've seen nothing to indicate he could be potentially harmful. If anything, he remains exactly the same now as he had last week."

"I'm shocked to hear you say that," James scoffed. "I thought you were loyal to Harley? He's taken a sexual interest in her. There's no telling what he might do to either of the women. Is that what you want?"

"Not one of the more intelligent remarks to come from your mouth," Conrad snarled. "If I believed for a second that he would harm Harley, I'd kill him myself. Before you three decide to wage war against an armed and skilled fighter, I think I should be allowed the opportunity to speak to him."

There was another moment of silence from those within the room. That they didn't even want to consider letting Conrad have a rational conversation with Damon first spoke volumes, as if they were hoping for an escalated altercation with him.

James glared at Harley, quickly losing patience. "He's your servant, goddammit," he scoffed, becoming enraged. "How do you feel about him wanting to ***share feelings*** with Damon?"

"I support Conrad and what he feels is in the best interest of the group," Harley announced without hesitation. "And he's ***not*** my servant!"

There were several moans from the men, apart from Brian, who appeared hesitant about what he must have witnessed.

Ivy suddenly glared at Harley, turning angry. "Are you insane?"

Harley exchanged glares with Ivy. "I suppose I could be, but I've never known Conrad to be wrong about a person's character," she announced boldly. "Besides, that'll give them time to recover before getting their asses kicked again if they try something stupid."

"If he puts his hands on me, I'm holding you responsible," Ivy lashed out, then stormed to the back and disappeared behind the curtain partition.

Chapter 25

Conrad walked through the darkened woods along the slightly muddy path and entered the clearing just before the shower building. Damon casually sat on the bench outside the small building, one foot propped, his forearm resting across his knee, his head against the wall. He opened his eyes only briefly, eyed Conrad, and again closed them without a word.

"Might I have a word with you?" Conrad asked as he approached.

Damon didn't bother opening his eyes. "I'd rather not," he muttered.

Conrad sat on the other end of the bench, staring out into the clearing. "I consider it important."

Damon eyed him, then groaned while straightening. "What do you want?" he finally muttered.

"Obviously, after tonight's incident, there are some who have concerns over your state of mind," Conrad informed him.

"I need a fucking cigarette," Damon scoffed.

"I'm serious."

"Me too," Damon huffed, then glared at him. "What's wrong with my state of mind?"

"I'm not sure myself, but there must be some concern, or they wouldn't have come after you tonight," Conrad informed him.

"How do you know ***they*** came after ***me***?" Damon asked, curious.

"I just have a feeling they did," Conrad replied. "I can't say I trust any of them myself."

"And you trust me?" Damon scoffed with a slight chuckle.

"Not completely, but you haven't put up much of a fuss about chores and helping out," Conrad remarked. "Even though I'm confident you could easily survive on your own."

"I have my reasons for staying," Damon muttered and shut his eyes.

"I don't suppose you care to share those reasons?" Conrad asked.

"No."

"Might I make a suggestion?"

"Could I prevent it?"

"No."

"By all means--make a suggestion."

"Make amends with our fellow castaways," Conrad announced almost boldly. "It would be in everyone's best interest."

"I'll take it into consideration."

"You do that, mate," Conrad announced while standing and offering a smile.

"We're not mates, Conrad," Damon scoffed while glaring at him. "I don't have ***mates***, and I don't care to make any."

Conrad nodded with noted disappointment. "I see," he replied, then turned to leave.

§

Harley wasn't too surprised when Conrad returned to the barracks without Damon. She also wasn't surprised when he told her their talk didn't go exactly as he had hoped. Regardless of what he told her, Conrad downplayed the entire conversation to those in the barracks, hoping to soothe tensions and give everyone time to regain some common sense after spending half the afternoon buzzed. It was possibly after midnight when Randall finally returned from his walk, and Harley decided to turn in for the night. It had been a long day spent cramped in the barracks, and doing next to nothing was exhausting. She just wanted the day over with. Conrad, Lester, and Brian also went to their bunks, while Shawn, Tyler, and James taught Ivy how to play poker, possibly intending to include her in their next game.

Despite it being late and their bunkmates attempting to sleep, the four playing poker at the barracks table were unapologetically loud and bold. Maybe it was because they were drunk, or maybe it was because Damon wasn't there to keep them from getting out of hand. As Harley restlessly tossed under the covers on her cot, she could hear the three loud, drunken men making lewd comments and even sexual innuendos to the happily buzzed young woman. The thing that troubled Harley most was Ivy giggling and responding with her own suggestive remarks. Sexually charging men isolated on an island was not only dangerous for Ivy, but it also endangered Harley. When they finally realized Ivy was secretly sharing company with the captain, they could turn their sexual frustrations on her instead.

Conrad had worked hard to establish boundaries to keep Harley and Ivy safe, and one drunken evening could potentially erode everything he'd accomplished. Harley rolled onto her back and stared at the mostly dark ceiling, fearing for their future if they weren't rescued soon.

Chapter 26

Day Eight. After breakfast, Randall was in a hurry to leave, as he had been cooped up in the barracks most of the day yesterday, apart from his late evening walk. Considering he took his MRE rations with him for lunch and dinner, no one expected he'd return until much later. Harley wondered where the man went all day, but considering he was showing peak crash signs of cocaine withdrawal, lethargy, and intense irritability, he'd probably found a way to cope with whatever he was going through while out in the woods. It was best to leave him alone. Brian left on his morning rescue ship patrol, which entailed lots of fishing. Anymore, he brought enough fish back for Conrad to fry up for dinner for the entire camp. Shawn, James, and Tyler headed to the showers as part of their after-breakfast ritual, since none of them had showered yesterday due to the storm.

While the men hit the showers, Ivy went 'fruit hunting', and even though Harley had offered to go along, Ivy said she wanted to be alone. She didn't mention if she'd be back in time to walk down to the beach with them for the afternoon. Harley was convinced Ivy wasn't actually looking for fruit but hooking up with Shawn somewhere within the woods, which would be the only reason she actually wanted to be alone. Harley and Conrad were once again alone in the barracks. While Conrad began his usual morning routine of stress cleaning, Harley stripped the linen from both her and Ivy's beds. Today, they would wash their sheets, as best they could, in the hand-crank washing machine in the shower building. It was a huge step above a tub and a washboard from the dark ages. She heard Conrad leave the barracks, presumably to shake out his dust cloth, since they wouldn't be doing the sheets until later. She certainly wasn't going anywhere near the shower building while the three men showered.

When Harley heard Conrad return only a moment later, she was a bit surprised. He usually beat his dust cloth thoroughly against a tree on the other side of the fire pit. Harley gathered her bundle of linen and rounded the curtain. She immediately hesitated when she saw Damon standing within the small kitchen area, pouring the last of the coffee into a large cup. Harley tried to relax, though she was slightly anxious about seeing him after whatever had happened last night. She carried her dirty linen across the room and deposited it near the cabinet that held the clean linen.

"You returned," Harley remarked, immediately wishing she had just minded her own business.

"Like a rash, I just keep coming back," he scoffed, clearly irritable.

Harley couldn't help but glance at him. Indicated by the way his hand fidgeted, Damon needed his nicotine fix, particularly now that he had coffee without his usual morning smoke. He alternated rubbing his temple and patting down his pockets for his phantom pack of cigarettes. Harley hesitated by the cabinet and stared at the neatly folded linen. She knew she shouldn't say anything, but the awkwardness and strange behavior of the guys only an hour after his disappearance last night weighed on her mind. Damon was a necessary evil to keep the balance in their dysfunctional camp. She finally glanced at him as he removed an MRE pouch from the crate.

"You're staying, aren't you?" she heard herself ask in an oddly timid voice, then wanted to kick herself the moment the words left her mouth.

Damon eyed her, possibly more surprised by her words than she was. He seemed to hesitate before tossing the MRE pouch on the counter and minding his coffee.

"Can't exactly say I'm wanted here," he remarked, removing his lighter from his pocket, then groaning at the involuntary action. "That was made abundantly clear last night."

"That's because ***they*** have their own agenda," Harley informed him, the words tumbling out before she could stop them, her internal anxiety spilling out of her mouth. "And you're standing in their way."

"What makes you think I don't have my own agenda?" Damon asked, replacing the lighter in his pocket before involuntarily producing it again. He softly cursed and shoved it back in his pocket.

"I don't care if you do," Harley replied without hesitation. "You're the better option."

Damon just about gave himself whiplash while shooting a surprised look at her. He studied her a moment while instinctively reaching in his pocket for his lighter, but stopped himself. He tilted his head while raising his brows, suddenly curious.

"Do ***you*** want me to stay?" he asked in a tone that made her heart skip a beat.

Harley knew what she had to say but feared saying it. She feared the implications of her own words. Her body trembled at the way he looked at her and the thoughts that might be going through his head.

"Yes," she replied softly, unable to take her eyes off him. "I want you to stay."

For better or worse, she said it. After responding, Harley's heart pounded with anticipation of what she was sure would come next. The sexual proposition. In that brief moment, a thousand responses raced through her mind. One thing was abundantly clear: if it came down to it, she'd submit to him, if that's what it took to keep him at the camp. Harley was thinking of the greater good, as Ivy had originally suggested, but it was more than that. She couldn't imagine what their existence would be like without Damon keeping the playing field level. Harley didn't want to find out. Despite the rapid-fire conversations she held in her head, nothing could have prepared her for what happened next.

"Okay," Damon replied, then casually leaned against the counter and opened his MRE pouch.

Harley stared at the man who appeared almost indifferent now, although oddly relaxed. He seemed more interested in what his MRE pouch contained than anything ***she*** had to offer. Harley wasn't sure if she was relieved or insulted. She was positive he would proposition her, but was caught off guard when he didn't. Damon noticed her puzzled look.

"Did you want the tea and sugar?" he asked, attempting to read her look while indicating the pouch, as if that was what he took away from her gaze.

"Uh, yeah, sure," Harley replied, almost dumbfounded. "I saved my coffee and Tabasco sauce for you. It's in your nightstand drawer."

"Yeah, I saw. Thanks," Damon remarked, then set the tea and sugar packets on the counter. "If you're going to the beach this afternoon, ask Lester to check the lobster traps. Save me the trip."

Chapter 27

Later that afternoon, Harley, Ivy, Conrad, and Lester sat on the beach blankets, sunning themselves. Well, Lester wasn't so much sunning himself as fighting uncontrollable tremors. He periodically wiped sweat from his brow, despite it not being all that hot. It was a beautiful, warm, sunny afternoon with a gentle, cool breeze coming off the ocean, but not hot enough to make Lester profusely sweat. He might have caught something after their near-death experience that left them soaking wet and exhausted. Harley hoped he wasn't coming down with pneumonia. He looked sickly. Conrad was also watching Lester, although he didn't appear so much concerned as sympathetic. He handed the ship's steward a bottle of water.

"Sip this," Conrad informed him. "You'll feel better."

"Thanks," Lester whispered, accepting the bottle with a trembling hand. He managed a tiny smile and snorted a laugh. "No hiding it now, huh?"

It wasn't sickness but severe alcohol withdrawal. Conrad offered a tiny, reassuring smile.

"We all have our demons," Conrad assured him. "One day at a time."

Lester nodded and sipped the water. Although it was unclear whether it actually helped his nausea, Conrad's few encouraging words may have helped most. In the distance, they could just barely make out Brian in the rowboat, fishing and keeping an eye out for passing ships. Harley was still stuck on her earlier conversation with Damon in the barracks. Each time she thought about his lack of reaction, she was more and more uncomfortable with the things she had been thinking. She wanted to talk to Conrad about her conversation with Damon, but what was there really to discuss? That she suddenly couldn't get Damon out of her head was really starting to work on her. What did it mean? They'd been on the beach nearly an hour, and Ivy seemed more anxious than usual, considering the peaceful afternoon in the sun. She kept looking around and couldn't seem to relax.

"Where are those guys?" Ivy asked while scanning the woods' edge behind them, possibly anxious to see Shawn. "I thought they were joining us."

Maybe it was love. Despite having a low opinion of Shawn, Harley would still be happy for her friend. Something new and exciting to take Ivy's mind off their current situation would be a bonus. When Shawn, James, and Tyler finally arrived on the beach, all three looked out of sorts and out of breath as well. Ivy was the first to notice them, as she was constantly scanning the woods' edge. Her expression dropped to something resembling bewilderment, then concern. The others looked back as the three men approached.

"Is something wrong?" Conrad asked, also noting their expressions.

"There's been an accident," Shawn informed them while fidgeting and seeming tense. "Damon returned as we were getting ready to leave. We decided to discuss the gun situation with him."

"He wouldn't listen and kept walking away," James added.

"Don't sugarcoat it," Tyler scoffed to his friends, then looked at the others. "He made a wrong turn and fell from the cliff."

All four stared at the three men with surprise. Harley's heart suddenly sank as a strange pang of grief swept over her like a gut punch. She couldn't believe Damon was gone. If she hadn't asked him to stay, he might still be alive. Harley felt as if it were all her fault.

"Fell?" Conrad asked, surprised, with an odd note of something resembling suspicion.

"There was nothing we could do," James insisted.

"Personally, I think it's for the best," Ivy announced, matter-of-factly, surprising Harley, Conrad, and Lester with her callousness.

Harley was still rebounding from Ivy's heartless comment when she saw the way Conrad was glaring at the men through narrow eyes. Harley immediately knew Conrad didn't believe Damon had actually fallen to his death, and that was concerning.

§

Only an hour later, Harley and Conrad sat on the army blanket and watched Tyler, Shawn, James, and Ivy as they swam in the ocean without any sadness or remorse regarding Damon's death. None of them seemed to have a care in the world. When Lester decided to check on the lobster traps. Harley was still wrestling with her emotions after learning about Damon's ***accidental*** fall. It bothered her more than she cared to admit. In addition to feeling guilty for asking him to stay, she suddenly missed him and found herself replaying the way she'd kissed him in the middle of a monsoon, the night he saved Conrad. She also caught herself thinking about how good he looked shirtless on the beach the day before. Now that the two of them were alone, Harley focused her attention on Conrad.

"Do you really think Damon fell?" Harley asked what was bothering her most.

Without looking away from those frolicking in the water, Conrad drew a deep breath, held it a moment, and then shook his head.

"Men like Damon don't have accidents," Conrad muttered. "That being said, I don't know that those three half-wits could come up with any intelligent plan to arrange an accident, let alone overpower someone with that much military training."

"Any thoughts?" Harley asked.

"One or two," Conrad replied. "The three of them are too lazy to explore, so they probably don't know about the hangar or the cliff on the peak." His stare remained fixated on the swimmers. "And they'd never surprise someone like Damon out in the open like that anyway. There's a cliff beyond the freshwater pond above the latrine. That one, they may have stumbled upon." Conrad finally looked at her. "I think I'd like to take a little walk out there later this afternoon and have a look around. Look for signs of a struggle. Something that might indicate what actually happened."

"Mind if I tag along?"

"I was hoping you would," Conrad remarked. "Watch my back. Make sure I don't have an ***accident***."

When Ivy playfully screamed, Conrad and Harley returned their attention to the young woman splashing around in the water with the three guys, screaming, giggling, and clinging to them. The act itself would mean nothing under normal circumstances, but being stranded on an island where the men outnumbered the women four to one, it was a bold and risky move. Conrad frowned at Ivy's excessively flirtatious behavior and finally looked back at Harley.

"Have you spoken to her about all the flirting?" Conrad asked.

"I brought it up, but she thinks I 'worry too much and need to lighten up'," Harley remarked.

"I'd rather you stayed tense and on edge," Conrad muttered. "I'd prefer you ***didn't*** put your guard down around those guys either, especially now that Damon is gone. He seemed to keep the guys in check, so to speak. Ivy is playing a dangerous game, and she doesn't even realize it."

"I think she likes the attention," Harley remarked.

"Yes, that concerns me too," Conrad muttered, then glanced across the beach where Lester held up an empty trap. "I guess we're not having lobster for lunch today."

"I thought we were having the fish you smoked yesterday," Harley remarked.

"Someone pilfered my smoked fish," Conrad informed her. "All five of them."

"Probably more of a ***something***," Harley reminded him. "You shouldn't have left them outside in that cooler."

"No, I'm convinced it was ***someone***," Conrad remarked. "The cooler was latched. Nothing was tampered with, and it wasn't overturned or damaged in any way."

Harley eyed him somewhat suspiciously. When they saw James emerge from the water and head toward them on the blanket, both assumed he was coming for some bottled water in the cooler. Instead, he grabbed his towel and dried off a little before focusing his gaze on Harley.

"Could we take a walk, Harley?" James asked. "I'd like to speak to you--alone."

Harley considered it for a moment, and despite being less than interested in taking a walk with him, especially if he had something to do with Damon's accident, she agreed.

Conrad made a face while watching Harley walk across the beach with James.

"I know our relationship had gotten off to a bad start," James remarked, then stopped and turned to face her.

Despite wanting to lash out irrationally at James about their non-existent relationship, she sucked up her building anger and remained silent. She knew her expression conveyed her true feelings, but James was too self-absorbed to notice. Perhaps he just didn't care.

"But considering the current situation, I think we need to progress our relationship," James informed her.

"Progress the relationship?" Harley asked, a slight hiss in her voice, while resisting the urge to smirk and chuckle manically. "You mean you want us to have sex?"

"I'm afraid I must insist," James remarked in a slightly commanding tone.

"You must ***insist***?" Harley repeated his words, almost shocked by what she was hearing. How could he not see the psychotic glint in her eyes?

"It's in your best interest, Harley," James informed her. "Those horny bastards are starting to take an interest in you. If they know you're with me, they'll leave you alone."

Harley casually looked past him at Ivy playing in the surf with Shawn and Tyler, then returned her gaze to James. "You're right," she scoffed. "They can't seem to take their eyes off me."

When her eyes shifted back to him and narrowed, James must have finally felt the sarcastic dig. He became frustrated and possibly angry.

"I'll be sharing a woman's company," James announced with a slight hiss in his tone. "If not with you, then with Ivy." His smug, arrogant smile was almost enough to infuriate her. "So you'd better make up your mind."

"I've already made up my mind," Harley snarled in response. "I don't like you, James. You're controlling, self-absorbed, and manipulative. And your lack of sympathy regarding Damon's ***accident*** as a direct response to your actions is deeply disturbing." Harley's eyes narrowed, and her sneer was venomous. "If Ivy wants you, she can gladly have you."

James stared at Harley, appearing shocked that she dared speak to him like that. He didn't handle rejection well, and that was fine by Harley.

"You're making a mistake," James snarled, anger and possible embarrassment in his tone. "And your father isn't going to be very happy when he hears about this."

"By all means," Harley hissed back. "Go crying to my daddy about it."

"You like to pretend you're so different from every other 'daddy's girl'," James launched in response. "But you'll be crying a different song when he cuts you off." His eyes then narrowed as he pointed back at Conrad, who was now standing. "And he fires your favorite servant."

Harley folded her arms across her chest without taking her eyes off James. She wanted to put on a tough front, but his words cut through her. He knew how to hurt her. James then turned and stormed off, heading back to the others who were playing in the surf.

Conrad quickly approached, appearing concerned, obviously having heard the heated words. "What happened?" he asked. "Are you all right?"

Harley snorted a laugh. "I think he dumped me."

§

Conrad and Harley left the beach earlier than the others, not bothering to tell them they were heading back. It was possible the others didn't even realize they had gone. Lester remained, since he would be heading out in the rowboat when Brian ended his shift. Rather than go back to the barracks, Harley and Conrad continued past the shower building and beyond it to the freshwater pond. The path to the cliff was easy to find, as it was freshly trampled. Conrad indicated the path as they walked.

"This is the way they came," Conrad informed her. "Several sets of footprints. I'm positive those size thirteens are Damon's."

Harley felt a cold chill sweep over her despite the humid jungle. She gently rubbed her cold arms as her heart seemed to ache in response. She was frightened by what they might find as they got closer to the cliff. When they finally reached the cliff, which was almost entirely concealed by trees, Conrad stopped and looked around. Harley didn't see anything, which made her wonder what had Conrad's interest.

"What did you find?" she asked.

"Nothing," he informed her, then straightened and met her gaze. "Which is suspicious in itself."

"Nothing is suspicious?"

"There aren't any signs of a struggle," Conrad remarked. "They said they confronted him. Are we supposed to believe Damon simply walked away, took a wrong turn, and just happened to fall from the cliff?"

"Did they chase him?"

"Do you honestly think Damon would run from them?" Conrad asked, then shook his head. "Doubtful. Besides, if they had been running, the footprints would be heavier." He then approached the cliff edge. "There aren't any skid marks near the edge either."

"So they pushed him?" Harley asked, a quiver in her voice as her heart pounded while thinking about Damon's final moments.

"Unless we're to believe Damon suddenly became careless and made a wrong turn, as they would like us to believe," Conrad replied.

Harley joined Conrad by the edge and peered down at the water below. Not nearly as high a ledge as the cliff by the hangar, it was still a long way down to the water below. She stared a moment longer, frightened by what she might see, but there wasn't any sign of Damon. Dead or alive.

"What do we do?" Harley asked, again rubbing her arms while shivering.

"There's not much we can do," Conrad replied, sounding almost defeated. "Even if we somehow reasoned with Brian and Lester and got them to believe us, we're still no match against Shawn, Tyler, and James." Conrad released a deep, tense sigh. "Unfortunately, even if they came right out and admitted they killed Damon, what could we do about it while stranded here? We can't exactly lock them up."

"We could push ***them*** off a cliff," Harley muttered just barely loud enough that Conrad heard her.

"Only as a last resort," he replied.

Harley shot a look at Conrad, her mouth falling open in stunned disbelief. Thankfully, he didn't give her a chance to speak.

"It would be in our best interests if we keep our theory to ourselves and monitor them from a safe distance," Conrad insisted. "We need to bide our time until we're rescued."

"In other words, they get away with murder," Harley remarked. "There's no way to prove it was anything other than an accident."

"Unfortunately, that's correct."

Chapter 28

The sun was setting, and Randall still hadn't returned from wherever it was that he had gone, but they had already assumed he wouldn't be back for dinner. He seemed to be returning later and later with each passing day. Lester had the second shift in the rescue rowboat but would be returning any minute, now that it was dark. As Shawn, James, Tyler, and Ivy started a private game of Texas Hold'em, James was putting all his effort into flirting with the young woman, which didn't bother Harley in the least. It would actually be quite amusing when he finally discovered that Ivy had a thing going with the captain. Harley's relationship with Ivy was already fractured after saying she'd hold her responsible for anything bad Damon did. Still, after her callous comment about being glad Damon died, she decided she no longer wanted anything to do with the young woman. Such behavior was not something Harley could easily forgive.

Harley's stomach turned as she watched the four laughing and having a good time, despite the fact that a man tragically died as a result of their 'for the good of the group' confrontation. As if they weren't directly responsible for Damon's accident. If it even actually was an accident. There was certainly no proof that it hadn't been, but that didn't mean it was. Dead men tell no tales. Her disgust and distaste for the four had reached its boiling point, and she couldn't stand being in the same room with any of them right now. Harley approached Conrad, where he sat on his bunk reading his book for possibly the third time since they'd been stranded.

"I hate the feel of salt water in my hair," Harley informed him. "I'm going to take a quick shower before turning in."

Conrad practically sprang from his bunk, appearing almost alarmed. "I'd prefer if you didn't travel to the showers alone," he insisted.

"Why not?" she asked, surprised by his sudden burst of paranoia.

"I don't trust any of them," Conrad informed her. "I think I should walk you there."

They left the barracks and walked along the path in the dimly lit woods to the shower building. Both were distracted, although possibly for different reasons.

"We don't have any proof those three actually killed Damon," Conrad remarked. "But their lack of sympathy certainly speaks volumes."

"Do you really think they're capable of plotting and carrying out an assassination?" Harley asked. "Especially against someone like Damon."

"They're capable all right," Conrad insisted. "Fear is a powerful motivator, and it can be extremely infectious. He was a direct threat to them and their power over the rest of us." He remained in thought. "I just haven't worked out ***how*** they could have pulled it off. They're not exactly the sharpest tools in the shed."

His comment gave her something to think about. Even she realized the balance of power would now go unchecked without Damon around. Conrad and Harley reached the remote and quiet shower building and entered.

"I'll only be a minute," she insisted.

Conrad chuckled and made himself comfortable on the bench inside the latrine, outside the shower portion. "Sure you will."

"The water's too cold to enjoy it," she reminded him. "And there aren't any lights in there, so it'll be almost completely dark in the shower."

"Want me to check for snakes and spiders first?" Conrad asked.

"No, I'll be fine," she insisted and removed a candle from her bag. "I've come prepared. Nice, romantic candlelit shower for one."

A few minutes later, Harley was rinsing the shampoo from her hair by the dim light of her single candle. A candlelit shower was aesthetically pleasing, but the small flame cast shadows on every wall and made the dark corners even creepier. While she showered, Conrad talked to her from the latrine side. He hadn't been his usual, positive self since practically accusing the three men of killing Damon. Despite hearing him, Harley was off in her own world. When she thought about Damon, she couldn't stop the tears. She allowed herself a few moments of weakness while no one was around to see her crying. She quickly pulled herself together, washing the tears from her face. Once she was finished, Harley shut off the shower, grabbed her towel, and dried herself.

"So what do we do now?" Harley called out to Conrad, resisting the urge to cry some more.

"Survive," Conrad replied. "One day at a time."

After she finished drying off, Harley slipped into fresh army shorts and a tank top. She mostly used her own clothes during the day and slept in the army clothing. After putting on her shoes, she left the shower area while drying her hair. Conrad quickly straightened and sprang to his feet from the bench as Harley appeared through the opening. As they headed out of the building, Conrad was about to speak when they heard movement from within the woods. Both looked around and listened a moment. When they didn't see or hear anything, Conrad looked back at Harley, appearing uncharacteristically stern.

"I need you to make me a promise, Harley," he announced.

"Of course, anything."

Conrad placed a hand on her shoulder and stared into her eyes with a seriousness she'd never seen before. "If I tell you to do something, no matter what you think, do it without question."

"You're scaring me," she remarked, now concerned.

Without warning, Conrad pulled her into his arms and held her against him. "I'm scared too," he informed her. "If something were to happen to you, I--I don't know what I'd do."

Harley returned the embrace, despite how much it frightened her. "You don't have to worry," she replied. "I'll do whatever you ask."

"Thank you," he whispered and finally pulled away, meeting her gaze. "I know it's not my place to order you around, but just this once, I must insist."

"After practically raising me, you've earned the right," she reminded him.

"It's getting dark," he informed her. "We should get back to the barracks."

They headed down the path back to the barracks. Despite not hearing anything, Harley had a strange feeling she was being watched. If Conrad felt the same, he didn't react. It only took them a couple of minutes to reach the clearing and the barracks. When they heard soft moans, both hesitated and looked around the mostly dark area. Tyler was pressed against Ivy from behind, bending the enthusiastic girl over the wall to the burning pit, while he aggressively groped her breasts beneath her shirt. Although both were fully dressed, the sight was shocking all the same.

"What the--?" Conrad gasped, apparently loud enough that they heard him.

Tyler jumped away from Ivy and looked at Harley and Conrad with some embarrassment. Ivy gasped with surprise and hurried back into the barracks, looking a little ruffled. Despite being flustered, it was obvious she was a willing participant.

Tyler gently cleared his throat and sat on the edge of the fire pit. "You guys weren't gone that long," he remarked. "I thought you'd be gone longer."

"Obviously," Conrad muttered.

They heard something rustling within the woods not far from the barracks, alarming all three. Randall suddenly appeared, carrying an armful of wood. He was flushed, drenched in sweat, and out of breath. He spotted them before dumping the wood near the fire pit.

"Sorry, I'm late," Randall announced, as if he hadn't been gone since after breakfast.

Without another word, Randall hurried into the barracks while all three stared after him.

"Randall is seriously losing it," Tyler remarked, shaking his head. "Just the other day, he was babbling about some injured cat he'd found. Then this morning he's talking about a young girl he's been courting."

"The guy's obviously having hallucinations from drug withdrawal," Conrad informed him. "He's your friend. Perhaps you and James should check on him. Make sure he's okay."

"We might be friends," Tyler remarked, then held his hands in the air. "But his problems are his problems. We're all going through shit right now."

"Nice to know you've got your friend's backs," Conrad scoffed.

Randall emerged from the barracks with a towel and a fresh change of clothing and hurried past them toward the showers. Conrad watched him leave, deep in thought. After Tyler returned to the barracks, Conrad looked at Harley.

"I'm going to check on Randall," Conrad insisted. "Make sure he's all right." He then eyed her with noted concern. "Will you be okay while I'm gone?"

Harley nodded, then watched Conrad proceed up the path, taking his time so Randall wouldn't realize he'd been following him. By the time Conrad reached the shower building, the shower was already running. Rather than announce himself, Conrad entered the building just as Randall walked into the showers, clearly naked. Conrad sniffed the air and immediately cringed. There was a foul smell wafting from the pile of dirty clothes Randall had left on the bench. Conrad quietly approached the shower portion and peered in on Randall while he showered. Although it was dark, scratches, brush burns, and bruises were visible along Randall's back, legs, and arms. Randall might have fallen down a hillside or something, but Conrad's expression revealed doubt. As Conrad left the shower building, the faint cracking of a branch caught his attention. He squinted, looking into the darkened woods, and scanned the area.

§

Harley rested on her bunk behind the makeshift partition of army blankets with her back against the wall and attempted to read the only book that even mildly interested her. She heard Conrad call to her from the other side of the partition.

"Harley? You decent?" Conrad asked.

Harley sat up straight and lowered her book. "Yeah, come on in."

Conrad passed between the makeshift partition, approached, and sat on the cot beside her. Harley eyed his odd expression and knew that something he'd seen had him somewhat disturbed.

"There's something not right with Randall," Conrad softly informed her.

"Why do you say that?"

"I saw him as he was going into the showers," Conrad informed her, then met her gaze. "He had scratches and brush burns on his back, legs, and arms."

"Did he say what happened?" Harley asked.

"He didn't see me, and I wasn't about to make my presence known," Conrad insisted.

"He probably fell," Harley remarked. "Plenty of places to do that around here."

"Perhaps," Conrad replied and again sank into thought. "But from the way he's been acting, I suspect something happened before he fell."

Harley stared at Conrad with a curious look. "Withdrawal, particularly from the hard stuff, can easily produce hallucinations," she reminded him. "Who knows what dark world he's living in right now. For all we know, he might think people are out to get him."

Conrad snorted a tense laugh. "With this group, that might not be a hallucination," he remarked, then turned almost stern. "I want you to avoid him, especially if I'm not around."

Chapter 29

Day Twelve. It had been four days since Damon had his ***accident***, and Harley noticed a rapid escalation in just about everything around the campsite. Over the last four days, Shawn had Brian and Lester out in the rowboat in twelve-hour shifts, now covering the overnight as well. Harley wasn't sure whether Shawn was just being an authoritarian or purposely keeping the two men isolated from the rest of the group and, maybe, even from each other. In addition to fishing and checking the lobster traps, he had the two men hauling water twice a day to the barracks. What really seemed odd, though, was the increase in disappearing fish. At times, the fish vanished even before they were cleaned, and often when Conrad was only away for a few minutes.

Not surprisingly, without Damon around to do most of the work, nothing was getting done. Despite Shawn barking orders and treating Lester, Brian, and Conrad like slaves, he didn't ask James or Tyler to help. And the captain certainly wasn't pulling his own weight either. Even Ivy didn't do anything around camp anymore. Apparently, playing queen to the captain's king had its perks. Although Harley and Ivy still traveled together to the shower building for their morning showers, they didn't talk much. When Ivy did talk to Harley, it was usually to complain that Conrad wasn't doing enough or to try to order her around. Naturally, Harley didn't let Ivy bully her, but that usually resulted in Shawn getting involved and ordering Conrad to do the bullshit Harley had refused to do.

If the bullying and laziness weren't bad enough, Conrad discovered someone had gotten into the MRE crates and opened every pouch, removing the best items and leaving the scraps. All the sugar packets, crackers, and desserts were missing from every single pouch. Although Harley knew Ivy wasn't responsible, she was positive she had seen Ivy secretly scarfing down a candy bar earlier that afternoon. Harley was convinced the culprit was the captain. Being Ivy's dutiful boyfriend, he wanted to give her all the goodies from the MRE bags. Maybe he wouldn't feel that way if he knew Ivy had been sneaking around with Tyler. A couple of times, Harley's plans for an hour in the pond resulted in her and Conrad catching Tyler and Ivy performing lewd sexual acts in the water. Of course, Ivy never saw them.

Then there was Conrad. He was becoming increasingly paranoid over her welfare, even though the men weren't displaying any sexual aggression. It had gotten so bad that he rarely left her out of his sight. But Randall's behavior was possibly the most concerning. Despite supposedly being out all day collecting firewood, he brought back less and less, forcing Conrad to scrounge for whatever he could so he could keep cooking and finding new ways to make fish exciting.

§

That morning, Harley just about reached her breaking point while in the shower building with Ivy. Harley barely used a dollop of shampoo to wash her longer hair, attempting to conserve what little she had left in the bottle. They were nearly out of shampoo, even with the men using soap on their hair so the women could have what was left. Even though Harley and Ivy had originally divided the remaining bottles evenly between them, Harley noticed Ivy had a nearly full bottle, which didn't seem possible. She watched as Ivy used a shocking amount of shampoo to wash her hair for a second time. How did she have so much shampoo, especially to wash and repeat while using so much? Apparently, Shawn's queen got everything she desired, even if the rest of them went without.

Harley frowned with disgust, knowing there was nothing she could say or do about it except silently fume. She snatched her towel, wrapped it around her wet body, and headed for the bench inside the doorway. Horror suddenly swept over her as Shawn strode past her, completely naked and fully aroused, into the shower. He didn't give Harley a second glance, not caring that she was there or even if she had been naked. Shawn approached Ivy, circled his arms around her from behind, and pressed against her. She cried out with surprise, then laughed and giggled. Harley stared at the scene for only a moment with her mouth hanging open, her body practically trembling with fear at what she was witnessing. It wasn't as if they couldn't see her. They ***knew*** she was there!

Harley darted into the latrine and changing area. She was so shaken, she didn't even bother drying off. She fumbled with her clothes, hurriedly slipping into them. Being wet and her trembling hands made the task of dressing a thousand times more difficult. Harley barely had her shoes on when she heard moaning and giggling coming from the showers. Harley darted from the showers, unable to control her spiking anxiety as her entire body trembled. Her legs felt unusually weak, and there was a loud ringing in her ears. By the time she reached the barracks, the shock had worn off, and anger had taken its place. She actually wanted to strangle someone. Harley stormed into the barracks, nearly startling Conrad with her dramatic, grand entrance.

"Harley," Conrad announced, looking surprised. "Is everything okay?"

"No," Harley scoffed while practically tossing her towel across one of the chairs. "Shawn invited himself into the showers with Ivy and me!"

"He what?" Conrad exploded, eyes wide with a cross between horror and anger. "Even if you forgot to lock the door, he should have heard the water running."

"Oh, he heard it," Harley assured him while touching her aching head. "He and Ivy were going at it before I even had my shoes on."

"Are you saying she purposely left the door unlocked?" Conrad gasped.

"Oh, I'm sure of it," Harley scoffed. "I could have killed him. Or her. I don't know which."

"That's disgusting and completely disrespectful," Conrad erupted, becoming more enraged the longer he thought about it. "And it's against our rules."

"There aren't any more rules," Harley scoffed as her anger consumed her, which only made the ringing in her ears louder. "Especially not when it concerns King Shawn. Two weeks! It only took two weeks of being shipwrecked for morals to decay and decency to corrode."

"Not two weeks," Conrad corrected her. "Four days. Things started going downhill the moment Damon had his little ***accident***." He shook his head with disgust. "I'm going to have it out with our illustrious captain about his behavior."

"Yeah, then you'll have an accident too," Harley scoffed. Her own words were enough to quiet her rage. She didn't need Conrad doing anything stupid.

"I can't sit by and do nothing," Conrad reminded her. "He needs to be held accountable. I won't have your safety compromised because of his animal lust."

Harley frowned and shook her head while raking trembling fingers through her wet hair. "You should have seen the way he strolled in there, naked and fully aroused, dick swinging like some prized stud. Not a care in the world," she huffed. "Walked in right past me like he owned the place and everything in it."

Conrad stared at her a moment, then groaned softly before snatching a kitchen knife, looking like a killer from a horror movie. "Fuck talking," he snarled, all patience lost. "***He's*** about to have an accident."

"Put that down," Harley groaned. "Rather than talk to him or ice him, I think we need to bring it up in front of the others. Publicly shame him."

"We'll try it your way first," Conrad huffed, angrily tossing down the knife with a metallic clatter. "But if that doesn't work, he's getting a poisonous snake in his bed."

Chapter 30

Later that afternoon, Harley felt a little better after Conrad suggested she swim in the pond while he fished. He sat on a rock near the edge of the large pond with one of the ship's two fishing poles while Harley swam near the waterfall so she wouldn't scare the fish away. Her clothes were lying on a nearby rock while she swam in her two-piece bathing suit. Harley swam closer to the waterfall, enjoying the loud, hypnotic sound and the churning water. She looked back across the pond and watched Conrad with his pole at the other end, her view partially blocked by trees. Harley pushed her wet hair back and enjoyed the heavy spray of water against her body. When she opened her eyes, she thought she saw something move within the jungle. Harley stared into the woods, attempting to catch a glimpse of what she'd seen. At this point, she almost preferred a wild animal over one of her fellow passengers. When she didn't see anything, she looked back across the pond where Conrad remained fishing. Harley once more scanned the jungle, wondering what she'd seen.

§

A little after five o'clock that afternoon, Brian stumbled into the barracks half asleep. Shawn put them on five in the morning until five in the afternoon shifts, so no one had to row in and out of the ocean after dark. It was just before dinner, and Conrad and Harley had been attempting to create yet another fish meal. Conrad looked at the exhausted man and attempted a pleasant smile, although it was getting harder over the last couple of days.

"Hungry?" Conrad asked.

"More tired than anything," Brian replied. "What do you have?"

"Fish cakes," Conrad announced cheerfully.

Brian groaned and collapsed into one of the chairs at the table. "Bring it on," he announced with a dreary sigh.

Conrad served him a plate of fish cakes, waiting with anticipation for Brian's reaction. Brian showed no enthusiasm as he cut into the fried glob.

"Some strange behavior is going on around here," Brian announced while forcing the first bite.

Conrad joined him at the table. "Oh?"

"On my way inland, I saw Ivy and Tyler getting it on at the beach," Brian informed him. "But Lester told me he walked in on Ivy and Shawn in the showers. Didn't even lock the door. Neither were very discreet and didn't even attempt to hide it."

"Yes, I've noticed," Harley muttered.

"How long until they find out Ivy's burning the candle at both ends?" Conrad huffed, then shook his head. "Pretty soon, the two of them will be fighting over her."

"Well, it gets worse," Brian continued. "According to James, he's been sharing her as well."

Harley rolled her eyes and shook her head. "I didn't hear that one, but I'm not surprised."

"Morals are fading fast," Conrad informed Brian. "In a way, I suppose I'm grateful she's juggling them. It keeps Harley out of harm's way."

"I don't like it, and I don't approve, but it's completely up to them what they do," Brian remarked, then snorted a laugh. "Personally, I'll do without rather than take turns like she's some sort of amusement park ride."

"That's graphic," Harley muttered.

"Sorry," Brian replied while managing a tiny smile. "I think I have shipwreck fever." He then eyed Conrad. "I'd heard the rumor from Lester that our illustrious rich boy James has been paying Ivy for her services."

"I don't understand her," Harley remarked. "I thought she liked Shawn, but now she's having sex for IOUs."

"The money was probably too much of a temptation for her," Conrad muttered.

"It's the 'use now; pay later' option," Brian scoffed. "If James decides he's not going to pay her, she's screwed ***twice***."

"I doubt he'd do that," Harley remarked. "He might be an asshole, but he's not a cheap asshole."

"Unlike our captain, who invited himself into the showers this morning while Harley was still in there," Conrad informed Brian. "Harley said he put himself on full display in front of her, and then hooked up with Ivy before she even had time to run out the door. Naturally, it was quite upsetting."

Brian looked from Conrad to Harley with his mouth hanging open in surprise. "That's disturbing," he remarked, then shook his head. "Shawn always had asshole tendencies, but I never would have thought he'd go so low. Honestly, I only trust the two of you and Lester anymore." He seemed to consider everything he'd heard and seen lately. "For a guy who's been getting laid regularly, the captain's been barking orders and running our asses off an awful lot. I think he's up to something and wants to keep Lester and me out of the way."

"I think you're right," Conrad announced. "Something is going on around here, and we weren't invited." He hesitated while studying Brian for a moment. "Can I count on your support when I approach the captain about his behavior in the showers this morning?"

"Definitely," Brian replied, then shook his head. "I mean, as far as I'm concerned, I'm out of a job anyway. I only take Shawn's bullshit because I want to get home, and signaling a rescue ship seems to be our best option."

"Lester supports us, too," Conrad informed him.

"I haven't seen Randall in a while," Brian remarked. "Think he *fell* from a cliff in the same way Damon had?"

"No, he's still around, but he's returning less and less," Conrad replied. "It's odd, but I think he's the one who's been stealing my fish."

"Really?" Brian asked, surprised. "What makes you think that?"

"He smells often of fish," Conrad replied.

"What would he do with them?" Brian asked, then snorted a laugh. "I mean, I'd hope never to see another fish as long as I live."

"I couldn't say."

Brian pushed the dish away. "Thanks for the dinner," he announced. "You do good work disguising fish, but I just can't eat any more of it. I really need to get some sleep."

§

That night, something woke Harley from her light sleep. She opened her eyes, and to her horror, she saw James entering the partitioned-off area where Harley and Ivy had their bunks. She considered screaming, but he veered off to Ivy's bunk, stripped naked, and climbed under the covers with her. Although Ivy welcomed him into her bunk, there was no foreplay and no kissing. James was instantly on top of the young woman. Harley couldn't believe what she was witnessing, and, judging by the sounds she made, Ivy got little to no enjoyment out of it. James grunted like a pig as the cot creaked with each movement under their combined weight. He grunted a few more times, then let out one exaggerated groan, and it was over. Two minutes after he'd walked into their sleeping quarters, he was already slipping back into his clothes and leaving. It took him longer to dress than it did to ***relieve*** himself. Ivy just turned on her side and went back to sleep. Harley was stunned, if not horrified, by what she'd just witnessed.

§

Day Thirteen. The very next morning, Harley followed Ivy up the wide path to the shower building, not that she had any intention of showering with her bunkmate ever again. Ivy walked briskly, attempting to avoid her, but Harley remained in hot pursuit.

"It was bad enough having Shawn invade our shower yesterday morning," Harley lashed out. "But I don't appreciate your disgusting acts in our sleeping quarters with my bunk just five feet away!"

"Lighten up," Ivy scoffed while rolling her eyes. "You really need to get laid."

"No thanks," Harley snarled. "You seem to be doing enough of that for everyone these days."

Ivy spun to face her, forcing Harley to stop abruptly. "Hey, it's your fault I'm in this situation," she snapped hotly.

"Seriously? This is my fault?" Harley demanded. "How the hell do you figure that?"

"James wanted you," Ivy huffed in anger. "He still does. You wouldn't put out, so now he's paying me. With as lousy as he is in bed, it's a damned good thing too."

"Hey, you're the one who accepted his offer. I'd say the decision was all yours," Harley lashed back. "Don't put blame anywhere other than on yourself." She then pointed a warning finger at her. "And if you ever pull another stunt like that in front of me again, I'll empty that piss pot under my bunk on both of you!"

Harley spun and stormed back in the direction of the barracks. She heard something move in the woods and suddenly stopped, looking around. She thought it was Ivy, but she was already gone. Harley stared a moment longer before continuing on her way.

Chapter 31

Day Fourteen. The following afternoon, Harley and Conrad walked the path down to the beach. Both seemed pretty anxious after spending the last two days trying to avoid the others. Lester was sleeping off his overnight shift in the rowboat, and Randall disappeared right after breakfast, as usual. Harley skipped her morning shower, since she and Conrad would be on the beach that afternoon. Conrad wanted to check the lobster traps and add more chum to bait them. It was hard to believe when Lester said they were empty again that morning, yet all the bait was gone. Harley had no idea where, what, or who Ivy was doing anymore. Servicing three men was almost too much for Ivy to keep track of herself. How she was able to keep her affair partners from learning about one another remained a mystery.

At least there hadn't been any repeat performances in Harley's sleeping quarters. And with good reason. Despite much scrutiny and protests, Conrad moved his bunk to the back, next to Harley and Ivy. When Ivy expressed discomfort with Conrad being in their quarters, Harley merely responded, "Now you know how I feel," and left it at that. As they stepped out of the tree line onto the sand, both stopped short. Harley and Conrad nearly did a double-take at what they witnessed. On a faded army blanket on full display, right where anyone walking the path could see, Ivy lay tangled with the three naked men like some bizarre game of Twister. Shawn was beneath her, hands gripping her hips as she moved. James knelt behind her, his body pressed close. Tyler leaned in from the side, his mouth on her neck while his hand roamed freely.

All four naked bodies glistened with sweat and sand. Low grunts, moans, and flesh slapping flesh carried clearly on the breeze. It was abundantly clear that all three men were more than okay with sharing Ivy. Despite being in the rowboat almost on the edge of the horizon, Harley could almost see the whites of Brian's eyes as he witnessed the beach orgy from afar. Harley held back her gasp as heat flooded her face, followed by a sick twist in her gut. She was somehow unable to look away, as if watching a train wreck unfold in slow motion. Ivy arched with a gasp that sounded almost theatrical, her head falling back. James muttered something crude, which made Tyler laugh, the sound sharp and ugly against the gentle crash of the waves.

Harley's stomach turned. She spun on her heels without a word and stormed back along the path, returning to the barracks. She heard Conrad running after her, attempting to catch up.

"This behavior isn't going to stop unless we put an end to it," Conrad announced, his voice tight, almost strangled.

"They're doing this to make us uncomfortable," Harley lashed out. "They're seeing what they can get away with. Each time we ignore their deviant behavior, they push a little further. They're trying to break us!"

"Actually, I think they're just a bunch of clueless perverts with fractured moral compasses," Conrad remarked. "None of them are smart enough to pull off some sort of elaborate scheme to break us."

"Nobody's that stupid, Conrad," Harley huffed without slowing. The image burned into her eyes. Ivy laughing, the three men taking turns, no shame, no privacy, no regard for anyone else on the island. Her skin crawled. "They know damned well Brian can see them from the boat, yet they chose a location out in the open within his view. If Damon were alive, they'd never act this way."

By the time they reached the barracks, Harley's hands were still shaking. She stopped, drew a deep breath that did nothing to steady her, and turned to Conrad.

"I tried reasoning with Ivy, and this is what I get in retaliation," she just about shouted. "We're done cooperating with those assholes. No more free ride for them while the rest of us work our asses off so they can have orgies on the beach right in front of us. They've stolen provisions and pushed us around while giving us nothing in return. Their worthless asses can starve to death, for all I care. I'm done. If you can get Lester and Brian to back us, all the better. We mutiny tonight!"

§

When Shawn, James, Tyler, and Ivy showed up for dinner that evening, sporting their exotic tans, Harley, Conrad, Brian, and Lester were sitting at the table or relaxing on their bunks. Shawn glanced around, then looked at Conrad.

"Where's dinner?" Shawn asked. "Brian brought back a bunch of fish this afternoon." He then looked from Brian to Lester, possibly surprised to see both in the same room at the same time. "Why isn't someone out on the water with the rowboat?"

"It's your shift," Brian informed the captain, a slight hiss in his tone.

"As for the rest of us," Conrad announced. "We already ate." He then shrugged, with little care, without looking up from his book. "If you want something to eat, I suggest you find it and make it yourself."

"You're getting out of this relationship exactly what you put into it," Harley informed them, then sneered. "***Nothing***."

"We're officially on strike," Lester added as he flipped through his magazine, where he remained casually reclined on his bunk.

"It seems as if you need us and not the other way around," Conrad informed them, then returned to his book and turned the page.

Shawn sneered at them and headed for the crate of MREs. When he opened it, he found the crate empty.

"Sorry about that," Conrad announced with a soft sigh. "Apparently, the same person who stole all the sugar, crackers, and desserts came back for the rest."

Shawn became angry with the four. "You had better get back out there and gather more food," he demanded. "Or else we're all going to starve."

"No," Conrad announced with a sigh and finally looked up. "We won't ***all*** starve. Just the four of you." He then shrugged. "But I'm sure your orgies on the beach will keep you going until a rescue arrives. Well, providing one of you is sitting in the rowboat waiting for one."

"Is that what this is about?" Ivy demanded. "You're ***jealous*** of our beach activities?"

"Jealous? Are you fucking kidding?" Harley snarled, ready to lunge for the young woman. "We've discussed your lewd activities and putting yourselves on display for the rest of us to hear and see. Show some fucking decency and maybe an ounce of self-respect."

Conrad sprang to his feet and glared at Shawn. "This isn't a goddamned dictatorship," he announced, his anger and rage finally surfacing. "This is a partnership. If you four fucks can't pull your own weight, then you're no longer welcome to live with us."

"***We*** live with ***you***?" Shawn demanded. "Who died and made you lord and master?"

"Probably the same people who put you in charge," Conrad informed him. "Even your own men have had enough of you."

"That's mutiny!"

"Your ship sank!" Conrad shouted in an earthshattering tone Harley had never heard before. He'd reached his breaking point. "You're captain of jack shit! Your free ride is over! Come back with a couple of fish, some bananas, a few coconuts, and maybe we'll resume negotiations, but starting tonight, we're on strike. You can fend for yourselves or starve."

"And cover the fuck up!" Harley shouted in anger. "Keep your sex acts private, you fucking bunch of animals!"

Chapter 32

Day Sixteen. It took almost two days for Shawn, Tyler, James, and Ivy to finally cave in. They couldn't manage gathering any food for themselves, let alone firewood. Conrad took perverse pleasure in watching them squirm, requiring them to bring wood, water, and food to the camp. Ivy attempted to make peace with Harley, but Harley held onto her grudge, throwing the shower scene and beach orgy in her face. Ivy tried to play it off as an honest mistake, but their orgy hadn't been 'accidental' as they claimed. They had an entire island to find a secluded spot, but purposely chose the highly traveled stretch of beach for their orgy, knowing the others would see them. When pleading didn't work, Ivy tried crying, hoping to play on her emotions, but she wasn't buying it.

Harley wouldn't hold Ivy taking money in exchange for sex against her, just as she wouldn't hold her servicing three men at once against her. The deliberate display in common areas for all to see was what she couldn't forgive. They wanted to demean them by putting their sex acts on display in front of everyone, like some sick game. That was what Harley couldn't forgive.

§

Day Twenty-one. Five days later. Shawn, Tyler, and James, once again thinking they were above Lester, Brian, and Conrad, had completely reverted back to the way things were prior to the strike. Shawn didn't bark nearly as many orders, but the three men again did nothing to help out around camp. Ivy still considered herself the queen bee and placed herself upon a pedestal above Harley, because she was the envy of the three 'men in charge'. The only thing that had changed was the blatant orgies for everyone to see. The four still met up in the showers, on the beach, and in the pond, but they gave prior notice, in possibly the rudest of ways, when they would be in each of the places. Although she didn't appreciate the sexually graphic nature of the announcement, Harley was glad she was forewarned. Brian and Conrad, on the other hand, were opposed to the public orgies, whether they saw them or not. Lester didn't seem to mind, possibly getting his jollies from a spectator's point of view.

§

Day Twenty-four. Three days later. Conrad, Brian, and Lester had been holding secret meetings since the day of the strike. Harley lost interest in them because it seemed as if the men were being a little paranoid. Things weren't perfect, far from it. But Harley was okay with it since Shawn didn't order the men about anymore, even if they were still doing the same routine they'd been doing back when they were being bossed around. Although Conrad refused to leave Harley's side, except for bathroom breaks and shower stops with only a thin metal wall between them, his paranoia continued to increase, even escalate. He thought Harley was in danger, even when she was within his sight. Conrad was starting to talk nonsense, claiming that Shawn, James, and

Tyler were planning another accident--***his*** accident. He believed they wanted him out of the way so they could control her. Harley worried about Conrad so much that she started hearing things rustling around in the woods and even imagined him talking to people when there was no one there.

Conrad's paranoia and mood swings were also affecting Harley's sleep, as she was afraid to close her eyes even for a second. She wasn't sure if Conrad was getting any sleep either. Every time she opened her eyes, he was sitting up in his bunk, pretending to read, but he was always somewhere else. Maybe he was fine, and she was the one going crazy. Only time would tell. With still no sign of a rescue in sight, everyone seemed to go through a period where they lacked hope. Harley clung to her friendship with Conrad to keep her balanced, but she feared that it eventually wouldn't be enough.

Chapter 33

Day Twenty-nine. It was nearly sunset, and Harley once again turned in early. Not just to avoid the lewd behavior among the four swingers, but in the hopes that she and Conrad would actually get some much-needed sleep. Unfortunately, that never seemed to happen. Harley lay awake on her bunk in the partitioned area while Conrad actually slept, for a change, in what used to be Ivy's bunk. Ivy seemed to prefer her bed amongst her three boyfriends these days. Conrad tossed and moaned softly in his sleep, catching Harley's attention. She glanced over at his bunk and watched him. She didn't want to wake him, even though he was having a bad dream. He needed the sleep. Conrad suddenly gasped and just about shot up in bed. He sprang from the bunk and looked around, looking right past her, not even seeing her. It was possible he wasn't even awake, just sleepwalking.

"Harley?"

Harley moved to her elbow and looked at him. "Right here," she announced, catching his attention.

Conrad spun to face her as she sat up. He hurried to her and touched her face with a look of concern.

"Thank God," he gasped. "I was worried about you. I must've dozed off."

Harley stood and faced him. "I'm fine, Conrad," she insisted. "You don't need to worry so much. It's affecting your sleep. I'm starting to worry about you."

"Where are the others?" he demanded.

"The usual," she replied. "Four on the beach having an orgy, one off in a row boat, one asleep, and one God knows where."

Conrad quickly took her arm. "This won't work," he insisted. "You need to leave."

"What?" she cried out, stunned. "And go where?"

"James is bored with Ivy," Conrad informed her. "He's been ***looking*** at you."

"According to you, they're all ***looking*** at me," Harley reminded him. "I'm worried about you. You hardly sleep, and you follow me around all day. It's not healthy."

"You need to leave--now!"

Harley stared at him with surprise at his outburst. "What? Be serious!"

"You promised to do whatever I said, no matter what it was," he reminded her. "You can seek shelter in the old hangar on top of the hill. I'll meet you there tomorrow evening with your things."

"Are you serious?" she demanded. "Stay all alone in that hangar?"

"You promised," Conrad reminded her. "None of the others even know it exists. They won't find you there. You have to go before they get back."

Harley stared at him, surprised by what he was asking. He was right, though; she did promise. She slowly nodded and left the back room. As she stepped outside the barracks, the sky was already darkening as the sun set. A harsh storm was nearly upon them, and the wind blew violently. Harley paused outside the barracks and looked at the sky.

"Great day to wig out, Conrad," she muttered.

Harley hurried up the path, hoping to make it to the hangar and avoid the approaching storm. As if mocking her, the rain began to pour, just about drenching her. Despite the pouring rain, she heard someone on the path. Harley turned and saw James several feet behind her.

"I need to talk to you, Harley," James called out to her.

"Maybe later," she announced. "I, uh, have something I need to do first."

As she hurried toward the latrine and shower building, she looked back and saw that James was still following her.

"Go away, James!" she shouted back at him.

"I ***need*** to talk to you!" he insisted.

Harley became alarmed and started running along the less-traveled path toward the pond. She couldn't lead him to the hangar, especially if she intended to hang out there. In fact, besides herself and Conrad, no one even knew about the old hangar. When she looked back, James was still following her, also picking up the pace. Harley ran faster, now frightened, dodging overgrown plant life and jumping over rocks and roots. As it poured violently, she ran through the clearing with the fresh water pond and continued up the hill. The wind whipped, and she could barely see the path any longer. Harley reached the top of the hill, disoriented. When she looked behind her, James was gone. The back of the hangar was fifty yards to the left. If James made it up the hill, he probably wouldn't spot the hangar, particularly in the pouring rain.

Already soaked, Harley ran toward the hangar and along the side toward the front. James suddenly appeared around the corner and shoved her against the metal siding. Harley struggled against his grip, almost breaking free.

"Get away from me, you bastard!"

James again shoved her harshly against the hangar, creating a loud, metallic thump as her head struck the metal. Harley's eyes shut while enduring the startling pain. She opened her eyes and stared into his unpredictable, harsh gaze.

"You're supposed to be mine," James snarled. "It's about time you've learned your place."

Harley managed to push him away with all of her strength, but he retaliated and slammed her against the hangar again, her head striking the metal with another loud bang. This time, she was frozen from the pain. Despite both being drenched by the rain, James kissed her harshly and attempted to grab her shorts. A shadow loomed over him from the left. James was suddenly pulled away from Harley and thrown against the hangar near her. The metal hangar wall thumped loudly and dented. Damon held James to the wall, placing the barrel of his gun between James's eyes. Harley stared with shock and surprise at the supposedly dead man. James was beyond shocked. He was horrified. A sly and devious smile crossed Damon's face.

"What's wrong, James?" Damon snarled despite being soaked by the pouring rain. "Seen a ghost?"

"Damon, I--"

"Shut up," Damon snarled.

Harley stared, wanting to run, but she was too terrified to move.

"Thought I was dead, huh?" Damon scoffed at James, who was possibly paralyzed with fear. "Fifty-foot cliff. Not much of a dive. I used to dive off the cliffs in Polignano a Mare, Italy. I'm also a great swimmer." His brows rose dramatically. "Do you think you could survive that fall if ***I*** were to push ***you***?"

"You were out of control," James insisted, finally speaking, attempting to control his fear. "We had to protect the others."

"Protect the others, my ass!" Damon shouted, then attempted a smile and once again appeared calm. "I know exactly why you wanted to get rid of me."

"Let's just forget about this whole ordeal," James insisted. "I'll give you five hundred thousand to forget about it. You can even have Harley."

Damon suddenly grabbed him by the throat while gritting his teeth. James gasped and struggled against his hand.

"I don't want your money," Damon snarled while eyeing him before slowly releasing him. His look was stern and harsh. "Take off your clothes."

James suddenly appeared horrified at the order. "What? You wouldn't--?" he gasped, then trembled, fearing the worst. "You're not that crazy! Take the girl!"

Damon again placed his gun to James's forehead. "Do it," he snarled.

James quickly removed his soaked clothes while trembling with fear. Harley eyed Damon and his gun, trying to decide whether to make a run for it. Even though James deserved whatever happened to him, she didn't want to witness ***that*** kind of assault. The rain continued to pour down, soaking all three as James removed the last of his clothes. Damon eyed James's naked body and raised his brow before meeting his gaze.

"That's ***really*** embarrassing," Damon remarked with a humored smirk.

"What are you going to do?" James asked, frightened and trembling at the thought of Damon's next move.

"I'm going to give you a five-second head start before I target practice on your ass," Damon replied, his smile mocking him. "You'd better start running--"

James gasped and ran for the path. Something snapped within Harley, and she ran in the opposite direction, not even stopping to look back. She ran through the wet jungle as fast as she could. Falling debris struck her while the rain stung as it poured down. When she was far enough away, she finally stopped and caught her breath. Harley looked back, but there was no one behind her. She looked around, trembling and attempting to make sense of everything that had just happened. The wind continued to blow harshly, and more debris pelted her. Harley didn't know where to go or what to do.

Chapter 34

It was one hell of a storm with blowing wind, pouring rain, and frightening lightning and thunder. Harley relived the trauma of the boat sinking with each storm. Rather than curl up in a ball and let it consume her, she slowly walked around the hangar and approached the small door near the large, closed bay door. With a trembling hand, she opened the smaller door and stepped inside the dimly lit hangar. As the storm raged outside, she stood just inside the doorway. Harley could see a light on within the office, and the old jeep was parked near the bigger door. A towel and dry clothing lay neatly folded on the hood of the jeep. Damon appeared in the office doorway across the large hangar and stared at her.

"If you intend to stay, lock the door behind you," he informed her. "I don't want any more surprise visitors tonight."

Damon disappeared into the office as quickly as he had appeared. Harley stared at the open office doorway a moment, then turned and locked the hangar door. She took the towel and dried her hair, face, and arms as she uncertainly approached the office. The small office, now clean and neatly organized, was well lit with a large, kerosene lamp and a fire burning in the wood-burning stove. It was very homey. Damon sat casually behind the desk and read an old, thick book. Harley stood, soaking wet, in the doorway and stared at him for a long moment. Damon briefly looked up, then returned to his book.

"There's hot water in the kettle on the wood burner," Damon informed her. "Hot chocolate, tea, and coffee are in the locker on the top shelf."

"You knew I'd come back?" she asked, shivering from her wet clothes against her body while the heat from the fire burning in the stove felt warm and inviting.

"Where else would you go?" Damon replied, almost lacking interest. He shut the book and leaned back in his chair. "You certainly can't go back to the barracks and confront James, so I suppose I'm the lesser of two evils." He chuckled, amused. "Imagine that?"

"A bit risky."

"Only in your mind," Damon replied, then indicated her wet clothes. "You may want to change into those dry clothes. Pneumonia would be dangerous." He offered a tiny grin. "I won't peek, I promise."

Less than ten minutes later, Harley returned to the office in the dry clothing Damon had left for her. Damon was reclined in his chair, his feet propped on the desk, and an open book in his hands. The cover read, "Aviation Mechanics". Harley uncertainly walked across the office to the stove, enjoying the warmth against her still damp skin. She poured some water into a cup, then added hot chocolate mix. After thoroughly stirring it, she took a sip and shut her eyes.

"God, that's good," she whispered, not realizing she said it aloud.

"All the comforts of home," Damon replied, then looked above his book, indicating the only cot within the office.

"Feel free to use the bed," he announced. "I have a sleeping bag I can put on the floor."

Damon returned to his book, barely paying any attention to her. Harley appeared uneasy as she watched him, despite his blatant disinterest.

"I'd like to hire you to protect me from James," Harley blurted out before she could stop herself.

Damon lowered his book and stared at her, showing little reaction and making no comment.

"I'll pay you double what James was paying you," Harley added.

"Don't be ridiculous."

Harley stepped closer to him, even though her body trembled and every instinct within her told her to stay away from him. "He's insane," she insisted, feeling her entire body tremble at what had happened earlier. "I need your help."

"I don't want your money," Damon announced so casually that it was almost chilling.

Harley tensed and, feeling insecure, attempted to rub away the tiny goosebumps on her arms. "What ***do*** you want?" she asked, now nervous, afraid of the answer.

Damon shut his eyes and groaned softly. "I'd kill for a cheeseburger," he replied.

Harley stared at him for a long moment and had to wonder if he'd gone completely mad. He opened his eyes, caught her look, and chuckled.

"I don't want anything from you," Damon informed her. "I don't take advantage of bad situations." He casually shrugged. "James isn't going to harm you as long as you're with me. He knows I'll kill him. Happily. Free of charge."

Harley uncertainly sat on the cot and stared at him. "You'd do that for me?"

"It would be more of a personal pleasure," he informed her. "I really just need an excuse."

"Thank you for helping me," Harley whispered, fighting her tears. The last thing she wanted to do was show weakness in front of Damon, even if he already knew she was weak. "I'd hate to think what might have happened if you hadn't intervened."

"It's not necessary to thank me," Damon informed her. "I don't tolerate sexual violence. Had he actually touched you, he'd be dead right now." Damon again indicated the cot. "Why don't you get some sleep? I'm sure you had a long day."

Harley finished her hot chocolate, set the cup near the bedside, and uncertainly slipped under the covers. Damon set his book aside and unrolled a sleeping bag just below the bunk, being the only available space in the small office. After he turned down the lantern, the wood-burning stove still gave off enough light to see the interior of the room. Harley watched Damon as he slipped into the sleeping bag below her. She couldn't believe he was alive and feared taking her eyes off him, not wanting him to vanish like some bizarre hallucination.

Chapter 35

Day Thirty. Shortly after sunrise, Damon opened the large hangar door, light spilling inside. Harley couldn't take her eyes off Damon. He projected an odd sense of balance she hadn't felt in weeks. It was almost as if he were thriving under the isolated island conditions. His calm restored an internal peace she had been unaware she'd lost. His movements and mannerisms made her brutally aware of how far Conrad had sunk since the camp fell apart. Part of her wondered if she'd fallen apart as well and just hadn't realized it. As Damon approached the ladder to the plane's open engine compartment, Harley studied the fighter plane with its wings taking up a large portion of the hangar.

"Isn't she a beauty?" Damon asked, grinning like a schoolboy.

Harley couldn't even remember the last time she'd seen anyone smile. That Damon was the one smiling was almost surreal.

"You don't honestly think you'll get this thing to run, do you?" Harley asked, attempting to get her mind off Damon's commanding and oddly sane presence.

Damon scaled the second ladder to the cockpit and climbed inside. The engines fired and vibrated the entire hangar. He immediately shut it down and looked at her while grinning.

"Running is easy," he announced, then snorted a laugh. "Flying's the hard part."

Damon climbed from the cockpit, scaled partway down the ladder, and then jumped the rest of the way to the floor, landing near her. Harley was a bit curious and climbed the ladder. She peered into the fighter jet's cockpit and stared at the claustrophobic space. The 'no frills' padded seat looked like the worst seat in coach on some generic airline with all the comforts of a roller coaster. Once seated, the pilot would essentially straddle the yoke that would possibly be snug against his crotch, and his legs would disappear beneath the controls at least up to his knees. There were many controls in front, no more than arm's length from where the pilot sat, as well as controls on either side, which would be classified as armrests. Once the canopy was lowered, a man with Damon's broad shoulders would probably be packed in like a sardine. The rear trainer's seat had a little more legroom and seemed a little wider, but was still quite claustrophobic and offered the same roller-coaster comforts.

"Do you know how to fly?" she asked while climbing back down the ladder.

"I've flown single-engine prop planes before," he informed her. "It's not exactly the same, but it's very similar. I've been reading the flight manual. I think I've got the basics."

"You're taking a big chance," she reminded him.

"What have I got to lose?"

"Your life," she replied with a snort and a shrug.

"Not much to live for here," Damon reminded her. "I certainly can't spend the rest of my life in solitude. I'll go insane. It's worth the risk."

"Why did you remain here alone?" she asked, confused by his decision to choose solitude. "Why didn't you come back?"

Damon casually leaned against the ladder and folded his arms across his chest. "James, Shawn, and Tyler attempted to kill me by pushing me off a cliff," he reminded her. "Almost succeeded too. It was in my best interest to remain dead."

"How did you survive?" she asked.

"Not my first time diving off cliffs," Damon informed her with a sly sort of grin. "And I did a lot crazier shit in the military. Although I'll admit, I didn't quite stick the landing as well as I could have, making me a wounded puppy for a week or more." He shrugged, seeming almost disinterested. "I thought about returning to the barracks after I healed and taking each of them out one by one." Damon chuckled, humored. "Not having any cigarettes made me a little cranky. But I realized going after them would have been like shooting fish in a barrel. Not exactly sporting."

"Attacking you was only the beginning of their descent into insanity," Harley informed him. "And they're not the only ones. Conrad became completely paranoid over my safety. For the past week, he barely left me out of his sight to use the bathroom." She groaned and ran slightly trembling fingers through her hair. "Randall has an imaginary girlfriend, probably the product of drug withdrawal, and Ivy put a 'for rent' sign on her ass."

"Yeah, I've witnessed their gang bangs while passing through on several occasions," Damon informed her, then snorted a laugh. "I have a pretty good idea what's been going on with the others since my tragic death."

She eyed him almost suspiciously. "You seem to be handling things rather well," Harley remarked. "If anything, you seem more relaxed now. Not as ***warm*** as you were before we were stranded."

Damon seemed amused by her comment. "I had a job to do," he informed her. "But after I was terminated, almost literally, I went back to being myself."

"I assume you threatened their authority," Harley remarked. "Is that why they wanted you out of the way?"

"That's only part of it," Damon informed her. "Shawn didn't like the power shift, and Tyler was pissed that he couldn't harass you and Ivy."

"Actually, we took care of Tyler the first day we were stranded," Harley informed him.

Damon snorted a laugh. "You mean after I punched him in the balls so hard that he couldn't walk right the rest of the day?"

Harley stared at him a moment, slightly surprised. Tyler's reaction to their confrontation suddenly seemed to make more sense.

"Is that what happened?" Harley asked, then chuckled softly. "I suppose that does make more sense."

"The real threat was your ***boyfriend,*** James," Damon remarked. "On the first day at the barracks, he wanted me to threaten and bully the others into submission so he could be in charge and give the orders. Typical spoiled rich asshole." Damon then hesitated and eyed her. "No offense to you or your daddy's money."

"None taken," Harley replied, then eyed him. "James was telling everyone you were making sexual comments about Ivy and me. He tried to convince everyone that you might harm one of us."

"I would assume, after last night, you realize that wasn't the case," Damon replied.

"Actually, I didn't believe him," Harley remarked, then shifted almost uncomfortably. "You had plenty of opportunities and didn't act upon any of them."

Damon studied her a moment, a tiny smile crossing his face. "I appreciate your confidence," he replied. "Actually, James was the one making inappropriate remarks about you and Ivy. When I thought he was just shooting off his mouth, I let it slide, but when I thought he might actually do something, I took offense. I have two younger sisters, so I don't tolerate that sort of behavior." He casually shrugged. "I'm not sure whether I punched him before or after he fired me. Doesn't really matter, I suppose."

"He knew you'd get in his way," Harley remarked. "That's probably why he wanted you out of the picture."

"Enough about that asshole." He patted the jeep while grinning slyly. "Want to go for a ride? I'm in the mood for bananas for breakfast."

"I haven't had those in weeks," Harley replied, pleased with the idea. Her look turned concerned. "Although I'm not so sure about your driving skills. Last time I drove with you, my soul left my body."

Damon smiled and chuckled. "Good times," he announced cheerfully. "Don't worry, we'll take the back way, so we don't disturb the others. The road isn't nearly as steep or rocky."

Chapter 36

Damon hadn't been wrong about the road on the opposite side of the clearing. It was a pleasant drive, and he didn't feel the need to drive at top speed, allowing Harley to relax and enjoy the ride. She couldn't believe how only a few minutes driving in the open jeep washed away weeks of tension. Damon even found a second pair of sunglasses to keep the wind out of her eyes. Harley caught Damon eyeing her a couple of times. It had been a long time since she smiled, really smiled, and actually enjoyed life. The wind whipped through her hair as the jeep bounced along the path, and for a few precious minutes, the island didn't feel like a prison. Damon finally stopped near a row of banana trees. He climbed into the back, removed a rope with a hook attached to it, and slung it around an upper branch. Damon then looked at Harley and smiled.

"Be right back."

Harley watched Damon skillfully climb the rope, making it look almost easy. While clinging to the rope, he cut two small bunches of bananas from the tree, one green and one yellow, and then climbed down. It only took him a few seconds to work the hook loose. He picked up the ripe bunch of bananas and handed her one.

"Breakfast?" he asked with possibly the most charming smile she'd seen in over a month.

Harley gratefully accepted the banana while grinning. They ate breakfast as they continued their drive along a narrow, bumpy path.

"I've had this entire side of the island to myself," Damon informed her. "None of the others explores very far. I have my own lobster traps set up, and I even figured out how to make a coconut-based butter. You'll love it."

She stared at him a moment while he drove. "I swear you've been having a good time."

"A well-deserved vacation," Damon replied, humored. "Makes you appreciate what's before us. First, a business stop. Then I'll take you someplace fun."

"Business?" she asked with some surprise. "What business could you possibly have here?"

"You'll see," he replied while grinning.

As they drove into a slightly larger clearing, Harley saw a crashed twin-engine cargo plane overgrown with plant life, tucked into the jungle. Damon stopped the jeep, and both got out, approaching the mostly rusted plane. Both wings were torn off, as well as the landing gear, when it crashed. There was heavy damage to the front, but the cockpit and fuselage seemed intact. Harley was slightly apprehensive as she followed Damon into the plane's body through the opening that lacked a door. The interior was possibly twice as creepy as the exterior. The jungle seemed to sneak its way into the plane as well. Since it was a cargo plane, there weren't any seats other than in the cockpit. What she saw were mostly crates, some smashed beyond recognition, while others near the wings and tail section remained intact.

As they approached the cockpit, Harley saw the skeletal remains of the pilot and co-pilot still strapped into their seats. She gasped with surprise, although she shouldn't have been surprised to see the remains. The pilot had remnants of his shirt hanging from his shoulders while his pants and boots were mostly intact. It wouldn't take years for a body to decompose in the jungle, but it was surprising that their bodies remained strapped in their seats. Certainly, the island wildlife would have pulled them from their harnesses shortly after the crash, but that didn't appear to be the case. Damon removed the fully intact leather bomber jacket from the co-pilot and handed it to her.

"You'll need this more than he will," he insisted.

The pilot was missing his jacket, which she soon realized was the one Damon wore. Harley noticed the pilot was wearing a holster with a semiautomatic. Damon removed the shoulder holster with the weapon and extra magazine still intact.

"That'll definitely need to be cleaned before firing," Damon informed her with an almost humored smile.

Harley insecurely clung to the leather jacket while looking around the cargo hull. She then looked at the jacket with old, dried blood stains and remembered it came off a dead man. Harley grimaced and held it away from her body. She wasn't sure how she was going to clean that. She then nodded toward the crates in the back.

"What's in all those crates?" she asked.

"Dinner," he replied cheerfully, passed her, and removed the lid from the closest crate. He removed a can and showed it to her. "Fathom Food Products. We have enough supplies here to last us months."

"Anything's better than fish," Harley remarked under her breath.

Damon filled a knapsack with several cans, possibly taking a variety for the next couple of days.

"Think we should tell the others about the supplies?" Harley asked, almost cringing when she heard herself say it aloud.

Damon glared sharply at her. "No, absolutely not," he scoffed. "They'll come in here and clean out everything, hoard it for themselves, and scream 'rationing'." He sneered his distaste. "Shawn will keep all the good stuff for himself and his minions while leaving the scraps for everyone else. No one's starving, so I'm keeping this find to myself. Call me selfish and cruel all you want, but I'm not playing by the captain's skewed rules anymore." He then gave a nod to the plane's fuselage. "Feel free to see if there's anything you want or need. There's a bag back there with smaller clothing that you might be able to use."

Harley again clung to the leather jacket, despite feeling icky about it, and walked to the back, past a crushed crate, to find the bag Damon had mentioned. Some old-fashioned shorts and shirts were possibly a little too big for her, but they would work. She took the entire bag without examining the contents further.

"Maybe it is selfish not to share your find," Harley remarked as she returned to him. "But shortly after you had your accident, someone raided the remaining MRE pouches. Bastard opened every pouch, removed all the good rations, and left the gross stuff."

"Rationing food and water when it's not necessary is a form of control," Damon informed her. "It's the only play Shawn has in his playbook." He then offered her a warm smile. "Welcome to the fun side of the island. You're in for a treat. A real spa day. Come on."

§

A few minutes later, the jeep stopped near a clearing on the far side of the island that contained a small pond. Damon indicated the water and smiled proudly. Although beautiful, the pond was much smaller than the one with the waterfall near the barracks and was probably not nearly as deep, making it less ideal for swimming and more for bathing. Larger rocks formed a natural barrier around the pond, with plenty of palm trees and other dense foliage, making it secluded and almost romantic.

Harley gave him an odd look. "It's just a pond."

Damon sprang from the jeep and rounded it to her side. "It's not a pond," he corrected. "It's a spring."

He motioned for her to follow him. Harley climbed out of the jeep and walked alongside him to the spring, where they paused by the edge.

"Try it," he insisted.

Harley kneeled before the water and placed her hand in it. It was hot! The appearance of the nearly clear, still water was misleading. It was as hot as bath water and twice as inviting. She looked at him with mild surprise, then smiled.

"It's hot!"

"It's a hot spring," Damon informed her. "Very relaxing." He then indicated the spring. "Go on. Take a dip. I promise I won't peek. I'll be by the jeep reading my flight manual."

Harley watched Damon head back to the jeep and sit on the back tailgate. She realized she was putting a lot of faith into this man by swimming naked in the spring, but she was dying to bathe in something other than cold water for a change. She rooted through the bag from the plane wreckage and found some soap. A few minutes later, Harley was happily washing, humming contentedly. Once she finished, she rested against the rocky ledge, shut her eyes, and nearly fell asleep.

"I wouldn't advise falling asleep," Damon announced over her.

Harley woke, gasped, and turned in the water to see Damon crouching near her in the spring.

"You promised," she gasped, somewhat offended that he'd betray her like that.

"I wasn't watching," Damon insisted. "I became concerned when you stopped humming. I'm pretty sure I heard something in the woods. I don't know if it's a someone or a something." Damon handed her the towel. "There's plenty of wildlife around this area. It's not safe to remain long."

Without lingering, Damon returned to the jeep, keeping his back to the spring, giving her some privacy to dry off and change back into her clothes.

Chapter 37

Damon drove the jeep along a bumpy path, then onto the beach on the far side of the island, where he picked up speed. Harley enjoyed the feeling of the wind whipping through her hair as they cruised close to the surf. When she caught him looking at her, she smiled. A few minutes later, they were driving back up the path to the top of the hill. Damon drove the jeep into the hangar and parked. After shutting it off, he looked at Harley in the passenger seat and offered a tiny smile.

"I need to do more work on the plane before dark," he informed her. "Will you be staying here tonight?"

"I certainly can't go back to the barracks," she reminded him. "Besides, this is the most relaxed I've been in a long time." She then hesitated, her smile fading. "Although--"

"What's wrong?"

"I'm worried about Conrad," she replied, then grimaced. "I hope he's all right."

"We can visit him at the showers later tonight," Damon informed her. "He's usually there around nine o'clock without fail."

"You seem to know a lot about our movements," she remarked. "Spying?"

"It gets boring at night," Damon informed her. "Besides, I like knowing what's happening around me."

Harley eyed him somewhat suspiciously. "You weren't hanging around the showers when I was in there, were you?"

"Of course not," Damon announced, offended. "That would be low, peeking through holes in walls. The pond, on the other hand--"

Damon jumped out of the jeep and walked toward the plane. Harley stood and sat on top of the seat.

"What's that supposed to mean?" she demanded.

"The pond is out in the open," Damon informed her, then shrugged. "Not my fault if someone's swimming while I walk past."

"And you just happened by?" she asked, raising her brows.

Damon picked up a wrench and began working on the engine without responding to her question. Harley climbed out of the jeep and walked toward him.

"Should I trust you?" she asked.

"If I intended to harm you, I would have gotten around to it last night," he assured her, briefly glancing at her before returning his attention to the plane. "You've been alone with me all day. Have I done anything to cause distrust?"

"No," she replied without hesitation. "But I'd be lying if I said you hadn't made me uneasy at times in the past."

Damon leaned against the plane's wing and studied her. "What did I do to make you uneasy?"

"You didn't 'do' anything," she informed him. "It's just the way you looked at me at my aunt's wedding. You always stared like there was some dark, sinister motive behind your eyes."

"I was just having fun with you," he assured her. "I assumed you were stuck up like all James's other rich girlfriends."

Harley snorted a laugh. "I guess he wasn't exactly saving himself before our introduction."

"No, I assure you he wasn't," Damon muttered. "Running around like a mutt in heat, actually."

Harley leaned against the ladder and smiled gently. "Guess I had good reason not to like him."

Conrad entered the hangar with Harley's bag and immediately stopped, staring at Harley with Damon.

"Harley--?"

Harley spun and stared at Conrad, surprised to see him. She ran to him, threw her arms around his neck, and hugged him. He dropped her bag, returning the embrace, and then pulled away, studying her.

"Are you all right?"

"I am now," she replied. "Damon saved me from James last night."

Conrad eyed Damon as he approached. "I sort of knew something must have happened when he returned out of breath, frightened--***and naked***."

Damon chuckled as he slapped Conrad's shoulder. "I thought you'd get a kick out of that," he replied.

Conrad returned the humored smile. "Been looking after my girl?"

"Of course, mate," Damon announced. "I'm going to need another mattress, though. That floor's murder on my back."

"You just stay on that floor," Conrad scoffed. "I'll find a way to get you a mattress."

Harley shifted suspicious looks between the two men. "What's going on?" she demanded.

"James was becoming unpredictable," Conrad informed her. "Damon and I'd been talking every evening since the night before his ***accident***. We thought you'd be safer here with him."

Harley shifted glares between both men. "You knew Damon was alive the whole time?" she demanded.

"Not the whole time," Conrad replied.

"But the two of you have been talking?" Harley demanded.

"Guess I forgot to mention that," Damon replied.

"Yeah, I guess so," Harley scoffed, then indicated Conrad. "Is he paying you?"

"No, I owe Conrad my life," Damon informed her. "He warned me about Shawn, James, and Tyler's intentions to harm me. It saved my life. It's what mates are for."

"Oh, so now you're mates?" Harley demanded while folding her arms across her chest. "Several weeks ago, the two of you couldn't stand each other."

Conrad smiled and placed his arm around her. "James was sadly mistaken when he said it didn't matter that we'd come from the same country," he informed her. "It's a British thing."

"I can't believe you'd trust anyone at this point," Harley remarked. "Especially another man."

"I have good reason to trust him with you," Conrad informed her. "You'll have to trust my judgment."

"I will."

"Good." He then eyed Damon, appearing almost enthusiastic. "What's for dinner?"

"Beef stew."

"Sounds terrific," Conrad replied, then walked around the plane, running his hand along the welded area. "How's she coming?"

"I need a little more time to work on the engine," Damon replied while leaning on the wing. "Several lights still come on."

"Do you really think you can fly it?" Conrad asked, glancing back at him.

"I guess we'll find out."

"What if you can't keep her up?" Conrad demanded. "Then what?"

"Then there'll be a spectacular crash at the bottom of the cliff," Damon replied while grinning, almost humored at the comment. "How are the others?"

"Acting strange as usual," Conrad replied. "Randall's gone most of the day. It's bizarre. I'd like to know what he's up to."

"I'd leave him alone, if I were you," Damon remarked. "You don't want to put up his defenses. He's suffering massive drug withdrawal. He could turn violent."

"I've considered that."

Chapter 38

Sunset. Conrad left just before dark, probably heading for the shower building. After he left, Harley and Damon sat on the jeep hood near the cliff edge to enjoy the amazing sunset from the best view on the island. Damon was casually stretched out, completely relaxed, while Harley hugged her knees to her chest, dealing with some of her insecurities. Both stared out at the ocean and the rapidly darkening night.

"I'm glad Conrad seemed better tonight," Harley remarked with her cheek resting on her knees. "I was starting to worry about his mental health."

"He's a tough son-of-a-bitch," Damon informed her, then fell silent for a moment. "No disrespect intended, but the two of you have a strange relationship. Most girls from old money aren't close to their servants. In fact, they barely consider them people."

"Well, Conrad isn't my servant," Harley reminded him. "And even when he was the family butler, he was always more like a father to me than just someone on staff. He's the only reason I've tolerated my actual father during my parents' divorce. As long as I'm civil to my father, I get to keep Conrad."

"James told me all about your close relationship with Conrad," Damon informed her. "He intended to fire Conrad right after the two of you got married."

Harley shot a look at Damon, her eyes wide with horror. "Did he say that?"

Damon didn't even bother looking at her and nodded. "Yeah, he's old money," he remarked. "He despises personal relationships with servants. Well, except the ones he's banging on the side."

Harley stared at Damon's profile for a long, stunned moment. "So you're saying he's more of a dick than I ever imagined," she remarked.

"Well, he did organize a hit on me," Damon reminded her. "So, yeah, he's a bigger dick than you could have imagined."

"I'm worried about the others," Harley remarked and shook her head. "I can't believe how fast their morals declined. I mean, they plotted your murder one week after being shipwrecked. Within two weeks, they were having orgies on full display for anyone to witness. What's next? Cannibalism? Where does it end?"

"It could all wear off in another month, if they're given a chance to settle into their new reality," Damon informed her. "There's probably a feeling of hopelessness at play with their behavior. Depression in a situation like this is understandable."

"Honestly, I would have handled all of this a lot better if Shawn, Tyler, and James hadn't been stranded here with us," Harley informed him. "I mean, the island is actually quite beautiful. We have food, water, and shelter. It's just the personalities involved that are the problem." Harley then glanced at Damon. "Were you depressed too?"

Damon was silent for a moment before shifting uncomfortably. "There were a couple of nights when I held my gun to my head," he finally replied.

Harley stared at him, shocked that someone like Damon would even consider taking his own life. Damon didn't look at her, possibly because he was uncomfortable sharing his personal thoughts and feelings.

"But I couldn't see myself going out that way," he remarked. "I'd rather go down in flames in that old plane. That's more my style." Damon drew a deep breath while staring out over the ocean. "Working on the plane and studying the flight manual really took the edge off of my depression. Gave me purpose--satisfaction."

"Those of us handling it the best seem to have hobbies and purpose," Harley remarked. "All James, Shawn, and Tyler have is Ivy to occupy them."

"When sex is all you've got, the novelty wears off fast," Damon remarked. "Which probably explains the escalation in their sexual thrill seeking. Getting into a routine and keeping busy is what everyone needs. Physical work helps keep the mind occupied."

"Conrad and I cleaned the barracks every morning after breakfast," Harley informed him. "At noon, he'd fish at the pond while I swam. Then we'd create new fish dishes for dinner. Clean up from dinner, take a walk, and he'd take a shower. That was my entire day."

"Banana runs every morning, soaking in my personal hot tub after breakfast, and working on the plane," Damon announced. "Then a walk at noon, back to the plane, and read an hour before bed."

"Noon?" she asked, picking up on his words.

Damon didn't look at her but smiled slyly. "Good a time as any for a walk."

"Past the pond, I suppose?" Harley scoffed.

"Just sightseeing."

"I'll bet," she muttered.

"I quit smoking," he reminded her. "I needed something to occupy myself."

"I suppose I should admire you for keeping your hands to yourself," she huffed.

Damon glanced at her and laughed softly. "I've been celibate nearly a year ***by choice***," he informed her. "I'm the king of restraint."

Harley stared at him with some surprise at the admission. "I didn't know men could go that long without," she remarked.

Damon looked at her while lightly cocking his head. "Says the twenty-two-year-old virgin."

Harley shifted uncomfortably, hating that he knew private details about her lack of a sex life. "You've got me there," she remarked. "Why celibacy?"

"The usual," he replied with a shrug. "Tossed over for another man. Tired of being used. Showing vulnerability only to have my heart ripped out of my chest and stomped upon."

"There's a complex side to you," Harley remarked, unable to look away from him. "Who would've thought--?"

"Not completely cold and heartless," he informed her. "Is your opinion of me ruined forever?"

"Yes," she replied, then flashed a smile. "But that's not a bad thing."

They stared into each other's eyes for a long moment. Damon smiled and playfully placed his hand over hers.

"It's getting late," he announced. "I'd better get you home before Dad finds out I kept you out this late."

Damon slid off the hood of the jeep, then assisted her off and into his arms. Once she reached the ground, he didn't release her, keeping her practically pinned between him and the jeep. Harley couldn't help but stare into his eyes, feeling slightly vulnerable and somewhat conflicted. Part of her wanted to kiss him, but she feared sending the wrong message, especially considering their highly stressful situation. Without a word, Harley placed her arms around his midsection and rested her head on his chest, clinging to him. Damon groaned softly and held her, resting his cheek on top of her head.

"I needed that," Damon whispered.

"Me too," she replied, refusing to let him go.

§

That night, Conrad slept in his bunk in the dimly lit barracks, relocated back to gen pop. When the door opened, and Randall entered, Conrad slowly woke and saw his wayward castaway shut the door behind him. Lester stirred in his sleep, turned on his bed, and placed his hand over his nose from something foul-smelling. As Randall walked past Conrad's bunk to his own, Conrad also smelled the foul stench that was overwhelming. He cringed from the stench and then noticed the bloodied scratches on Randall's neck. Randall grabbed his towel and his toiletry kit and headed back out, undoubtedly for the shower building. Lester and Conrad watched the man leave, then exchanged looks from across the barracks.

Chapter 39

Day Thirty-one. Harley stirred on the cot within the small hangar office well before sunrise, not sure what woke her. Indicated by the darkness beyond the tiny window, it was pre-dawn. Small embers in the wood-burning stove provided just enough light to make out the walls, desk, and Damon in his sleeping bag directly beneath her cot. Even though she could barely see his face, Harley stared at Damon's outline. She was grateful he was alive and even more grateful he was with her. Damon jerked sharply in his sleep, accidentally striking the cot with his foot, which had to be what woke Harley a moment earlier. Damon suddenly gasped, then groaned, now awake. He sat up within his sleeping bag and held his head a moment. There was no telling what nightmare he was reliving. Once his heavy breathing subsided, he turned and sat with his back against the cot.

"Are you okay?" Harley whispered, breaking the silence.

"Sorry I woke you," Damon replied softly, sounding defeated.

"Bad dreams?"

"Yeah," he replied.

"Want to talk about it?"

"I don't want to keep you awake," Damon informed her. "Go back to sleep."

"I can't sleep," she easily lied as she propped herself up on her elbow, placing herself closer to his back.

Damon groaned softly and ran his fingers through his hair. "I dreamt I was the only one who made it off the yacht," he softly replied. "I have that nightmare at least twice a week. I'm probably the only loner who doesn't like being alone."

"Well, you're not alone," she reminded him, making the conscious decision to place her hand on his shoulder.

Damon placed his hand on hers and affectionately caressed it. "Thanks for staying with me," he whispered while gently pulling her arm around his neck, wanting the closeness.

Harley held her breath a moment, then sighed softly. "If you promise to behave--"

"King of restraint," he responded a little too quickly.

Harley pulled her arm away from him and moved over on the cot, leaving some room for him. It was going to be a tight fit, but she probably wanted the closeness almost as much as he needed it. Damon practically pounced on the cot, given no choice but to mesh against her, facing her, and pulled the cover over them. He placed his arm around her and immediately clung to her, nearly crushing her head against his chest. Although she liked the way it felt being against him and in his arms, Harley was plagued by the image of James jumping on Ivy, grunting like a pig, and then leaving in under three minutes. She subconsciously shuddered at the thought.

"Am I making you uncomfortable?" Damon asked softly close to her ear. "I didn't mean to do that."

"No, you're not making me uncomfortable," Harley lied. "I just can't get the image out of my head of Ivy and James going at it in the cot next to me that one night. It kind of freaked me out."

Damon suddenly tensed. "He did that?" he asked. "While you were sleeping in the cot near them?"

"Yeah," she whispered and couldn't stop herself from shivering. "He was like an animal. It was disgusting."

"He's a pig," Damon scoffed. "I think the term is 'three pump chump."

Harley attempted to pull her head back and meet Damon's gaze, but it was difficult. "There's a name for it?" she asked, surprised.

Damon chuckled softly and pulled her head back against his chest. "He'd successfully disappointed dozens of women in the year that I worked for him," he informed her. "He certainly never got any repeat customers, that's for sure." He chuckled again. "By the looks of it, he has a small pecker too."

"Well, Shawn's was certainly bigger," Harley muttered.

Damon suddenly pulled back and attempted to meet her gaze. "What the hell were you people doing in the barracks after my tragic death?"

"Shawn strolled naked into the shower for his rendezvous with Ivy," she informed him, then sneered. "Didn't even wait until I'd left."

"Probably hoping you'd join in," Damon scoffed as he again pulled her head against his chest. "Fucking pigs. They wouldn't have been pulling that shit if I'd been there."

"No, probably not."

"Want me to beat them impotent?" Damon asked.

Harley snorted a laugh. "No, that's okay," she replied, then hesitated. "You were kidding, right?"

"Well, just temporarily impotent," Damon informed her. "It would be permanent, if that helps."

Harley couldn't help but laugh as she affectionately nuzzled his chest. "Is this some sort of bizarre courting ritual?" she asked.

"Is it working?" Damon asked with a soft chuckle.

"I'm pretty sure you became my boyfriend the night you saved Conrad's life when the yacht sank," she informed him, realizing what she'd said right after she said it.

"Is that so?" Damon asked, humored.

"With the understanding that you're patient about the physical stuff," Harley remarked, then tensed slightly. "Are you patient?"

"King of restraint," he again replied, then kissed the top of her head, apparently pleased, and once more nuzzled her with renewed enthusiasm. "I knew you liked me better than James."

"As if there were any doubt," she muttered.

§

Immediately after breakfast, Conrad followed Lester along the narrow path in the woods, maneuvering in and out of vines and vegetation. It almost seemed as if they were lost.

"Are you sure he came this way?" Conrad asked while looking around the unfamiliar area.

"Positive," Lester replied. "I'd seen him go this way before. I'm dying to know where he goes, but I didn't want to follow him by myself."

"I'm curious myself after last night," Conrad muttered.

"Did you see those scratches on his neck?" Lester asked, then shook his head. "And what was that smell?"

"Urine, I believe," Conrad replied.

"That's what I thought too," Lester remarked. "But it smelled really strong. I'm telling you, this guy's not right. I think he found an injured animal or something." He again shook his head. "He claimed the scratches came from his girlfriend while they were ***mating***."

"Mating?" Conrad asked, surprised. "Is that your term or his?"

"Those were his words," Lester remarked. "I overheard him talking to Tyler this morning."

"I hope he isn't performing disgusting acts with some animal," Conrad gasped.

"Judging by those scratches, I'd say the animal put up a good fight," Lester muttered.

"I just don't get it."

They finally appeared in a small, completely enclosed clearing thick with jungle. The path seemed to continue on the other side of the clearing, but they would have to crawl through some thick underbrush to get through. Both men exchanged looks, uncertain about crawling on their hands and knees through the thick brush. Lester groaned and shook his head.

"I'm not giving up," Lester informed Conrad, determined to continue. "I'll go first. See how far it remains cramped. Don't follow until I signal you. I want maneuvering room, just in case."

Conrad nodded and watched Lester crawl through the opening in the thick brush. Something was heard moving outside the area, and it wasn't Lester. Conrad looked around, startled by the sounds. Lester suddenly cried out, alarming Conrad. Lester scrambled out from the thick brush while screaming and holding his bleeding neck, blood seeping between his fingers. He quickly made it to his feet, his eyes wide, and grabbed Conrad with his free hand.

"Go!" Lester cried out.

They heard a low snarl within the thick brush not far from them. Conrad grabbed Lester's arm and pulled him back the way they'd come. Both men ran along the narrow path, trying to reach the main trail as the sounds of rustling palm fronds echoed around them. Lester gasped, stumbled, and fell to the ground. Conrad turned, ran back for his fallen man, and crouched over him. Lester's shirt and hands were drenched in his own blood, having bled out from the gashes on his neck. Something thrashed around nearby. Conrad looked around but couldn't pinpoint the direction it was coming from. He slowly straightened while shifting his gaze around him, then turned and ran for the main trail.

Chapter 40

The army jeep pulled up alongside the hot spring and parked. As Harley climbed out of the vehicle, Damon paused and looked around, possibly having heard something. Harley removed her towel, clean clothing, and toiletry kit from the jeep and headed toward the larger rock near the spring. When she looked back, Damon followed her with his own things. She eyed him while raising a suspicious brow.

"What do you think you're doing?" she just about demanded.

"We need to make this a quick trip," Damon informed her while removing his shirt without hesitation. "We'll have to bath together."

Harley stared at him, her eyes wide and her mouth hanging open. "I don't think so," she announced. "You said you'd be patient with the physical aspect of this relationship."

"If I were going to try something, Harley, I would've gotten around to it by now," he insisted.

"That's not the issue," she remarked. "You and me naked in there together, that's the problem."

"Do you want to bathe here or in the freshwater pond closer to our beach?" Damon asked, raising commanding brows. "Something feels off, so if we stay here, it's going to be brief. Certainly not enough time for me to properly ravish you."

Harley groaned, not appreciating the last part. "Fine," she huffed.

When Damon removed his pants and briefs, Harley looked away. He looked at her turned head, laughed, and entered the water. Harley looked back at the spring after he sank up to his neck. Damon didn't even hesitate to remove the soap from the rock and casually began washing. Harley fidgeted a moment, attempting to convince herself she was doing the right thing.

Damon glanced at her and appeared almost humored. "You don't have to take your undergarments off if you don't want to."

"Makes me a prude, huh?"

"No, you're entitled to your modesty," Damon replied. "Honestly, I just want you to get in here so we can finish and leave.

"I don't know why I think it's such a big deal," Harley muttered. "It's not as if you hadn't peeked before."

Damon appeared disinterested and continued to wash. "You're wasting time."

Harley stared at his turned back while he washed. She groaned, then quickly removed her clothing and climbed into the hot water. She sank under the water to wet her hair, then surfaced and pushed her hair back. Damon turned and eyed her only briefly, even though the water concealed her up to her neck. He smiled and handed her the soap.

"That must've been a big step for you," he teased.

"Just keep your distance, mister."

Damon laughed softly as Harley snatched the soap and moved away from him. Her modesty humored him further.

"Behave," she scoffed. "You can still lose your boyfriend status."

"I am behaving," Damon insisted. "I just feel honored that you trust me this much."

"I don't really have a choice, do I?" she huffed. "Besides, you haven't tried anything yet."

"Yeah, I'm practically a saint," he muttered while frowning.

Harley swam back to the large rock and set the soap down. A large, black spider crawled only inches from her hand, nearly touching her. Harley screamed and sailed backward in the water as Damon turned to see what made her scream. She suddenly turned and jumped into Damon's arms. The moment their naked bodies collided, Damon practically froze. Harley wasn't even aware of their predicament and pointed at the rock.

"Did you see that!" she cried out. "Kill it! Kill it!"

Damon looked where she pointed and saw the spider meander away without a care. "It's just a spider," he insisted while she practically climbed his body, frightened of the spider.

Harley glared at him with hostility at his callous remark, then gasped when she realized she was clinging to him, their naked bodies pressed and locked together by her legs wrapped around his thighs. Damon remained motionless while holding her in his arms as they stared into each other's eyes in shared silence. She suddenly realized why he was so heartless with his comment. There was a much bigger issue. Harley's heart was pounding from more than just her near-death experience with the fat spider. Her cheeks reddened when she realized she was pressed against Damon's naked body, and she knew exactly what was poking her. Rather than spontaneously pull away, her body suddenly ached for him instead, and she wasn't sure how to turn off the feeling. Her eyes strayed to Damon's mouth, and that was all the encouragement he needed.

Damon lowered his mouth to hers and kissed her tenderly and with surprising warmth. Her heart was pounding from the kiss, and she couldn't stop herself from responding with a little more eagerness. Damon answered back with a little more passion and even some aggression, kissing her as if his life depended upon it. Harley clung to his neck and just about crawled up his body, clinging to his lower body with her legs. As she partially slid down his body, Damon sharply groaned, and she suddenly felt something she'd never felt before. Harley immediately knew there was partial penetration, causing her to gasp with surprise more than anything. Something in her subconscious told her to just go with it, but Damon jumped away from her the moment she gasped. He quickly put several feet between them, appearing concerned, embarrassed, and strangely out of breath.

"Sorry," he practically cried out, then ran trembling fingers through his wet hair as he shook his head. "I'm really sorry. Guess I'm not the king of restraint after all."

Harley knew he didn't do anything wrong. She was the one who jumped on him, resulting in some unintended penetration. Oddly enough, she actually didn't mind. It felt--***good***. Harley was about to respond when they heard branches rustling nearby. Whatever was out there sounded big. Both tensed and looked to the woods.

"Something's out there," Harley gasped, surprised.

"We have to go," Damon insisted.

Within a matter of seconds, both were out of the hot spring and dressing, barely taking time to dry off. Damon grabbed their towels and toiletry kits, tossing them into the back of the jeep as Harley climbed into the passenger seat. They could hear something big moving around, and it sounded close. Seconds after Damon jumped behind the wheel, the jeep burned out on the dirt lane. As they sped away from the hot spring, Harley looked behind them. Something on four legs moved within the woods just a few yards from the spring near where they had been parked. Harley gasped, alarmed, as Damon looked in the rear-view mirror.

"What was that?" Harley cried out.

Damon shook his head. "I don't know," he replied. "A wild boar, maybe."

"Have you seen any before?"

"No," Damon replied. "Besides birds and snakes, I haven't really seen any wildlife."

Chapter 41

After getting out of the vehicle within the hangar, Harley hung their wet towels over the jeep's roll bar. She then grabbed the bag containing her dirty clothes and toiletries and walked around the front of the jeep. Damon immediately leaned against the vehicle, raked his fingers through his hair, and stared at the ground, seeming distracted and uneasy. It was then that Harley realized something was wrong.

"Is everything okay?" she asked, cocking her head. "You seem distracted."

"You must think I'm a real asshole," he muttered, unable to look at her.

Harley stared at him, her mind rapidly playing back everything that had happened that morning. She squinted at him, attempting to make sense of his words. "Why would I think that?" she asked.

"I said you could trust me, yet I seized the first opportunity to jump on you," he muttered.

Harley stared at him, somewhat baffled by his words. "What are you talking about?" she asked. "You reacted as well as anyone could expect under the circumstances. I mean, I was the one who jumped on you." She then shrugged. "I also gave you non-verbal consent to kiss me. You didn't do anything wrong."

Damon lifted his eyes and met her gaze, his concern evident. "Are you aware of how close you were to losing your virginity?" he asked.

Harley considered the question, then shrugged. "I'm guessing about another five inches or so," she casually replied.

He stared at her, almost shocked by her reaction. "If you're aware of that, why aren't you more upset with me?" Damon asked.

"It wasn't your fault," Harley reminded him. "I jumped on you. Gravity was at fault."

Damon stared at her a moment, attempting to figure her out, then managed a tiny laugh and shook his head. "There's something not right with you," he remarked. "I've had girlfriends get mad at me for far less."

"Maybe I appreciate you more than they did," Harley remarked.

Damon groaned softly and shook his head while hiding his smile. "Talk like that turns me on," he remarked. "I don't think I've ever heard a woman say those words to me before."

Harley smiled, embarrassed by her own thoughts. "What's the weather forecast for tonight?"

Damon considered the question, walked to the front of the jeep, and looked out across the open field. "It's going to be clear, light winds, mostly full moon, and pleasantly warm," he replied, then glanced at her. "Why?"

Harley shrugged while maintaining her smile. "I was thinking maybe we could sleep out under the stars with that million-dollar view of the ocean near the cliff," she replied. "If you think it's safe."

"Safe as long as you don't sleepwalk," he reported, a tiny grin crossing his face. "Sleeping bag for two?"

"I was thinking just a couple of blankets," she replied. "More room."

"You're aware of the seriously romantic overtones," Damon remarked. "Is this some sort of test to make sure I can behave?"

"No," she replied. "I just want my first time to be special and romantic."

It was possible Damon stopped breathing as he stared at her. "Please, don't tease," he finally replied, seeming tense. "I'm already out of sorts."

Harley uncertainly moved closer to Damon and placed her arms around his neck. Despite feeling her entire body tremble, she looked into his eyes and smiled timidly.

"I could resist the physical attraction I felt while watching you splash around in the ocean that first afternoon," Harley remarked, then held her breath a moment. "But the emotional attraction I feel for you is far stronger than I am."

Damon groaned and sharply pulled her against him, nearly startling her with the abrupt action. "I was sure I repulsed you," he replied somewhat softly.

"Repulsed is a strong word," Harley informed him. "You worked for James. That automatically made you intolerable."

"And now that I'm a free agent?"

"When you told off James that first day at the barracks, my opinion of you completely changed," she informed him.

"I knew I should have popped him in the mouth," Damon groaned, seeming almost pleased with himself. "Unfortunately, I thought that would have been rude."

"Yeah, it probably would have been," Harley replied, but maintained her smile. "Just promise me something."

"Anything," Damon replied while moving his mouth closer to hers.

"Promise you'll take things slow tonight," Harley remarked. "I want my first time to be something special.

Seeing how James treated Ivy traumatized me a little, but I'm willing to trust you."

Rather than kiss her, Damon pulled her head to his chest and nuzzled her. "You don't have anything to worry about," he whispered, then kissed the top of her head. "I wanted you from the moment I met you at your aunt's wedding. I'm not rushing anything."

Harley pulled back just far enough to meet his gaze, staring at him with some surprise. "You did?" she asked.

Damon chuckled softly and gently caressed her face. "I'd have to be dead not to have been attracted to you," he reported, then smiled almost insecurely. "But I knew you'd never be interested in someone like me, and James was right, your father would hate me."

Harley shrugged with little care. "I don't care much for my father, so I guess it all evens out in the end."

Damon stared at her a moment, then grinned and chuckled before kissing her quickly on the lips. "Well, I have a date to prepare for," he announced. "I should check those lobster traps."

"Want me to come along?" she asked.

"No," he replied. "You just stay here and relax. There's a dirty magazine in the desk drawer." He then winked at her. "Read a couple of articles."

Chapter 42

Sunset. The jeep was parked out by the cliff, while Harley and Damon occupied the blanket on the other side, with a perfect view of the ocean. Both were still partially dressed, with Harley sitting between Damon's legs while he held her from behind, kissing her neck and shoulder while affectionately caressing her abdomen below her bra. Harley caressed Damon's arms around her, enjoying his hot breath and warm lips on her bare skin. Despite the seriousness of the romantic moment, Harley couldn't hold back a few stray giggles. His beard tickled. When her bra seemed to come off magically, her giggles were replaced with soft moans. She loved the way he gently fondled her from behind, taunting her with each touch and caress. As his hands firmly traveled her body, she writhed her back against his chest and ran her hands along his arms. The feeling growing deep inside her was so intense that she wasn't even sure what to make of it.

"Do you trust me?" he asked softly between kisses.

Harley groaned, then released a sigh. "I trust you."

Damon maneuvered around her, warmly kissed her lips, and gently lowered her to the blanket, partially moving on top of her. As his hands continued traveling her body, she tensed slightly, waiting for the part where he jumped on her, as James had with Ivy. The moment she tensed, Damon dialed back any escalation, allowing her to relax once again. Harley felt as if he were taunting her, refusing to press forward yet kissing, fondling, and even rhythmically pressing against her. Her body ached for more, arching against his as she pawed at his chest and arms, and her legs rubbed against his thighs, inviting him in. Her head was spinning, and her body aching, unlike anything she'd ever felt before. A drunken sensation while remaining completely sober. By the time he slipped her out of her panties, Harley was practically begging for his touch. A tidal wave of never-before-felt sensations shot through her entire body as he delicately explored her. Gently probing and moaning soft words against her skin.

§

Harley nuzzled her face against Damon's bare chest beneath the blanket under the stars while both panted heavily. Damon held her against him, a permanent smile on his face.

"I can't remember a better evening," Damon remarked while caressing her shoulder. He attempted to look at her, but her eyes were closed. "Are you okay?"

"Never better," Harley replied, then groaned softly and lifted her head, meeting his gaze. "Not at all what I was expecting."

Damon chuckled while clinging to her. "What were you expecting?"

"I don't know, but not that," she replied with a soft laugh. "I guess I just assumed there'd be some kissing, some groping, and then you'd get on top."

"Well, you seemed receptive to the full foreplay experience," Damon remarked. "I certainly wasn't passing up that opportunity. I didn't hurt you, did I?"

"No, not at all," she insisted.

"I was never anyone's first before," Damon informed her. "I hope I made a good impression."

Harley lifted her head and met his gaze with a sly grin. "Yes, and I'd love for you to impress me some more."

"Give me an hour, and I'll show you some exciting new positions," Damon insisted, pleased with her response. He looked up to the sky and smiled while caressing her against him. "I never had outdoor sex before. A first for me. It's very freeing."

"If you're sure no one explores the other side of the island, maybe we can have our own private picnic on the beach tomorrow afternoon," Harley suggested.

"I would absolutely love that," Damon replied, then chuckled softly. "You really enjoyed being intimate with me?"

"Honestly," she announced. "I wish we'd been doing that since day one."

"With me?"

Harley managed a tiny chuckle while nuzzling him. "Of course with you," she replied. "I'm happy you were my first, Damon."

"I'm glad you gave me a chance," Damon replied softly.

They just about dozed off in each other's arms when Harley's eyes popped open, concern on her face.

"If we don't meet Conrad at the shower building, do you think he'll come up here looking for us?" she asked.

Damon groaned softly. "I hadn't thought about that," he remarked. "Maybe we should put some clothes on, just in case."

"We could walk down to the shower building and meet him there," Harley suggested, then offered a playful smile.

"Then he won't come up here anymore tonight. Resume our sleepover under the stars."

"I like the way you think," Damon replied.

Chapter 43

Harley and Damon looked around the dark shower building with the use of Damon's kerosene lamp from the hangar. Both were surprised that there wasn't any sign of Conrad.

"I don't get it," Harley remarked, nervously looking around. "It doesn't even look as if anyone showered here tonight. The floor is dry."

"Yeah, I noticed that too," Damon replied, then looked back at Harley. "We should probably check the barracks and make sure he's okay."

"Maybe I should go alone," she announced. "I'm sure James told the others you're not dead by now. If you show up, they may try to finish the job."

Damon studied her while cocking his head. "That's a rematch I've been looking forward to," he reminded her. "And considering there aren't any cliffs for them to push me off of in the barracks, I like my chances."

"What if you hang back by a minute or two?" Harley suggested. "Let me read the room first."

"You have one minute," Damon informed her in a stern tone. "And the barracks door stays open, or I come in with guns a blazing."

"Deal."

It was only a short walk down the hill from the showers to the barracks. Despite the nearly full moon, the trail remained dark in the woods, so Harley was thankful for Damon's kerosene lamp. Even though she was granted a one-minute head start, Damon led the way. Once they reached the clearing, Harley took the kerosene lamp while Damon waited at the end of the path. There were lights on within the barracks, so someone was definitely home. Harley opened the barracks door and paused in the doorway. James, Tyler, and Shawn were playing poker at the table while Ivy relaxed on her bunk and read an old magazine. Considering that either Lester or Brian would have been out on the rowboat, it wasn't surprising to any of them that someone entered. The three men casually glanced at the door and were a bit stunned to see Harley, dropping their cards in the process.

Harley had no idea what James told the others about what happened the other night, but she was sure he didn't tell them he'd chased her down and attacked her. Of course, with morals on the decline, maybe they wouldn't even care if he had. Judging by their reactions, he definitely didn't tell them that Damon was still alive. When Ivy saw the reaction of the three men, she looked at the door as well, saw Harley, and sprang up on her bunk.

"Harley?" Ivy gasped. "Where have you been?"

Ivy's question was a bit surprising, which meant even Conrad didn't tell anyone that he knew where Harley was the last two days, either.

"Oh, so you actually noticed I was gone," Harley scoffed, then indicated James. "Well, after James nearly bashed my head in and tried to rape me, I decided to lie low for a while."

Shawn and Tyler looked at James, somewhat surprised by the accusation. James was horrified by her words but easily brushed them off.

"That's a lie," James snapped back in response. "I never touched her."

"The evening he came back to the barracks naked?" Ivy asked, mildly horrified.

"I'm surprised you even noticed," Harley scoffed. "He probably just slipped back in line for your little foursome, while you let him degrade you until he felt better about himself."

Ivy insecurely rubbed her shoulders while glancing at the three men at the table. Shawn and Tyler appeared uncomfortable with the foursome comment. Shawn then gave Harley a sympathetic look.

"You should have come to me immediately," Shawn informed her. "We had a discussion when we were first shipwrecked that there would be a zero sexual harassment tolerance policy from day one." He straightened proudly. "James will be punished for what he did. You'll be safe from harassment, I promise."

"***You*** promise?" Harley scoffed, then snorted a laugh, sounding like a psychopath. "***You***? The pervert who entered the shower building completely naked, dick in hand, not giving a damn about my privacy, so that you could fuck Ivy. ***You*** think you have any moral high ground here?" She then looked around the barracks. "All four of you are morally reprehensible." She then glared at the three men. "And the three of you should be in jail for sexual harassment, sexual assault, coercion, and attempted murder."

James, Tyler, and Shawn suddenly tensed, though they quickly tried to act innocent. James sank in his seat, obviously knowing something he had failed to tell his comrades. If they had known Damon had survived, they would have reacted very differently.

"Those are some pretty serious accusations," Shawn announced, insulted and irritated.

Damon casually leaned in the open doorframe with his arms folded across his chest. "Didn't you tell me I should stay outside to avoid a confrontation?" he asked Harley. "Or did you just want to have all the fun?"

Tyler and Shawn looked as if they'd seen a ghost while James sank even lower in his chair.

"Damon--" Shawn gasped, his eyes wide as he turned pale.

Ivy gasped in horror and jumped back a step when she saw Damon. Harley ignored Damon's comment and maintained her glare on the three men.

"The three of you pushed Damon off a cliff because you wanted him out of the way," Harley scoffed. "He was a direct threat to your reign of terror."

"Mostly, I was just in the way," Damon remarked, remaining oddly calm, which was even scarier.

"Jungle law dictates capital punishment for anyone found guilty of attempted murder," Harley informed them, then sneered at Ivy. "And also any accomplices."

Ivy gasped, frightened by her words. "I didn't know they tried to kill Damon," she cried out. "I didn't have any part in what they did."

"It was those two," Tyler cried out, terrified, while indicating Shawn and James. "I didn't know what they were up to until it had already happened."

"Fuck you, Tyler," James shouted at his friend. "You wanted Damon out of the way as much as the rest of us."

"You have to understand, Harley," Shawn announced while twitching and trembling, possibly fearing for his life. "Damon was out of control, and he was armed. He was planning on killing the three of us so he could have you and Ivy for himself. We had to stop him."

"And who told you all this?" Harley demanded and then indicated James. "The man who bashed my head in and tried to rape me?"

Ivy shot concerned looks at the three men, fearing them for possibly the first time. Shawn and Tyler glared at James, who suddenly turned defensive.

"It wasn't just me," James cried out while eyeing the two men at the table with him. "The two of you wanted to get rid of him just as much as I did and for your own selfish reasons."

The three men started shouting at one another, hurling accusations out of anger and fear.

"Quiet!" Damon bellowed loudly enough that the barracks vibrated. All eyes were suddenly on Damon, who looked around. "Where's Conrad? Let's just get him and get the hell out of here."

"Conrad and Lester never returned," Tyler informed him somewhat timidly. "We'd hoped they'd come back before dark."

"What do you mean he never returned?" Harley gasped. "Where did he go?"

"They went off together earlier," Shawn informed her, not seeming very concerned. "We haven't seen Randall either. We didn't think it was wise to search for them in the dark, so we planned on waiting until morning."

"Or maybe the three of you arranged another accident," Harley snarled.

A slight gasp escaped Ivy's throat as she shifted her gaze to the three men. Brian entered the barracks looking exhausted and dirty from his twelve-hour shift in the rescue boat.

"Where's Lester?" Brian demanded before looking around the barracks. "I've been waiting--" He suddenly hesitated and stared at Damon, his eyes wide in horror. "They said you were dead."

"Wishful thinking," Damon scoffed, turning back into the hardened man Harley knew before the shipwreck. He then looked at her. "We have little choice but to wait until morning."

Harley shifted uncomfortably but didn't question Damon's authority on the matter. She knew it wasn't safe to be out in the jungle after dark.

"What's going on?" Brian demanded. "What did I miss?"

"Lester and Conrad left this afternoon and never returned," Shawn informed him.

"They're probably just lost somewhere," James insisted. "Neither of them has any sense of direction. Randall's not psychotic, despite what you think."

"Well, there's definitely something not right about that guy," Brian remarked. "But I was actually wondering what happened with Damon."

"Ask your fellow shipmates," Damon scoffed. "I'll be back at dawn to help search." He then eyed Brian. "You're with me." Damon indicated the three men at the table. "I don't feel like having another ***accident***."

Brian's eyes widened as he shot a look at the three men, horror on his face. "Conrad was right, wasn't he?" he gasped, then looked back at Damon. "Those three pushed you from that cliff."

"Yeah, pretty much," Damon scoffed.

Damon nodded to Harley, gesturing toward the open doorway. Without a word, she joined him. James hurried after her and stopped her only a step before Damon.

"Harley, wait," James announced.

When she turned to face James with a look of annoyance, Damon glared at him. James managed a tiny smile and gently touched her arm.

"I'd like to apologize for the other night," James whispered. "I don't know what came over me. I swear to you, it'll never happen again. Please forgive me. Stay here with us. I promise things will be different."

"I have no intention of ever forgiving you, James," Harley informed him, matter-of-factly. "And everyone back home will know what kind of sick, perverted bastard you really are."

Damon slowly approached them, giving James an icy look. James glared at Damon, then looked back at Harley with annoyance.

"He got to you, didn't he?" James demanded.

Harley glanced at Damon, who was now ***her*** attack dog, then looked back at James.

"No, he didn't get to me," Harley informed him while shaking her head. "But he did charm the pants off me, and I jumped on him so fast--"

Damon grinned like a schoolboy as he took her hand and kissed it suavely.

"You bastard," James snarled in anger while glaring at Damon. "You got what you wanted from the start. You took Harley from me!"

Damon sneered at James, possibly ready to strike. "I couldn't take what was never yours." His mood immediately changed when he looked back at Harley and again extended his hand to the open door, indicating for her to go first.

Harley ran her hand along Damon's chest, smiled lustfully at him, and then left the barracks. Damon looked at James, grinned, and followed her. After they were gone, Ivy stared at James, Shawn, and Tyler, who immediately convened at the table, speaking in soft, angry voices. Their hostility seemed to be directed at James, who hadn't warned them that Damon was still alive. When Brian approached the conspirators, Shawn glared commandingly at his first officer.

"With Lester still missing, I'm going to need you to go back out with the rowboat tomorrow morning," Shawn informed him.

Brian removed the flare gun from the back of his pants, held it up, and glared back at Shawn. "With all due respect, sir," he announced, then sneered. "Fuck you, fuck your partners in crime, and fuck your orders." He nodded to the back. "I'm going to sleep in the back behind that privacy partition, where I don't have to see your faces. And if any of you so much as peeks around that curtain, I'm going to light you up with this." He indicated the flare gun in his hand before heading across the barracks. He glared at Ivy as he passed. "Oh, and fuck you too."

As Brian disappeared behind the partitioned area, Ivy insecurely folded her arms across her chest and looked back at the three men, who were suddenly at a loss for words. Shawn met Ivy's gaze, appeared sympathetic, and was about to speak when she vigorously shook her head.

"No," Ivy scoffed, a quiver in her voice. "Don't even try to explain your side of the story." She again shook her head. "I can't believe I let any of you touch me with your filthy, blood-stained hands."

Ivy bolted for the door.

§

Harley and Damon were halfway to the shower building when they heard someone rustling around on the trail behind them and closing fast. Damon removed his gun, maneuvered Harley behind him, and aimed his weapon. Ivy appeared on the path and jumped, immediately stopping when she saw the gun aimed at her.

"I'm sorry, Harley," Ivy called out, practically down to tears. "I swear, I didn't know they tried to kill Damon, and I had no idea James went after you."

Harley touched Damon's arm, indicating without words that he should 'stand down', and took a step past him, facing Ivy.

"I never believed you were in on the plot, Ivy," Harley remarked, then raised her brows. "But you were happy when you heard he was dead." She shook her head while squinting at her. "Just as Conrad and I had our suspicions, I'm sure you had your own regarding their oddly convenient story about Damon's accident, but you chose to follow them blindly. And for what? A little security? A little control? A little superiority over the rest of us?"

Ivy insecurely clung to her chilled shoulders and held back her tears. "Something like that," she whispered while sniffing. Ivy then gave a quick nod at Damon. "I could tell he liked you. You had him looking out for you, even if you refused to see it. You already had Conrad in your corner." She shrugged while trembling. "Who did I have? No one. I wasn't like you or the others. I didn't have money or a family name. I didn't even have Paul anymore. I needed to look out for myself." Tears filled her eyes. "When I started warming up to Shawn, I finally felt safe, but Damon refused to respect Shawn's authority."

"I don't respect or follow idiots," Damon informed her. "Idiots get good men killed."

Ivy lowered her head and wiped the tears from her eyes. "Which is where Tyler came in," she whispered. "There was a little more balance. I guess things just sort of spiraled after that." Ivy lifted her head and met Harley's gaze. "You're right. I finally felt secure." She frowned. "I finally felt deserving."

"Deserving?" Harley gasped, unable to take her eyes off Ivy. "They used you. Not just James. All three of them."

"I know," Ivy whispered, a quiver in her voice. "I picked a side, and it was the wrong side. When you disappeared, Conrad, Brian, and Lester shut down, isolating themselves from us. No one said what happened to you, and Shawn,

James, and Tyler didn't even seem interested in finding out. That's when I realized how wrong I'd been." She stared at Harley for a long moment. "I'm sorry about everything, Harley. I chose proving I was worthy of a man's love over a friend who accepted me as I was, not for what I could do for her."

Harley frowned, lost in her own thoughts a moment, before meeting Ivy's gaze. "You made some bad choices," she reminded her, then groaned. "But you *were* carrying around some pretty heavy insecurities before the ship sank." Harley sighed, then managed a tiny smile. "Chalk it up to a learning experience and, instead, appreciate the friends who don't require sexual trade-offs."

Ivy returned the smile and again wiped her tears while sniffing. "I appreciate that," she replied softly. "We'll find Conrad tomorrow, and things will be different from now on, I promise."

Harley nodded. "And, although he might be a little irritable at the moment," she announced. "Have an honest discussion with Brian. I think the two of you should stick together."

Ivy managed a tiny laugh. "Yeah, well, he already told me to fuck off," she remarked. "I don't see that happening."

"He's more reasonable and caring than you think," Harley informed her. "He'll keep an eye on you until we find Conrad and Lester."

"Will you return to camp then?" Ivy asked.

Harley glanced back at Damon, then met Ivy's gaze. "I think I'm going to stay with Damon," she replied, smiling. "Two's company."

Ivy snorted a laugh. "I get it."

Chapter 44

Day Thirty-eight. A little after sunrise that morning, Ivy swam naked across the pond, enjoying the quiet morning. She lazily floated on her back and sighed contentedly, as if she'd finally found freedom. There was just enough sun poking through the trees to warm her exposed body. Her peaceful morning was interrupted by the sound of someone or something moving around within the woods. Ivy dropped back into the water and listened while looking around. With Conrad and Lester having been gone twenty-four hours or more, her anxiety may have spiked over their disappearance. When she didn't see anyone, she should have relaxed, but her paranoia seemed to increase. She swam back to the small bank where moments earlier she had carelessly tossed her clothes.

Ivy climbed out of the water, dried off in record time, and hurriedly dressed. Still, she seemed to be alone. She turned and nearly collided with Randall, who was only a couple of feet from her. She let out a startled gasp, not expecting to see him. No one had seen much of Randall the last few days, so his condition was somewhat surprising. His eyes were sunken and had unusually dark circles beneath them, and he was dirty, with several days' stubble on his face. More surprising were the moderately fresh scratches on his neck. They weren't so fresh that they were bleeding, but they were red and angry-looking. An evil, twisted smile crossed his now thin, pale face. Ivy attempted to relax and managed a tiny, nervous smile.

"Randall, you startled me," she gasped, adding an uneasy laugh.

"I'm sorry, I didn't mean to," he replied almost cheerfully, which in itself was creepy.

"I'm finished here," Ivy informed him while attempting to remain polite despite her twitching body. "The pond's all yours, if you want it."

"Great," Randall replied, his creepy smile never faltering. "Thanks."

Ivy tried to maintain her smile despite being creeped out by her wayward fellow castaway. She gave a tiny wave, then walked past him to leave the pond area without acting as if she wanted to make a hasty escape. Randall picked up a rock and suddenly struck her on the back of the head. Ivy gasped and immediately dropped to the ground.

§

Harley sat on the passenger seat of the jeep, only an hour after sunrise that morning, and watched as Damon checked the magazine in his gun.

"I don't see why it's so terrible for me to want to go along," Harley practically pouted. "Conrad is my best friend. I should be going with you."

Damon replaced his gun in his holster and looked at her. "I know how you feel about each other, but you're still not coming along," he informed her. "If there's something out there, I don't want you getting hurt."

"I suppose you're trying to be charming, but I don't get into all that macho male dominance bullshit," she informed him.

Damon pulled her out of the jeep, into his arms, and kissed her quickly on the lips.

"I'm not stopping you from going because this is ***man's work***," he assured her. "You can't go because I'm selfish. I want you here where you're safe." He kissed her again, prolonging it a moment, before pulling away and avoiding looking at her. "Besides, there's no telling what we might find. Because Conrad is your best friend, I don't want you exposed to something traumatic."

Harley shuddered at the thought, knowing he was right. If something happened to Conrad, she wasn't sure she could handle seeing him dead.

"Fine," she huffed softly, attempting to make it sound as if it were her idea. "I'll stay here just this once. But be careful, okay?"

"I will."

Damon again pulled her into his arms and kissed her with a little more passion. Her heart skipped a beat because it had that 'just in case I don't return' feel. Damon then handed her the gun and shoulder holster he'd removed from the dead pilot.

"I cleaned the gun and ensured it's in working order," Damon informed her. "You have two magazines. That's thirty rounds. Fifteen in each magazine. Do you know how to shoot and load a semiautomatic?"

Harley frowned and nodded, accepting the gun in the holster. Damon kissed her quickly, then turned to leave while still holding her hand. He paused, then turned to face her. Harley didn't like the serious look in his eyes.

"I just want you to know," Damon announced somewhat timidly. "I love you, Harley."

Harley jumped into his arms and clung to him. "Prove it," she whispered close to his ear. "Come back to me."

Damon clung to her as if he'd never let her go, but then he did.

Chapter 45

As Damon approached the barracks on the path from the shower building, Brian hurried across the clearing, meeting him halfway and looking concerned.

"Am I ever glad to see you," Brian announced. "Shawn went to the pond this morning hoping to smooth things over with Ivy, but she wasn't there. He claimed he found fresh blood. Tyler and James went with him to look for her."

"How long ago?" Damon demanded.

"Fifteen minutes at most," Brian informed him. "But what if Shawn lied about what he found at the pond? Ivy refused to speak to any of them last night, and she wanted to avoid them this morning. Considering what they did to you and with Lester and Conrad missing--?"

"I doubt they'd do away with Ivy," Damon insisted. "Hormones dictate she's more valuable to them alive."

"If not them, then what's out there?"

"I'll tell you what's out there," Damon scoffed. "Randall. That's what's out there. He's suffering severe withdrawal. Probably hallucinating and everything." He shook his head. "I never should have kept to myself these last few weeks.

That captain of yours lacks any common sense and leadership skills."

"He's not my captain," Brian snapped back. "Lester and I have been colluding with Conrad ever since your little accident."

"Then maybe I can actually trust you," Damon remarked before indicating the path to the distant pond. "Let's see if we can catch up with "The Three Stooges."

§

Ivy slowly woke to bright sunlight on her face. Her head was pounding, and she had a difficult time opening her eyes. When she finally did, she could barely focus. She lifted her head and looked around with some disorientation while tenderly touching the back of her head. She cringed with pain, then saw the small amount of blood on her fingers. Ivy wasn't even sure what had happened. The last thing she remembered was talking to Randall and leaving the pond area. As her vision came back into focus, she realized she was in what could only be described as a massive nest, mostly made of fronds, some bamboo, and fur from other animals. One thing was abundantly clear: the nest was man-made. Ivy then noticed Lester on the ground not far from her, face down. She was relieved to see him, not just because he had been missing, but she wasn't entirely alone now.

"Lester--?" she announced softly and touched his shoulder.

To her horror, Lester was stiff and cold, indicating he'd been dead for several hours or longer. Ivy gasped and pulled her hand back while staring at the dead man. She tensed slightly, mustered her courage, and slowly rolled him over. As he fell onto his back, the stench of decayed flesh was overwhelming, almost causing her to choke. His body was hollowed out from his throat down to his groin. Ivy cried out and fell onto her backside. When she heard something growl from nearby, she slowly and nervously looked around with fear in her eyes. Despite not seeing anything other than the jungle, it didn't make her feel any better. She scrambled to her feet and bolted in the direction of the only path in the woods. She barely made it out of the nest when she collided with Randall. When their eyes met, she was instantly horrified.

"Going somewhere?" Randall asked, smiling that creepy smile.

"What'd you do to Lester?" she gasped while taking a step back.

"He had a little accident," Randall casually replied, then raised his brows. "Would you like to meet my girlfriend?"

"No," Ivy gasped without hesitation.

Randall suddenly turned angry and grabbed her arm, causing her instant pain. "You're being rude."

Ivy screamed and kicked Randall in the shin. When he bent over to clutch his shin, she thrusted her knee into his chin. His head jerked back, and he fell to the ground. Randall slowly stood, holding his jaw, and watched Ivy run from the small clearing. He hesitated only a moment before chasing after her. Ivy managed to jump over several roots and rocks without stumbling, running on pure adrenaline. She scaled a fallen tree with ease and landed in something soft. Ivy cried out with surprise and horror when she realized she was in quicksand. She screamed and attempted to pull herself out of the thick, sloppy substance, but was already engulfed up to her waist since she had been struggling.

Shawn, Tyler, and James arrived, having heard her screams, and stopped short of the quicksand. Ivy saw them and cried out. Shawn gathered some vines and began cutting them with his small pocketknife while Tyler and James attempted to form a human chain and reach for her. Randall suddenly appeared on the other side of the quicksand pit, eyed them, and smiled as if everything was perfectly normal.

"Hey, guys," Randall announced. "What's up?"

Tyler and James stared at Randall for a moment, immediately alarmed by his odd behavior and his physical condition.

"Help Shawn with Ivy," James muttered to Tyler. "I'll talk to Randall."

"Are you insane?" Tyler gasped, his eyes still wide as he stared at the man he no longer recognized. "He doesn't look right."

"Randall and I are friends," James insisted. "I'll be fine."

James slowly circled the quicksand and paused ten feet from his friend. Randall watched him with a cheap sort of grin on his face.

"How's it going, Randall?" James asked.

"Just fine," Randall replied. "How's it going with you?"

"You look tired," James remarked. "Want to come back to the barracks and get some sleep?"

"No, I have a lot of work to do."

"We have more than enough firewood," James insisted.

Shawn and Tyler threw the vine to Ivy, who was now up to her chest in the substance. She frantically grabbed for the vine while screaming.

"Just grab the vine, Ivy," Shawn demanded. "Try not to panic."

"Easy for you to say!" she screamed back.

They threw the vine again. This time, Ivy grabbed onto it, and the two men began pulling her from the substance with some effort. They dropped the vine and pulled her the rest of the way to solid ground by her arms as James moved a little closer to Randall.

"It's been rough on all of us, Randall, but we can help you," James insisted. "Come on. Let's go back to the barracks and get you something to eat."

"I've been eating," Randall informed him. "I'm fine. Would you like to meet my girlfriend?"

James studied his friend for a moment, then attempted to play along with his drug withdrawal delusions. "I didn't know you had a girlfriend," he remarked. "When did you meet a girl?"

"The morning after the typhoon," Randall informed him. "I found her. She'd been injured during the storm, and I nursed her back to health."

"Oh?"

"Tending to her injuries, bringing food to her," Randall replied, then chuckled. "First with MREs and then with extra fish and lobster the guys caught."

"You took the fish that went missing?" James asked, surprised.

"Well, yeah," Randall remarked. "My girlfriend was hungry. I had to give her something. She really liked the fish and lobster." His grin again increased. "Would you like to meet her? I know she'd like to meet you."

Tyler and Shawn pulled Ivy to her feet, then looked at James, who was now four feet from Randall. All three vigorously shook their heads.

"No, no, no," Tyler cried out softly to his friend. "Get out of there."

James looked back at Shawn and Tyler, motioning with his hand that he had the situation under control. Shawn and Tyler shook their heads and waved for him to join them. While his head was turned, Randall lunged for James, taking him down to the ground, biting his neck. James cried out with surprise as both men fell to the ground. Shawn and Tyler released Ivy and ran for the struggling men. Randall was on top of the thrashing man, who punched and kicked at him. Blood seeped from James's neck from where Randall sank his teeth into him. James finally managed to throw Randall off of him and scrambled to his feet while holding his bleeding neck. He looked at the blood on his hand, then back to Randall, with blood covering his mouth and running down his chin, and a psychotic grin.

"You're fucking insane!" James cried out.

Shawn and Tyler nervously pulled James backward and away from Randall while Ivy screamed almost hysterically at them.

"Let's get out of here," Ivy cried out. "We have to get out of here! Come on! Let's go!"

The three men continued to back up while keeping their eyes on Randall, looking half-crazed, casually walking toward them as if nothing had happened.

"We're dead," Tyler gasped.

James held his bleeding neck. "What the fuck is wrong with him?" he cried out, now angry.

They heard a strange snarling sound from nearby. Randall smiled deviously, apparently knowing something they didn't.

"Come on!" Ivy screamed. "Hurry!" She then turned and ran, not waiting for them.

Shawn smiled nervously and spoke in almost a calm tone. "Run--"

They turned and ran through the woods after Ivy.

Chapter 46

Late morning. Harley nervously paced the length of the hangar, arms folded insecurely across her chest as if holding herself together. Every few steps, she glanced at the closed door. Damon insisted on keeping the big door shut so she'd be safe while he was gone. Or so he said. Although he would never admit it, Conrad's disappearance made Damon a little paranoid, which made her nervous. She wondered if Damon secretly thought Conrad was dead but refused to share his thoughts with her. Harley's mind reeled, hashing every possible reason Conrad would be gone the entire night. He wasn't the 'outdoorsy' type. A horrible thought then struck her. She froze mid-step, a chill racing down her spine. What if Shawn, James, and Tyler ***had*** done away with Conrad? He wasn't nearly as big a threat to the trio as Damon had been, but he was turning Brian and Lester against them. That in itself may have earned him a death sentence.

Now, she was even more concerned about his disappearance. Harley approached the small hangar door, opened it, and stared down the runway to the cliff, unable to tear her eyes away from the scenic edge. Just last night, she was with Damon watching the sunset moments before he made love to her. Now, that moment would forever be scarred if she learned Conrad met some horrible fate that same day. Despite knowing there was nothing she could have done, Harley still somehow felt it was her fault for Conrad's disappearance. She should have been there, looking out for him as he had always looked out for her. Harley scanned the woods on either side. Of course, there was no sign of Damon or Conrad. What had she really been expecting? Harley frowned as she attempted to rub the chill from her shoulders.

"Damn it, where are they?" she muttered.

When she looked to her left, she saw Randall suddenly appear near the corner of the hangar. His stealthy appearance was enough to make her jump, but when he offered a creepy, unsettling smile, a cold wave of panic shot through her. She jerked backward, recoiling at Randall's psychotic smile. Her eyes strayed to the faint blood stain down the front of his shirt. No matter what the story was, it definitely wasn't good.

"Hello, Harley," Randall announced, sounding even creepier than he looked.

"Hey, Randall," Harley replied as her body stiffened in response.

Randall moved closer to her and the door. "Got a minute?"

It was almost as if he were her neighbor stopping by to say hello. Seeing her at the hangar he possibly didn't know existed didn't even seem to faze him. Nothing good would come from this conversation.

"I think my cake's burning," she replied, then darted back inside the hangar and slammed the door, immediately bolting it.

Harley heard a loud, metallic thud as Randall struck the smaller hangar door. She jumped back with a gasp and stared at the dent on the door, which must have caused him tremendous pain. She removed the semiautomatic from the shoulder holster and aimed it at the door. The door vibrated with another bang. The dent was now larger. If he didn't break his shoulder with those powerful hits, it'd only take a couple more to bust down the door. Harley considered her limited options. If he broke down the outside door, the flimsy interior office door would be nothing, and she'd have no way to escape. If she waited until he broke through, she'd have to take him down with the first shot, and she wasn't entirely confident with her shooting skills. Her only other option was to hide.

Harley ran to the plane, climbed the ladder, and jumped into the rear cockpit area. She hit the button to close the canopy, grateful it worked. If she were lucky, the tinted canopy glass would make it harder to see inside. She still felt exposed. She had to assume Randall would eventually climb the ladder looking for her. Harley squeezed into the small, cramped space under the front ejection seat, beneath the instrument panel. Although the area was incredibly tight, Harley managed to curl up in it. She attempted to control her heavy breathing while staring at the tinted glass canopy, just waiting for Randall to find her. She gasped as the banging against the small exterior door increased. When she heard the door break open and strike the opposing wall, Harley held her breath.

"Harley, I know you're in here," Randall called out, sounding almost playful.

As she heard things crash to the floor not far from the plane, Harley jerked and clutched the gun, aimed at the canopy, prepared to shoot if necessary.

"Come on out, Harley," Randall announced. "I just want to talk to you."

She heard several more things crash to the concrete floor. When she heard the ladder creak and felt subtle vibrations from the craft, she knew Randall was on the cockpit ladder. He was so close, she could almost smell him.

What *was* that smell? Harley remained still and tried to keep her breathing as quiet as possible while staring at the tinted glass canopy. When she saw a shadow loom over the cockpit, she knew he was at the top of the ladder looking in. Harley's heart was pounding as if it would burst from her chest from her spiking adrenaline. All he needed to do was find the canopy latch, and he would have access to the entire cockpit. She heard a thump against the canopy, but she couldn't see anything, since she was facing the rear seat and he would be above the front seat until the canopy opened. Harley then heard his hand screech as it slid over the glass, but he wasn't attempting to get in. Undoubtedly, he was trying to view the rear seat.

Harley heard him curse softly under his breath before he descended the ladder, again causing slight vibrations against the jet. The moment he hit the ground, he resumed tossing items around and calling out to her.

"I know you're in here," Randall playfully sang. "Come on out!"

§

The barracks door flew open as Ivy hurried inside and watched Shawn and Tyler help James to his bunk. Ivy ran across the room to the cabinet, removing towels and the first-aid kit. James groaned as he collapsed on his bunk.

"I'm fine, really," James insisted, although he sounded weak, breathing labored, shallow breaths.

Shawn stared at him while alternating between raking his fingers through his hair and shifting from foot to foot. "You don't look fine."

"I just need some rest," James replied while attempting to catch his breath.

Ivy cleaned the blood from around the bite wound on his neck and examined the extent of his injury. "I think the bleeding stopped," she informed the others.

"He lost a lot of blood, and that long hike didn't help," Tyler insisted. "Now that the bleeding has stopped, I think he'll be all right with some rest. We just need to keep the wound clean so it doesn't get infected."

"I'll clean the wound and dress it," Ivy informed them. "There's plenty of wound cleaner and antiseptic solution in the kit."

Shawn pulled Tyler aside, wanting to speak privately to him while Ivy tended to James's injury.

"That's a deep wound for a human bite," Shawn remarked softly.

"It's nasty all right," Tyler replied, then shook his head. "Looks like a wild animal bit him."

"If I hadn't seen it for myself, I never would have believed Randall did that to him," Shawn remarked. "I don't understand how he could do that much damage."

Chapter 47

Early evening. The hangar was only dimly lit with the large bay doors closed. There were overturned objects, tools lay scattered everywhere, and dozens of items were smashed. Despite the destruction, the hangar was eerily silent, and nothing moved. Within the fighter jet's rear cockpit, Harley slowly woke from where she remained curled in a small ball in the back beneath the console. She looked around the nearly dark, cramped space, disoriented. When she heard movement outside the plane, she remembered where she was and what had happened. Harley remained still, clutched her gun, and listened to the faint sounds outside the fighter jet.

"Harley?" Conrad called out.

Harley lifted her head and struck the underside of the control panel. She clutched her head, momentarily stunned from the pain, then wiggled her way out from the small opening. She was stiff and could barely work her way out. Everything hurt from her prolonged fetal position in the cramped area. She fought through the pain and fumbled to open the cockpit canopy. Every muscle in her body cramped and tightened as she straightened. It was even worse when she climbed onto the ladder and tried to climb down. Conrad turned, saw her, and hurried to her. Harley practically broke into tears as she threw her arms around his neck and clung to him.

"Oh, Conrad," she nearly sobbed. "I'm so glad you're alive!"

Conrad managed to pull away from her and looked around at the destruction within the hangar. "What happened here?"

Harley eyed the mess in the dim lighting. "Randall broke in and tore the place apart," she informed him as her body now trembled in fear. "You should have seen him. He was insane!"

"I sort of suspected he was the culprit," Conrad muttered, then looked back at her. "Where's Damon? Is he okay?"

"He went out looking for you and Lester early this morning," Harley informed him, then shook her head. "He should have been back by now. What happened? Where did you go?"

"***Something*** attacked Lester while we were following Randall," Conrad informed her, attempting to mask his sorrow. "Lester didn't make it. I'm convinced it was a cougar or a panther. Nothing human could've left wounds like that." He remained tense and unable to relax. "We'll wait here for Damon another hour until it's nearly dark outside. If he's not back by then, we'll join the others in the barracks."

"Maybe we should look for him," Harley suggested.

"That would just send him out after us again," Conrad insisted. "He knows to come here. This is where we should wait."

Harley's concern for Damon spiked, that heart-stabbing feeling of dread again rushing through her body, but she knew Conrad was right. They needed to wait for Damon to return to the hangar.

§

Ivy ran through the woods along the narrow, well-worn path beyond the shower building. She panted heavily while looking behind her several times with terror in her eyes. Something massive rustled along the path, running not far behind her. She screamed, panic-stricken, focusing on the path ahead of her.

"Ivy! Where are you?" Shawn could be heard calling from deeper in the woods.

"Ivy!" Tyler called out as well, seeming far away.

Ivy didn't stop or slow, dodging branches and jumping rocks. When she saw a snake hanging from a tree before her, she screamed, ducked, and narrowly avoided it. Even the snake wasn't stopping her. There was a loud snarling sound directly behind her. Before she could even scream at the sound, Ivy was tackled to the path. She cried out as she hit the ground, attempting to break free.

§

Only a few seconds later, Shawn and Tyler appeared on the same path and abruptly stopped, eyes wide and mouths hanging open. Ivy was sprawled across the path with blood rapidly seeping from her neck where her throat had been torn out. She wheezed and gasped her last breath. A low groan was heard not far from them. Shawn and Tyler looked back, slowly straightened, and stared at Ivy's blood-spattered attacker. A faint snarl was heard from somewhere within the woods, but their eyes remained fixed on Ivy's killer standing before them.

"Fuck!" Tyler cried out. "Run!"

Both men turned and ran along the path, but there was movement all around them. They turned and ran deeper into the woods, farther from the barracks.

§

The sun had already set, and the woods would soon be dark. Conrad stood by the small hangar door with Harley's gun in his hand and stared outside, conflicted by the decision they would soon have to make. Harley nervously paced the length of the hangar, alternating raking her fingers through her hair and rubbing her chilled arms, torn on whether they should actually leave. If Randall could break into the hangar, he could certainly break into the barracks. It didn't seem as if they were safe anywhere. At least in the hangar, she'd be there when Damon returned. A sharp, hollow pang of grief shocked her system. She ***hoped*** Damon would return. What if he ran into Randall? Randall was unhinged. How could Damon fight a half-crazed, psychotic demon? Harley cursed herself for the mental torture she was putting herself through.

If she'd stood her ground when Randall broke into the hangar and used the gun to defend herself rather than hide, maybe she could have stopped him. Then they'd no longer be living in fear of him.

"We'll leave a note for Damon and join the others in the barracks," Conrad informed her, remaining firm, knowing she would protest. "We're safer in numbers."

"Are you sure we'd be better off with them?" Harley asked, stalling for time, as if another thirty seconds would make all the difference.

"He broke inside once," Conrad reminded her. "There's only one way in and out of here. I know it doesn't sound like it, but we'll be safer with the others in the barracks."

Chapter 48

Harley and Conrad headed through the darkening woods, looking around cautiously as they hurried along the path. Conrad kept Harley's gun while she clutched a large wrench. As they approached the well-lit barracks, Conrad paused before the door and looked down. There were droplets of blood before the door. He looked at Harley and motioned for her to wait. He cautiously opened the door, peered inside while aiming his weapon, and then slowly entered with Harley following him. There was blood along the floor leading up to a vacant bunk, but the barracks were empty. Conrad approached the cot and observed a larger amount of blood on the pillow.

"That's James's bunk," Harley informed Conrad.

"Looks like he'd been hurt and was lying here for a while," Conrad remarked, then nodded at the bloody rag on the floor. "Someone was tending to whoever was injured in this bunk."

"But where are they now?" Harley asked. "Why would they move an injured person?"

"I don't know," Conrad replied, then looked at the bloody trail along the floor while clinging to the gun. "Wait here. I'm going to follow the trail."

"Wait here?" Harley gasped. "Are you insane?"

Conrad appeared to reconsider and took her hand. "You're right," he announced. "Stay close to me."

They followed the blood from the barracks, up past the shower building, and onto another, less-traveled trail. Conrad suddenly stopped and stared into the woods before them. What was left of fresh, human innards was almost hidden beneath some underbrush.

"Oh, my God--" Harley gasped, her heart pounding at the horrifying sight.

Conrad turned Harley and hurried her back toward the hangar, which was now the closer option, only taking a couple of minutes to reach it. Once they entered the hangar, Conrad found a heavy chain and used it to secure the door, adding a large clip to hold it shut. He turned and leaned against the door, shutting his eyes a moment, panting heavily and trembling.

"Was that James who'd been gutted on the trail?" Harley gasped, clutching the wrench nervously. "What did that? Randall couldn't possibly--"

"I don't know ***what*** did that," Conrad replied as he finally opened his eyes.

There was an urgent pounding on the door, startling both of them. Conrad jumped away from the door and aimed the gun at it as both stared, listening.

"Harley!" James cried out from the other side of the door. "Let me in! I've been injured!"

"It's James," Harley gasped just loud enough for Conrad to hear. "What do we do?"

Conrad took a step closer to the door, paused before it, but didn't open it. "James, what happened?" he asked through the door. "We found blood in the barracks."

"Hurry," James cried out. "You need to let me in. He's after me!"

Conrad motioned Harley away from the door. She took several steps back, gripped the wrench, and watched as Conrad removed the clip and unwrapped the chain. He opened the door only a couple of inches, just enough to peer outside.

"My God!" Conrad suddenly gasped, letting the door open the rest of the way.

James hurried into the hangar while clutching his bleeding neck. He was covered in a large amount of fresh and dried blood. Conrad shut the door behind him while James panted heavily, possibly from running a great distance. Harley took a step closer to him, but Conrad motioned for her to stop. Harley immediately stopped on his command, keeping her eyes on James and clutching her wrench.

"What happened?" Harley asked.

"Shawn and Tyler left the barracks to investigate something outside," James informed them, shifting looks between the two of them. "Ivy stayed behind to help me. That's when Randall came into the barracks and attacked her. I tried to stop him, but I couldn't get him away from her. I wasn't strong enough." James turned to face Harley. "He dragged Ivy from the barracks and killed her in the woods. I couldn't do anything to stop him. When he turned on me, I ran."

Conrad approached James from behind, attempting to rationalize his story.

"Ivy--" Harley gasped, horrified, realizing the pile of innards belonged to the young woman.

While standing behind him, Conrad placed his gun to James's head. James immediately stiffened.

"Care to tell the story again?" Conrad snarled, not believing him.

"I'm not lying," James insisted while remaining still, casting a sideways glance at the gun against his head.

"You didn't attempt to pull Randall away from her," Conrad informed him. "There was no sign of a struggle anywhere on the path, and that also doesn't explain the blood on you." Conrad was silent for a moment. "Remove your hand from your neck."

James slowly lowered his hand to reveal four deep scratches near the infected bite mark.

"It was you!" Harley cried out, taking a quick step back from him as she raised her wrench.

James suddenly whirled around and knocked Conrad against the plane with a loud thud, dislodging the gun from his hand and beneath the plane. James then grabbed Conrad by the throat and pulled him to his feet. Harley lunged for James and struck him across the back with the wrench. Despite the hard hit, it didn't even faze him. James tossed Conrad aside and turned his attention to Harley. She attempted to swing again, but James caught her wrist and thrust her backward across the hangar. She landed roughly on her backside and slid several feet, the wrench flying from her hand and across the floor. When Harley looked up, James was standing over her. She cried out, attempting to scramble away from him when he grabbed her by her leather jacket and pulled her to her feet. He slammed her against the nearby tool counter hard enough that the intense pain nearly paralyzed her.

When Harley managed to open her eyes, James smiled evilly at her through large, sharp teeth. She stared at him, so paralyzed with fear that she couldn't even scream.

"You--you killed Ivy," Harley stammered.

"Yes, I killed her," James announced, appearing pleased with himself. "I tore her throat out." He ran his tongue along his sharp, bloodstained fangs. "After Randall bit me, I could feel something coursing through my body. I've never felt so powerful. Like a superhero."

"Superhero?" Harley gasped. "You ***killed*** Ivy!"

"I had to," James insisted. "But I won't kill you." A low chuckle escaped his throat. "I chose you. You're the only mate I want, and I finally have the power to make you mine."

Harley's eyes were wide, unable to look away from his fangs as she trembled. "***What*** are you?" she gasped.

Conrad suddenly appeared alongside James and placed the gun against his head. "Dead," he replied and pulled the trigger.

There was a loud pop right before James's head snapped to the side from the bullet penetrating through his cheekbone and exploding out the opposite side of his face. Harley screamed with surprise, unable to do little more than stare in horror as James fell to the floor. Harley stared at his motionless body as blood quickly spilled into a small pool around his face. For a moment, Harley and Conrad exchanged looks, unable to comprehend everything that had just happened. A loud thumping suddenly echoed along the hangar roof. Both looked up at the high, curved metal ceiling and listened only a moment before hearing it again. Before they even had time to react to what they heard, there was a loud bang at the small door. Harley softly cried out as both looked at the door. It vibrated again and dented. Conrad grabbed Harley's arm and pulled her to the jeep. She didn't know what the plan was, but she trusted his instincts. Conrad handed her the gun and started the engine.

"Shoot anything that moves," he ordered.

Harley climbed into the back of the jeep and positioned herself on the floor so she'd have a better sniper's position. Conrad backed the jeep away from the closed hangar doors as far as the fighter plane allowed. Harley gasped and took shelter on the floor, anticipating his next move. Conrad violently shifted the jeep into gear and stepped on the gas. The jeep burned out on the concrete floor and rocketed toward the big doors. Harley screamed while covering her head. The jeep struck the doors with enough force to partially rip them off their hinges. The hangar door closest to the smaller door just about struck Randall, who rolled across the ground. As the jeep rocketed from the hangar, Harley lifted her head and looked back in time to see Randall spring to his feet. She fired several times but missed.

"There's a road to the left!" Harley cried out.

Conrad turned onto the narrow path to the left without slowing. The jeep slid in the mud and jetted down the steep, rocky path. Harley bounced around the back of the jeep and cried out while attempting to hold onto anything that would stop her from flying out the back, while Conrad struggled to control the jeep.

"You call this a road!" Conrad shouted.

"Turn right," Harley cried out, remembering her wild ride with Damon their first day of exploring.

Conrad was about to question her order to turn right when he saw the shower building up ahead with little maneuvering ability. He gasped, then swerved to the right on what was barely considered a path, let alone a road. The jeep ran over a large, exposed rock and became airborne. Harley ducked while Conrad cried out in terror. The army jeep flew from the woods, airborne several feet off the ground, and landed roughly on the beach. Harley bounced from the back of the jeep and tumbled across the sand, rolling several times. Conrad slammed on the brakes, kicking up sand, and looked back. He jumped from the jeep and ran to her as she pulled herself to her feet.

"Are you okay?"

Harley spit out sand and grabbed the discarded gun. "Next time, I drive."

They hurried back to the jeep and jumped inside. Conrad drove along the beach, heading for the other side of the island, hoping to get as far away from Randall and whatever had been climbing around on the hangar roof. Harley looked at Conrad once she felt they were safe.

"What happened to James?" Harley gasped. "That wasn't him. That was a monster. Did you see him? He had fangs."

Conrad looked at her while driving. "Fangs?"

"Yes, like some sort of vampire or wild cat," Harley insisted. "And if Randall was at the hangar door, who the hell was on the roof?"

Conrad stared at the beach ahead of him as he slowed down. "Randall talked about an injured cat he'd found the morning after the yacht sank," he informed her. "Maybe it was some sort of wild cat that was on the roof."

"But that doesn't explain why James had fangs," Harley reminded him.

Conrad appeared to consider her comment, then briefly met her gaze. "Brian and I had discussed attempting to reach your mother's island with the rowboat."

"You're insane," Harley cried out. "Do you know how long that would take?"

"We can't survive long against a wild cat," Conrad reminded her. "There are only about seven rounds left in that gun. I'm not even sure that caliber weapon could stop a large cat." Conrad looked to the dashboard and frowned. "We're low on gas. We need to return to the barracks and take shelter."

"Are you crazy?" she gasped. "We're not safe there."

"We're not safe out in the open either," Conrad reminded her. "It'll have to do. We'll barricade the door and lower the blast shutters on the windows. Hopefully, the others will return there."

"Maybe they're already there," Harley remarked, although she wasn't convinced anyone was still alive at this point.

Harley's heart sank when she thought about Damon out there all alone. All his combat training wouldn't help against some wild cat.

"We'd better get to them," Conrad announced, returning Harley to their current, dire situation.

A gunshot rang out from within the woods. Both jumped with surprise and looked around. Conrad immediately stopped the jeep while Harley stood in the passenger seat, looking toward the woods with nervous anticipation. She prayed it was Damon. They heard the sounds of rustling branches and faint male cries. Conrad honked the horn, giving the survivor their location on the beach. Shawn and Tyler ran from the woods toward them while yelling and screaming.

"Go! Go!" Shawn cried out as both men dove into the back of the jeep.

Conrad stepped on the gas, burning out in the sand. Harley watched the woods as they sped away. Randall appeared on the beach, stopped, and watched them leave.

"What the hell was that?" Tyler cried out.

"Didn't look like a wild cat to me," Shawn shouted.

"We need to get back to the barracks," Tyler insisted.

"Are you crazy?" Shawn cried out. "James might be there!"

"James is dead," Harley informed him.

Both men appeared relieved and attempted to relax despite Conrad driving dangerously fast.

"What happened?" Harley asked both men while briefly turning to look back at them.

"James went insane and attacked Ivy," Shawn informed her. "He was like a wild animal. She tried to get away from him, but he chased after her."

"By the time we caught up with them, Ivy was pretty much dead," Tyler added while still panting from their long-distance run.

"We thought we were in the clear, but we ran into Randall right before you came along," Shawn remarked.

"He couldn't have gotten this far that fast," Conrad insisted.

"This is fucked up," Tyler scoffed.

The jeep sputtered and rolled to a stop not far from the beach path to the barracks.

Conrad angrily pounded on the steering wheel. "Damn it," he cried out. "Everyone out."

All four jumped out and hurried along the wide path toward the barracks. Harley was aware of every sound, making her heart pound faster and harder. The others were equally spooked, shifting gazes and aiming weapons at every chirp and twig snapping. The rapidly spreading shadows didn't help. Harley saw imaginary faces lurking in every shadow. She had to keep reminding herself to keep her finger off the trigger, fearing she might accidentally fire the weapon and alert the real threat to their location. Accidentally shooting herself in the foot also crossed her mind. Despite the growing darkness, they reached the barracks in record time. Considering their last encounter with Randall, they'd barely have enough time to fortify the building before he made it back. Even with the metal shutters down over the windows, it didn't mean they were safe, not by a long shot.

Chapter 49

Day Thirty-nine. It was just before sunrise, although it was difficult to tell beyond the shuttered windows in the barracks. A kerosene lantern remained dimly lit the entire night while the four slept in shifts. The blood on the floor and in James's bunk was a constant reminder of their dire situation. Despite none of them getting much sleep, all four were wide awake, sitting at the table, attempting to work out a new strategy for survival. Unfortunately, survival seemed rather bleak.

"We have enough food for a month or longer," Conrad informed them, "but our water won't last more than a couple of days."

"We certainly can't go back out there," Shawn insisted. "We were lucky to escape the first time."

"Food and water are of little consequence," Tyler remarked. "We're never keeping Randall out. He's like superhuman or something."

"Agreed," Conrad replied with a defeated sigh.

"And so what if we can keep him out?" Harley announced. "We're still stranded on this island. No one is going to rescue us if they don't know we're here. We'd be prisoners in this barracks until we die."

"Which is about three or four days after the water runs out," Conrad reminded her.

Harley hated that Conrad always had a valid argument when he was right. Conrad eyed the revolver on the table in front of Shawn.

"Where'd you get the gun?" Conrad asked Shawn, desperately needing to change the subject before everyone completely lost hope.

"I found it inside one of the footlockers," Shawn replied, then shoved it across the table. "It's practically useless. The sights are off. You'd have to be extremely close to kill anything, and there's only four rounds left."

"You'd better make them count," Conrad insisted. "If Randall comes back here--"

"If--?" Tyler chuckled uncomfortably.

"We'll need all the firepower we can get," Conrad insisted. "There are spaces alongside the shutters. We can break the glass and use it as kill holes. Four against two, and we have guns. If they attack the barracks, our chances are better."

"What about the rowboat?" Tyler asked.

"What ***about*** the rowboat?" Shawn scoffed.

"If one of us could get away from the island, perhaps we could reach our port of origin," Tyler insisted. "It can't be that far away. We were only sailing about fourteen hours before we ran aground."

"You're crazy," Shawn cried out. "It would take a week to get there by rowboat ***if*** you survive any storms that pop up. It's still storm season, you know. Plus, we'd need a ton of supplies."

"Brian thought it was possible," Conrad remarked.

"Brian couldn't get across a swimming pool without a map," Shawn scoffed. "I'm not stupid enough to attempt that sort of journey."

"I'll go," Tyler announced a little too quickly.

"What does a rich boy like you know about the ocean?" Shawn demanded.

"It's large and wet," Tyler scoffed. "I know how to row, and my solar watch has a built-in compass. Luck will have to do the rest."

"We have little choice," Conrad insisted, then shook his head. "We won't survive long while Randall is out there hunting us."

"You're both insane," Shawn scoffed.

"We'll throw some supplies together in a duffel bag and head for the beach as soon as it's light," Conrad informed Tyler.

"Are you going to help carry supplies?" Tyler asked. "I'm going to need at least a week's worth of water."

"Yes, I'll help you," Conrad replied.

"Me too," Harley added.

"You're staying here," Conrad informed her so sharply that there was no room for discussion.

"What? By myself?" she demanded. "Oh, that's really safe."

"I'll be here," Shawn reminded her, then snorted a tense laugh while shaking his head. "There's no way I'm going back out there. I'd rather die of dehydration than have my insides torn out."

"You're not going anywhere without me," Harley informed Conrad while standing, ignoring Shawn. "You need someone to watch your back in the woods on the return trip."

"You're not going out there," Conrad again insisted and also stood.

"I'm not staying here while you get yourself killed," Harley launched back, her voice rising as she faced off against Conrad.

"Don't argue with me, Harley," Conrad practically shouted. "I can't lose you. You're the only thing I love in this life!"

There was a strange silence the moment the words left his mouth.

"Right back at you," Harley replied softly without taking her eyes off her friend. "If something happens to you, do you think I want to be stranded on this island alone?"

"Again," Shawn remarked. "Not going anywhere."

Harley glared at Shawn. "That's even worse," she scoffed, surprising the captain. She returned her attention to her friend. "We should stick together."

"It's my nature to look after you, Harley," Conrad informed her. "If I'm looking after you, I'll be putting my own life in jeopardy. If I do this myself, I have a better chance of returning."

Harley stared at the man she'd loved since she was a little girl and attempted to hold back her emotions. "I don't want to be responsible for putting your life in danger," she whispered.

Conrad pulled her into his arms and held her in a warm embrace. Harley had a horrible flashback of Damon holding her right before he left. It felt like another 'final goodbye'. She clung to him and fought her tears. The thought of losing the man who was like a father and her best friend was too much.

"You've always been like a daughter to me," Conrad whispered while clinging to her like a security blanket. He pulled away just far enough to meet her gaze. "In a way, I always felt as if you should have been my daughter."

"I feel the same, Conrad," Harley insisted while holding back her tears and pretending to be brave.

He released her but didn't take his eyes off hers. "I have a confession to make," Conrad announced, then drew a deep, tense breath. "I was in love with your mother from the moment I'd met her. A good servant knows his place, and I thought she was happy with your father, so I was happy for her." He managed a tiny, tense chuckle. "I broke protocol by maintaining a secret friendship with her. When her marriage to your father took an ugly turn, I wanted to profess my love for her and take her away." He frowned while sinking into a darker time. "But I remained the dutiful servant and stayed loyal to your father." Conrad drew a deep breath and straightened proudly. "I was determined to protect you, where I failed to protect your mother, and stood up to your father when he tried to keep me from becoming your personal assistant."

"I didn't know that," Harley whispered, unable to take her eyes off him.

"I thought about telling your mother how I felt after she left your father," Conrad informed her. "But I didn't want to complicate things for her and lose my position as your assistant by pissing off your father." He hesitated a moment before managing a tiny smile. "At your aunt's wedding, I almost told your mother how I felt about her." His smile slowly faded. "If she felt the same, I'd have her, but I'd lose you. I chose you."

Harley practically choked on the lump in her throat and threw her arms around Conrad, holding him. "If we get out of this," she whispered. "I want you to tell her how you feel. You've sacrificed your happiness for everyone else. I want you to be happy."

"I am happy," he whispered. "Being here for you has always made me happy." Conrad finally pulled away, offered a tiny smile, and placed his hand on hers. "I'll be fine out there, I promise."

Harley knew he was just saying that to make her feel better. They had a chance of holding down the fort against Randall and his 'girlfriend', but out there--? She feared this would be her last goodbye, just as it had been with Damon, but she had to pretend it would be okay for Conrad's peace of mind. She nodded, giving in.

Chapter 50

An hour after daybreak, Conrad and Tyler stood on the beach, not far from the surf, staring at the ocean and the shore with confusion.

"Where's the boat?" Conrad demanded.

"It was here last night," Tyler insisted. "Brian went off with Damon this morning. He said he'd left it here. He always pulls it halfway up the beach in case the surf gets rough, so it doesn't get pulled back out."

"Maybe he came back for it," Conrad remarked, then shook his head before patting Tyler's shoulder. "We need to get back to the barracks. It's not safe out here."

"I hear you," Tyler muttered.

They turned and hurried back to the path at the jungle's edge. Randall suddenly appeared on the beach and tackled Conrad to the sand, landing on top of him. Tyler sprang into action and grabbed Randall around the neck from behind, attempting to pull him off. Randall tossed himself backward with all the agility of a gymnast, rolling both men across the sand. Tyler attempted to keep Randall from biting and scratching him while trying to push him off. Conrad removed his gun and aimed it at Randall, but Tyler and Randall were rolling around too fast for him to get any kind of shot that wouldn't result in him hitting Tyler. A loud snarl suddenly rang out from the woods, alerting Conrad. He spun and aimed his weapon. Horror was revealed in his eyes as he cried out while rapidly firing the gun.

§

Shawn lay on his bunk and watched Harley as she paced the entire length of the barracks since Conrad and Tyler left. Every memory she'd ever had growing up with Conrad seemed to play out in her mind on a vicious loop. All the happy memories had a way of making her sad. She didn't know what she'd do without him.

"Why don't you sit down?" Shawn practically insisted, interrupting her quiet thoughts. "They only left thirty minutes ago. They're probably just launching the rowboat now."

"It seems a lot longer than half an hour," she muttered, then approached a crack between the boards on the closed-off window and stared outside, as if that would help the situation.

Everything appeared quiet, though it didn't matter much. Things at the hangar had been quiet right before Randall arrived and tore up the place. It was another beautiful, warm tropical morning in paradise. How could the day be so beautiful when she felt as if her world was ending? It almost didn't seem fair. At least she had a decent view of the trail leading up from the beach. Harley again considered the possibility that Damon was already dead. If something happened to Conrad as well, it was almost too much to bear. That would leave her all alone--with Shawn. Harley looked back at the captain, who somehow managed to look relaxed despite everything that they'd been through yesterday. Her stomach turned, but she looked away, fighting the urge to retch at the thought of spending eternity with that man. Did he even care that Ivy was brutally butchered? All he seemed to care about was himself. She couldn't do it. Harley refused to go on without Conrad or Damon.

If it somehow became just her and Shawn, she'd find a way to end it all. They were never going to be rescued, and she wasn't going to live out the rest of her days with the man who tried to kill Damon because he couldn't handle having his authority challenged. Such a frail ego. How long until he plotted her death? Harley attempted to push those nauseating thoughts from her mind and looked back out the crack between the boards. Randall suddenly appeared before the window, staring back at her. Harley jumped back with a startled gasp, alerting the captain. Shawn leapt from his bunk and joined her at the window.

"What is it?" Shawn asked.

Harley backed away from the window. "Randall," she gasped softly.

Randall had seen her. He'd been looking right at her. He somehow knew she was looking out that crack in the window, almost as if he ***sensed*** her. A rock suddenly shattered the glass on the outside. Both cried out and jumped back a step with surprise.

"Arm yourself," Shawn cried out, clutching his gun.

Since she gave her gun to Conrad for his journey, Harley grabbed the axe, clutching it in both hands, and stared at the window. The front door suddenly vibrated, followed by a beastly snarl. Harley and Shawn spun toward the door as a second strike broke the lock. The door struck the bunk, keeping it from opening, but it didn't stop the assault on the door.

"Come on," Shawn shouted while running to the back of the barracks.

Harley was hesitant to follow him, knowing they wouldn't get very far on foot out in the open. Staying in the barracks seemed safer, although not by much. She groaned softly, giving in, and hurried after him. Shawn removed the brace that had kept the back door secure and flung it open. Both dashed into the destroyed section of the barracks and headed for the massive opening. As they ran out, they heard the loud crash of the bunk striking the floor. If Harley had stayed, it would have been all over for her. As she ran through the woods, only a couple of feet behind Shawn, axe in hand, she knew it was only a matter of time before Randall and his cohort caught up with them. She was delaying the inevitable. There didn't seem to be any way they survived. When Harley looked back, nothing was chasing them. Was it possible they managed to slip out unnoticed?

They reached the clearing before the pond. As Shawn made a sharp turn for the connecting path, Harley slid in the mud and tumbled into the water. Harley surfaced with a startled gasp and saw Shawn disappearing into the woods, possibly not even realizing she'd fallen into the pond, although he must have heard the splash. She saw the discarded axe on the path just within reach. Before she could jump from the water, she heard a loud rustling sound within the woods and nervously looked around. Despite not seeing anything, Harley sank deep into the water and swam beneath the surface for the waterfall. When she reached the other side, she surfaced between the waterfall and the rocky grotto. Through the loudly crashing water, she could see the path in the woods. Despite the deafening sound of the waterfall, Harley held her breath and remained motionless while mostly hidden.

Through the waterfall, Harley could easily make out Randall's silhouette emerging from the woods. He continued on the path Shawn had taken. She shut her eyes and allowed a tiny breath to escape. Then she heard that chilling beastly snarling she'd heard too many times in the last twenty-four hours. Her eyes opened, and she remained motionless in the water. Through the waterfall, Harley saw the distorted outline of something large running on four legs past the pond. Was it a wild cat? She remembered that day at the hot spring, catching a glimpse of something poking out of the woods as they drove away. Is that what she had seen? What was it?

Chapter 51

Harley ran without slowing through the woods, following the jeep trail Damon had taken her on while heading to the hot spring. She bolted into the small clearing that housed the wrecked plane. Harley barely hesitated or even slowed while darting inside the plane. She rushed to the cockpit, lunged past the skeletal remains of the pilot, and reached under his seat, snatching an emergency kit. She opened the box, removed the flare gun, and loaded it. Harley was about to leave the plane when the partially destroyed crate caught her attention. She tilted her head, now curious, and approached. The words 'Alcom Laboratories' were printed on the side. She peered inside the crate and saw that the bottom was lined with old straw bedding.

Harley considered what she was seeing only a moment before horror crossed her face. It wasn't just some injured wild animal Randall had found; it was an animal from some sort of laboratory! Perhaps even a genetically mutated hybrid of some kind! Harley hurried away from the plane wreckage with the flare gun and several extra flares. A thousand thoughts raced through her mind. She finally slowed on the path to the hot spring while nervously looking around. It was then that she heard a male moan. She jumped against a nearby tree, remained motionless, and listened. She heard the male moan more clearly now. Harley slowly crept through the woods along a smaller, less-traveled trail. She discovered a tiny clearing not far from a large rock formation.

In the middle of the clearing, she saw Shawn on his knees with his back to her, obviously in pain. Harley quietly crawled into the clearing toward him, not wanting to alert anything nearby to her presence. She suddenly detected the foul stench of rot, almost making her gag. That's when she noticed the severely decomposing remains of larger animals. Their juicy, fleshy remains were infested with bugs and maggots. There were heads and partial remains of animals Harley never even knew existed on the island. Perhaps they hadn't seen the larger animals because Randall's genetically altered girlfriend had already exterminated them long before they were shipwrecked on the island. She knew she had to grab Shawn and get out of there. Harley quickly scrambled closer to Shawn, needing to snap him out of his shock.

"Shawn," she whispered.

Harley moved around him when he didn't respond. She was about to nudge him when she saw his eyes were rolled back and his mouth hung open. Her eyes strayed to the long slit from his throat to his groin, revealing his hollowed-out body. She let out a startled gasp and flew backward, hitting the old bones. Harley immediately jerked and spun to flee when she saw Ivy's decapitated head, her lifeless blue eyes staring back at her. The girl's final moments of terror were frozen on her face, her mouth twisted mid-scream. Harley placed her hand on her mouth, held back her scream, and fought back her tears. She again heard the male moan, but it wasn't coming from the body pit. She looked past Shawn's motionless body, zeroing in on the sound.

Harley crept closer to the trees, keeping low and silent, and looked past them. She saw Randall on his knees in another small but lush and grassy clearing. His head was back, his eyes were closed, and he appeared to be in pain. Harley clutched her flare gun and sneered, hoping he was in pain. She hoped he was suffering, and if he wasn't, she intended to make sure he would be very soon. She quietly moved to a closer tree, now providing a profile view of Randall. When she saw Randall within a large nest of sorts, he was naked and appeared to be mounting someone doggie style. Harley squinted and strained to see who was with him. Her eyes suddenly widened in horror at the hideous cat-like creature.

The creature appeared almost human but coated with fur, long, large paws rather than hands and feet, and a long, mountain lion-type tail that swished as Randall 'mated' with her. Her pointy cat ears suddenly twitched, then pivoted in Harley's direction. When the cat creature turned her head, she stared at Harley with round, yellow, cat-slit eyes. The hybrid creature hissed loudly, revealing long, sharp fangs. Harley straightened out of reflex and gasped with horror, momentarily frozen. Randall immediately jerked and pulled away from his 'mate', focusing on Harley as well. Harley snapped out of her shock and fired the flare gun at the creature. The creature sprang upward into a nearby tree with startling and amazing agility. When the flare hit the nest, the dry material burst into flames.

With trembling hands, Harley frantically loaded another flare and aimed it at the trees, where the feline was now lurking. As she pulled the trigger, the creature jumped into another tree, the flare missing and jettisoning high into the air. When she looked back at the swiftly burning nest, she saw Randall, naked and charging at her. He snarled and growled, revealing his own set of sharp fangs. Harley cried out, seeing whatever Randall had now become, and ran through the woods for the path. When she reached the path, she heard movement and snarling behind her, but didn't dare look back or risk falling. Randall was close. Too close!

She jumped rocks and puddles with a level of speed and agility she never knew she possessed. She heard movement from the trees and the ground, seemingly all around her. Branches fell from the trees just behind her while twigs snapped on the ground. The creature snarled from somewhere above her, getting closer and possibly ready to pounce upon her.

Harley saw the edge of the woods and the bright, welcoming beach up ahead. She picked up speed and ran onto the deep sand, losing some traction, but maintaining her balance, and kept running. Something forcibly struck her from behind, throwing her face-first into the sand with something heavy landing on top of her. Without looking or thinking, Harley kicked free and flipped onto her back. Randall, naked, dirty, and foul-smelling, was already on his knees, hovering over her. His mouth opened to reveal four sharp fangs as he lunged for her neck. Harley could do little more than scream and throw her hands up in what would be a failed attempt to hold him back. Her hands barely made contact with Randall's bare chest when she heard the explosion of rapid gunfire.

Harley opened her eyes in time to see Randall's body jerk and jolt as several bullets tore into his exposed flesh. He was thrown off her and fell with a thump to the sand. Harley screamed and shielded her face. When the sound ceased, she jerked, sprang into a crouching position, and stared across the beach. Damon released the empty magazine from his weapon, slapped in a full one while seamlessly cocking the gun as he spun toward the woods, and fired at something she didn't see. She then saw the outline of the cat creature dart back into the safety of the woods. Damon ran to Harley, grabbed her hand, and pulled her to her feet.

"Are you okay?" Damon asked, pulling her away from the edge of the woods while keeping one eye on it. "I was afraid you were dead."

"Not yet," Harley gasped, then glared at him. "Where the hell have you been?"

"Trying to find that wild cat," Damon informed her. "When I got back this morning, I discovered the hangar torn apart, and the jeep was gone. I didn't know what happened to you or the others, and then I saw a flare in the sky just a moment ago."

Harley indicated the flare gun. "I ran into your 'wild cat," she remarked, then fumbled to load another flare. "We have to find Conrad and Tyler. Tyler was going to take the rowboat and get help, but Conrad never returned to the barracks."

"Tyler and Conrad wouldn't have found anything when they arrived on the beach," Damon informed her. "I sent Brian out in the boat when we discovered there was a wild cat of some kind."

His words felt like a punch to the gut, and she could do little more than stare at him. Reality came crashing back, but she refused to believe Conrad was dead.

"We have to find them," Harley insisted, now trembling. "That's not some wild cat running around out there. It's some fucked up lab experiment." She nervously clutched the flare gun like a lifeline. "Whatever it is, it bit Randall, turning him into a bloodthirsty monster. The same thing happened to James."

"James has been infected, too?"

"He was," Harley replied softly and shivered. "Conrad killed him. The others are dead. Ivy, Shawn, and Lester. We need to find Conrad and Tyler."

"We'll find them," Damon informed her. "But we need to keep moving. We need to get away from here. Whatever that thing was, I frightened it, for the moment, but it'll be back."

Damon clung to Harley's hand as they ran the entire length of the beach until they reached the area where the yacht sank over a month ago. They stopped when they saw blood and pieces of scattered innards on the sand near the surf. Damon pulled Harley against him as she gasped and covered her mouth. Her worst fear had come true. Conrad was dead!

"We need to get back to the hangar," Damon insisted.

"Conrad," Harley sobbed softly. "He's not dead! He can't be dead!"

Damon held her in his arms despite his spiking anxiety. "We don't know that he's dead," he insisted. "But we can't stay out here, exposed. We need to get to the hangar and take shelter."

"It's not safe there," she cried out, a heavy, cold weight settling in her chest as her last flicker of hope drained away. "It's not safe anywhere!"

"We can't stay here, Harley," he informed her in a stern tone. "We need to go. Now!"

Chapter 52

Harley entered the hangar behind Damon, her arms insecurely folded across her chest and her head lowered, mourning the loss of her friend. Even though she didn't want to believe it, she knew Conrad had to be dead. There was so much blood along the sand.

"We're not safe here," Harley insisted between sniffs. "That thing will come in here and get us."

Damon pushed the remaining hangar door open the rest of the way, then turned to Harley and nodded to the plane ladder.

"Climb inside."

"What for?" Harley asked.

"We need to get help," Damon informed her, revealing rarely seen panic. "We won't survive long if we stay here. I need to get my flight manual."

When she realized what Damon was suggesting, horror set in. "We can't leave," she insisted, coming back to life. "What if Conrad isn't dead?"

Damon stopped briefly, seemingly slowing time itself, and met her gaze, attempting to project comfort and calm despite his rising anxiety.

"We'll come back with an army and find him," Damon assured her before his look again turned commanding. "But for now, we have to get out of here. Flying out in this old tub is our only hope."

Damon urged her to the ladder, then hurried to the office for his flight manual. Harley knew he was right and placed her hands on the ladder. Her eyes then strayed to the small pool of blood on the hangar floor. Her heart suddenly skipped a beat. Where was James's body? She slowly released the rung and looked around. A small trail of blood led beneath the plane. Harley held her breath and slowly crouched down, looking at the landing gear beneath the plane. Her heart was pounding so hard, her ears hurt. There was nothing there. Harley stared a moment longer then straightened, her brows knitted in confusion. But where would he have--? She heard a soft groan behind her. Harley gasped while spinning around. James stood directly in front of her, blood seeping from both sides of his face where the bullet entered and exited.

"Going somewhere?" James hissed while grinning through bloodied teeth, his speech slightly slurred from the damage to his jaw. "We have important things to discuss, you and I."

Harley screamed and darted beneath the plane. When she straightened on the other side and looked back, James wasn't there.

"Harley--?" Damon called out from the office.

Harley gasped, fearing for Damon's life if she didn't warn him about James. She ducked back under the plane and saw Damon bolt toward her from the office. The plane shuddered slightly and creaked as James leapt from the wing and landed on top of Damon, tackling him to the concrete.

"No!" Harley cried out and bolted out from under the plane.

Damon struggled to hold James back with his hand, clutching his throat, as he attempted to sink his fangs into his face. One bite and it was over for Damon, who was rapidly losing the battle. James, much like Randall, appeared to have superhuman strength from the creature's mutated saliva. Harley refused to lose Damon, especially to James. She knew she only had seconds before Damon was overpowered. She looked around but didn't see any weapons of opportunity, not something that would defeat James's newly found strength. As Damon struggled against his attacker, Harley saw the handle of his hunting knife sticking out of the boot of his wildly thrashing legs. Harley practically threw herself to the concrete near them and grabbed Damon's foot, possibly startling him.

As she attempted to free the Bowie knife, Damon grounded his foot in a last effort to give her access to it. He was losing the battle, holding James back, and went with his last option. Harley yanked the knife from Damon's boot and straightened on her knees just in time to witness Damon shoving two fingers into the bullet wound on James's face. The action was enough to turn Harley's stomach, but it was effective. James cried out in agony, pulling back just enough to relieve the pressure. Damon refused to release his jaw, just about detaching it with a nauseating crunch. Harley raised the Bowie knife above her head and cried out while plunging it into James's back. He attempted to cry out in pain, but Damon still refused to release his broken jaw, clinging to it with two fingers.

James dug his claws into Damon's leather bomber jacket, unwilling to stop his assault. Harley ripped the knife from between James's shoulder blades and straddled his back. With her left hand, she grabbed a handful of hair, pulling his head further away from Damon's face, freeing Damon's fingers from his jaw. With what could only be described as a loud battle cry, Harley plunged the long, broad blade into James's temple, driving it straight through until it stopped at the hilt. James gasped, eyes wide and motionless, before falling limp against Damon's hand on his throat. Harley cast herself off James's back. Once she was clear, Damon tossed James's lifeless body to the opposite side. As Damon scrambled into a sitting position, Harley turned onto her backside, gasping for air, and staring at her handiwork. For a moment, neither could look away from the dead man, then finally exchanged gazes.

"You're scary," he announced while managing a tense chuckle.

Harley cast a look from James's broken, displaced jaw to Damon's bloodied fingers before meeting his gaze.

"Back at you."

Damon laughed softly while moving to his feet with a little added stiffness, then extended his bloodied hand to assist her from the floor. Harley eyed his blood-covered fingers, grimaced, and held up her hand, declining his help, before pulling herself to her feet. A metallic bang on the roof echoed throughout the entire hangar, alarming both.

"Get in the plane," Damon cried out.

Harley scaled the ladder and practically flung herself into the rear cockpit. Damon grabbed his flight manual and jumped on the ladder, slightly rocking the plane. Out of the corner of her eye, Harley saw a shadow move past the destroyed hangar doors.

"Hurry!" she cried out.

The cat creature suddenly appeared, clinging to the edge of the cockpit and hissing, her yellow cat eyes locked on Harley. Harley screamed and ducked down in the seat, having nowhere to go. The thick, heavy flight manual whizzed past Harley's head and struck the creature in the face. The creature's tail swished with anger, her attention now focused on Damon, who was on the ladder on the opposite side, his gun now in his hand. Damon fired two shots as she pounced across the cockpit for him. Both shots missed, and the creature knocked him off the ladder. Harley frantically fumbled to get out of the cockpit and accidentally hit the engine button. The engines fired with a loud, deafening sound, rattling the entire hangar. The cat creature sprang off of Damon and ran from the structure, frightened by the sound and the massive vibration it created. Although a little dazed from the fall, Damon pulled himself to his feet, climbed the ladder, and just about fell into the front seat. Harley could see that his jacket was sliced, but he appeared unharmed.

With the push of a button, the canopy shut like a lid closing on a casket. Harley gasped, now that she was crammed inside the small area.

"Seatbelts, please," Damon announced while trying to sound confident, but it was obvious he was struggling to keep calm.

Harley watched as Damon slipped into the flight harness. She gasped and nervously fumbled with her own five-point harness.

"Oh, God," she cried out, then clutched the seat and shut her eyes.

Harley was positive they would die a fiery death at the bottom of the cliff! At least it would be a quick death. Damon taxied the plane from the hangar, the long wings barely clearing the opening, and straightened onto the runway. They sat on the runway a moment as the engines fired louder and faster. Harley opened her eyes, hoping Damon had changed his mind, but they were soon taxiing down the runway. Harley again clung to her seat and now held her breath, somehow unable to close her eyes to the terror. The feline suddenly jumped into their path. Harley saw the creature and screamed, grabbing the stick before her and pressing a button. The fighter plane guns fired rapidly, exploding the ground around the creature. The feline darted out of the path of the gunfire and the plane.

It seemed as if she were gone until they heard a thumping outside the speeding plane. Harley gasped and looked around. The creature's tail disappeared beyond the wing. She was on the plane! A red light appeared on the control panel, and an alarm wailed loudly.

"Shit--"

"What's wrong?" she cried out.

Flames appeared from the plane's engine compartment in front of them.

"Nothing," Damon replied.

Harley screamed at the flames, then saw the cliff ahead. "Abort!"

"Too late!"

Damon pulled back hard on the stick, and the plane soared from the cliff and into the air. Harley screamed and stared at the ocean that was before and below them from their elevated view. For a fleeting moment, time seemed to stand still. The water was so calm and blue, and there were few clouds in the sky. Even though they were going to die, it was possibly the most breathtaking scene Harley had ever witnessed. For a split second, she felt at peace with the idea of dying. When the flames from the engine compartment became more intense, Harley suddenly realized how painful their death was going to be. Time sped up, and everything seemed to move faster. The feline suddenly peered in on them from the canopy above, her fangs exposed while hissing, and hanging on with her claws despite the speed. Damon jerked on the controls, alarmed by the sight of the creature they hadn't escaped. He turned his head and attempted to look back at Harley while cringing.

"Abandon ship," he cried out.

"What?" she gasped.

Damon pulled a lever, and the canopy flew from the plane, taking the feline with it, jettisoning the creature through the air. Both seats suddenly ejected from the burning plane, soaring upward at a tremendous rate. Harley cried out, clutching her seat and pinching her eyes shut. She heard a woman's shrill, high-pitched scream echoing in her ears, frightening her. As the seat began to drop at the same rapid pace, she couldn't resist looking down, seeing the ocean swiftly getting closer, and realized the woman screaming had been her. In the midst of her looming death, she saw a Navy ship out in the ocean with a helicopter flying near the vessel. Somehow, it seemed poetic that a rescue was so close by, now that she was going to die. Harley continued screaming hysterically, unable even to process everything happening in that moment. Why did it feel like it was taking so long for her to die? Had time slowed down?

The parachute suddenly opened, swiftly pulling her upward again like some crazy amusement park ride with no safety precautions. She continued to scream, although her rocketing chair of death finally leveled out and now descended more slowly. It didn't matter; Harley couldn't stop screaming. The plane roared through the sky, engulfed in flames, on a downward angle before crashing into the water with a tremendous splash, possibly breaking apart on impact. Harley looked to her left and saw Damon's parachute several yards away from hers. His head was back, and his eyes were pinched shut. Although he seemed to be handling the situation better, he certainly wasn't having fun. Damon opened his eyes just in time to witness the explosion from the water where the plane had crashed. Both parachutes gently fell into the rippling water not far from the shore.

Harley frantically released her harness and dragged herself onto the sand to avoid Damon's parachute, only a couple of feet behind her. After releasing his parachute, he stumbled through the surf behind her. Harley collapsed on her stomach and shut her eyes while Damon breathed heavily, sank to his knees beside her, and then collapsed onto his back.

"You okay?" he asked while trying to catch his breath.

Harley didn't lift her head, equally winded. "I'm never flying with you again."

Damon chuckled. "Spectacular crash though."

Harley lifted her head and glared at him while he grinned in response. She groaned softly and heaved herself partially on top of him, clinging to him as if her life depended upon it. Damon tightened his arms around her as both continued to pant from their wild ride in the flaming fighter jet. Harley's eyes suddenly popped open as she gasped. She pulled away from Damon and sat up, remembering what she'd seen.

"There's a ship in the ocean," she cried out. "And a helicopter. I saw them!"

Damon sat up, almost baffled, and both looked out at the ocean. Instead of a Navy ship, they saw two men in a rowboat rowing and riding the waves to shore. Harley heaved herself to her feet, barely able to keep her legs under her, and stared in stunned disbelief as Brian and Conrad waved and shouted from the confines of the small rowboat. Relief that her friend was alive hit her so hard that she could barely walk.

"Conrad," she gasped.

"Harley," Conrad cried out, a broad grin on his face as he continued waving.

As Damon made it to his feet, Harley sluggishly ran into the water toward the approaching rowboat, overjoyed that Conrad was alive. The cat creature suddenly lurched from the water alongside the small boat, capsizing it, and toppling Conrad and Brian into the shallow ocean. The soaked creature jumped on top of the overturned boat and shirked low while hissing at Harley. Harley immediately stopped, staring in horror that the creature had survived the massive plummet and managed to swim back to shore. As the feline pounced for Harley in the surf, Conrad leapt from the water and tackled her to the shallows. Brian, who surfaced on the opposite side of the capsized boat, struck the creature in the back with his oar, momentarily distracting it. The feline, spinning on the boat, unleashed its fury on Brian instead.

"Oh, shit!" Brian cried out, prepared to defend himself with the ore.

Rapid gunfire echoed from shore as Damon unloaded his entire magazine into the feline. The creature jerked from multiple bullets ripping through her hide before falling into the water in a bloody heap, floating rather than sinking. Harley scrambled to her feet while attempting to pull Conrad from the water with her. Both were coughing and gasping after inhaling the salty water. When they saw the floating, dead creature only a couple of feet from them, they pulled themselves to shore. Brian tugged on the capsized rowboat, pulling it to shore, unwilling to let it slip away. Conrad gathered Harley in his arms and clung to her while panting heavily.

"Are you okay?" Conrad whispered between gasps and coughs.

"No, but I'll live," Harley replied with a soft groan while clinging to him.

Without releasing Harley, Conrad looked at Damon and smiled. "Nice flying, Ace," he announced, with a soft chuckle.

"More like soaring in a fiery inferno," Damon remarked. "But we're still alive."

"I'm grateful for that."

When Conrad released Harley, she practically jumped into Damon's arms and clung to him. He held her head to his chest, sighed, and nuzzled her hair. A faint, pulsating thumping caught their attention. All four looked up and saw the U.S. Navy helicopter approaching from the ocean. Conrad and Brian frantically screamed and threw their arms in the air, waving to it. Damon chuckled softly and affectionately kissed the top of Harley's head before releasing her.

Chapter 53

The U.S. Navy helicopter circled the area once, then lowered to the beach, kicking up a sandstorm around it. Once it landed, four soldiers armed with automatic weapons leapt out, storming the beach before assessing that there was no threat. One soldier checked out the dead creature in the surf while the other three approached the four survivors.

"Are you with the missing charter yacht, Magnus Rattner?" the soldier asked.

"Yes," Brian immediately replied with a dramatic, relieved sigh.

"Coast Guard's been looking for you guys for weeks," the soldier announced. "A lot of people are going to be happy we found you." He then appeared curious. "Was that a U.S. Navy Skyhawk that nosedived into the ocean?"

"It was," Damon informed the soldier while managing a slightly ironic chuckle.

"We saw two people eject to safety," the soldier remarked, then eyed him. "Are you the crazy pilot?"

"Unfortunately, yes," Damon replied, still somewhat humored.

"Spectacular crash," the soldier announced, sharing his humor before looking at the others. "We were informed that there were ten people aboard the yacht. Are there any other survivors?"

All four lowered their heads and shook them.

"The rest were killed by a deranged passenger and a wounded animal he'd nursed back to health," Conrad informed the soldier.

"What the hell--?" the soldier standing over the dead creature by the surf suddenly cried out, aiming his weapon at it despite its obviously deceased condition.

The two remaining soldiers ran to join their comrade and looked over the dead creature.

"What the hell is that?" the second soldier cried out.

The soldier with the four survivors eyed his men and the dead creature from afar, then looked back at them.

"Wild animal?" the soldier questioned.

"That's the story we're sticking with," Damon informed the man.

"Is there any immediate danger remaining?" the soldier asked.

"All neutralized," Damon assured him.

"I'm sure the four of you can't wait to get back home, but the Coast Guard will probably have some questions regarding the deaths of your shipmates," the soldier insisted, then appeared almost sympathetic. "They'll probably want to recover the bodies."

"Understood," Brian replied. "We're more than willing to assist that recovery." He then hesitated. "What's left of them, that is. We're just grateful you saw the plane crash into the water and were able to find us."

"Actually, we were checking out a flare we saw maybe half an hour ago," the soldier informed him. "That's what brought us here."

"That was my flare," Harley remarked, then looked at Damon. "The one you saw from the beach."

"We'll take you to our ship and make you comfortable until the Coast Guard arrives," the soldier informed them. "We'll assist them in their recovery mission, and then they'll transport you home."

§

Although showers on the naval ship were expected to be brief, typically under five minutes, and the water pressure was terrible, Harley was grateful for a moderately hot shower. She wanted to linger but adhered to the requested restrictions. She wouldn't miss the showers in the shower building, but she was already nostalgic for the hot spring. The best hot tub at the fanciest hotel couldn't even compare with the scenic beauty of the natural hot spring. While thinking about it, Harley was also going to miss the pond and its tranquil waterfall. Her thoughts briefly strayed to Ivy, and she found herself fighting her tears. She didn't deserve what happened to her. In reality, the girl just wanted to be loved, but she chose the wrong men. Harley pulled herself together, slipped into her borrowed white Navy fatigues, and joined the others.

When Harley entered the briefing room and saw Damon in the crisp white Navy fatigues, she had to hold back her laugh. Damon sneered, obviously disgusted.

"Not a word," he muttered.

"Aye, Aye, skipper," Harley replied, unable to hide her grin.

Brian entered the room, looking completely at home in his tidy whities, and collapsed into a chair at the table. "I haven't felt this comfortable in over a month," he remarked while leaning back in the chair, possibly on the verge of falling asleep.

Sleep. Harley couldn't even remember when she last slept. It was probably close to forty-eight hours. It was her second night in the hangar with Damon. She invited him into her bunk, and he snuggled with her the rest of the night. There were only brief naps after that, while they feared for their lives. Conrad finally entered the room, wearing a white dress uniform and a white dress hat. Harley almost didn't recognize him. He looked at Harley, proudly tugged on the jacket, and grinned.

"Have you ever seen whites this white?" Conrad asked. "Not one wrinkle and perfectly lined creases. Whoever the officer is in my size, he's an artist with an iron."

"Welcome to the military, Conrad," Damon muttered. "You'd fit right in."

Conrad maintained his grin while brushing a speck of lint off his sleeve. "The shorts are a little over starched, though," he then remarked.

"Just how sensitive ***is*** your tushy?" Damon demanded.

When the ship's commander entered the briefing room, Damon snapped to attention, stopping short of saluting. Brian lurched from his chair, being equally respectful. Conrad maintained his usual demeanor, appearing ready to serve tea. Harley eyed the three men almost suspiciously. It was as if she'd entered another dimension. The ship's commander was certainly no Captain Rattner.

"As you were," Captain Lark announced, adding a tiny, humored smirk. He removed a bottle of whiskey and four glasses from a nearby cabinet and set them on the table. "Have a seat and a drink. I'm sure the four of you could use it."

As Brian, Damon, and Harley sat at the table, Conrad picked up the bottle and poured a double shot for each of them. Harley eyed him, raising her brows somewhat skeptically.

Conrad caught her look and grimaced. "Sorry, old habits," he remarked, then took a glass for himself and chose the seat on the other side of Harley.

Captain Lark sat at the head of the table, flipped through some papers, and then eyed the four. "My men pulled a wild cat from the ocean," he informed them. "Anything special you'd like to tell me about the wild cat that killed your shipmates?"

"If I had to guess," Damon announced in an almost emotionless tone, "I'd say it was a cougar."

Conrad and Damon were the only ones who maintained eye contact with the captain. Neither breaking under his gaze. The captain finally nodded and again looked at his paper.

"Can I count on the four of you to stick with that story?" Lark asked.

All four nodded.

"Any idea how this ***wild cat*** got on the island?" Lark asked.

"There was a smashed crate in an old wrecked plane," Harley informed him. "The crate had writing on it."

"Could you give my men the precise location of this wrecked plane?"

"I can," Damon replied. "Harley's never been to the plane. All her information is second-hand."

"No need to get your defenses up," Lark remarked while leaning forward across the desk. "Your wild cat is being incinerated. We'd just like to make sure everything else is incinerated along with it. The world is better off without such abominations."

"I very much agree," Damon replied.

"If you truly feel that way," Conrad announced while sitting rigid in his chair. "You may want to ***incinerate*** a few more ***abominations***."

"Oh?"

"Two of our dead shipmates were infected by the wild cat," Conrad informed him. "Maybe you'd like to ***sanitize*** the island a little before the Coast Guard arrives."

"If you could point us in the right direction, I'd appreciate it," Captain Lark replied.

Chapter 54

The four survivors were once again transported back to the island, where they assisted the Coast Guard in recovering the remains of their fellow passengers. Between the four of them, they were able to lead personnel to where each of their shipmates was killed. Randall and James were the only ones they claimed they couldn't find. In reality, the Navy already disposed of their infected bodies to keep anyone from getting their hands on their mutated blood for nefarious purposes. All four agreed they would tell the truth about Shawn, Tyler, and James turning on them and trying to kill Damon, but they agreed to spare Ivy's reputation post-mortem. She had been operating on survival instincts, and they were convinced she wasn't an accomplice to Damon's botched murder attempt.

It was close to sunset by the time the Coast Guard had finished collecting the remains and their personal effects and loaded them onto their ship. Despite being safe and ready to head home, Conrad was unable to lower his guard and stayed by Harley's side as if his life depended on it. Brian, on the other hand, was about as calm and relaxed as one could get. A couple of drinks, and he was ready to return to his regularly scheduled life. Harley wasn't sure what to make of Damon's mood. He seemed to have reverted to his old self and barely spoke since the Coast Guard arrived on the scene.

Harley stood alongside the railing on the Coast Guard's vessel and stared at the island in the near distance. It looked so much smaller from their position anchored in the ocean. The Coast Guard's men were still on the island finishing up their investigation, and it was uncertain when they would weigh anchor and head home. Harley decided to enjoy one final sunset on the horizon of hell's paradise. Their stay hadn't exactly been a pleasant one, but there were moments she would fondly remember forever. To the same extent, Harley was happy to be going home, but it was bittersweet. She no longer had to worry about her father pressuring her to marry James, but she didn't want to go back to her father either. Conrad approached her at the railing and handed her her cell phone.

"Your phone is charged," he announced. "Once it was back online, it sounded like a war zone with missed calls and text messages.

Harley accepted her phone and then looked at the man alongside her. Conrad changed back into one of his suits, among his personal effects he'd retrieved. The suit didn't have a single wrinkle. Knowing Conrad, he'd spent the last hour ironing it. When her phone rang, she didn't even look at the caller and immediately silenced it. She looked back at the distant island and sighed softly.

"I know how you feel," Conrad remarked, also staring at the island. "A month of our lives was spent there. Part nightmare, part paradise. I'll miss the paradise part."

"I'm not going home to my father, Conrad," she announced while straightening and eyeing him. "I've made up my mind."

"I thought as much," Conrad replied, a warm smile on his face. "I've been thinking about that. I wouldn't doubt that a lot of people will want to hear about our tale of survival. Maybe even write a book about it. I've already talked to Brian, and he's agreed to let me manage our television and podcast appearances. If you trust me, I think I can parlay those deals into enough money to keep us going until your trust fund becomes available. Neither of us will have to go back to your father."

Harley stared at him a moment, then grinned. "I trust you, Conrad," she announced. "More than anyone else, I trust you." She then hesitated. "What about Damon? Have you talked to him?"

"I approached him, but he seemed aloof and just a tad crabby," Conrad remarked, then cocked his head while eyeing her. "Any idea what's gotten into him since the Coast Guard arrived?"

"I don't have a clue," Harley replied with a dreary sigh. "Something's up, but I haven't had a chance to speak with him privately."

Conrad stared at her a moment, seemingly weighing things in his head. "Anything happen between the two of you while you were alone together in the hangar?"

Was he guessing, or did he actually suspect something had happened? Harley tensed slightly and suddenly didn't know what to do with her hands. Conrad easily read her body language and nodded.

"I see," Conrad replied. "It's understandable. Seeking companionship during a highly stressful situation."

Harley groaned softly and raked her fingers through her hair, then sheepishly met Conrad's gaze. "I suppose, now that we're returning to our previous lives, he doesn't have any use for me. Or any of us."

Conrad stared at her a moment in silent disbelief. "I was actually referring to you," he informed her. "Do you know why I trusted Damon to keep you safe when I didn't trust anyone else?"

"Of course," Harley replied. "Because the two of you needed to trust each other. You saved his life by warning him about the others."

"No, Harley," Conrad replied with a soft sigh. "Damon stepped up to protect you and Ivy from James and Tyler. As my paranoia increased, even after he let everyone believe he'd died, he kept watch over you. Over both of us, but mostly he looked out for you. Keeping you safe kept him going. He's in love with you."

"He told me he loved me," Harley remarked softly, drifting out, briefly reliving that tender moment in the hangar before he left. She then met Conrad's gaze. "I assumed it was just sort of 'while we're stranded' kind of thing."

"I don't think so," Conrad informed her. "The real question is, how do you feel about him?"

"I fell in love with the man I met on the island," Harley replied. "But I'm not sure he even exists anymore."

"Maybe you should find out."

Chapter 55

Although the Coast Guard ship was fairly large, Harley found Damon without too much trouble. He was one deck down, staring at the distant island, same as she had been. Harley approached, suddenly feeling tense around him. Her heart was pounding, and every nerve in her body seemed to be twitching. She didn't understand how she could be so nervous around the man who had pleasured her in every way imaginable only two days ago. She feared she didn't even know him. Everything had changed in one afternoon, and she wasn't sure where that left them. If what they had would be left behind with the island, Harley had no regrets, and she would happily give herself to him all over again. Damon straightened the moment he saw her, seeming equally uncomfortable.

"We didn't have time to talk in private since the Coast Guard arrived early this afternoon," Harley remarked, alternating between fidgeting with her pockets and the ship's railing. "We should talk."

"I knew this was coming," Damon replied, letting out a low sigh. "I'm aware of your father's reputation and his control issues." His attempt at a smirk more closely resembled a sneer. "Old money and guys like me don't mix. Your father would never approve of me."

"My father's thoughts and feelings don't matter," Harley informed him, her defenses increasing at the thought of Damon rejecting her.

"Once he cuts you off, his thoughts and feelings will matter plenty to you," Damon reminded her. "James told me all about your ***conditional*** family wealth and how your father controls every aspect of your life. I make a decent living, but it doesn't come close to the lifestyle you're accustomed to."

"I don't want a ***lifestyle***," Harley informed him. "I just want a ***life***." As she stared into his eyes, her heart pounded while exposing her vulnerability. "My father manipulates and intimidates everyone, and he'll do everything he can to maintain his control over me." Everything that had happened on the island over the last month flooded her thoughts. Her fear of losing Conrad, standing up to James, and a glorious sunset on the cliff with Damon. "But not anymore. I'm in control of my life."

Damon studied her, a smile creeping across his face. "I'm guessing that felt pretty good," he remarked.

She considered the comment, then smiled and nodded. "Actually, it was very satisfying to finally say it aloud."

"You realize you don't have to fight that battle alone," Damon reminded her. "You've got Conrad." He then hesitated as his grin increased. "And personal protection is kind of my specialty."

Harley chuckled, slightly tense. "If I can't afford Conrad, I certainly can't afford your services," she reminded him.

"I think you can," Damon replied. "I'm running a special on beautiful castaways this week."

"Oh?" Harley asked, unable to hide her smile. "What's your special rate?"

"A cup of coffee and a packet of Tabasco sauce."

Harley laughed while gently placing her hand on his chest. She met his gaze again, happy to see him smiling. Damon captured her hand and held it against his chest as his look turned serious.

"Be honest with me, Harley," Damon asked barely above a whisper. "Could you see yourself with a guy like me?"

"Unless you've changed your mind, I already started something with you," Harley remarked. "And I'd really like to see where that goes."

Damon groaned softly, pulled her into his arms, and kissed her quickly before nuzzling her. "I'm very happy to hear that."

Below the forward deck, the steady metallic clank and rattle of the anchor chain carried clearly along the open weather deck as the cutter weighed anchor. A long, deep, prolonged blast from the ship's whistle followed, vibrating through the steel plates under their feet and signaling they were finally underway, heading home. As they stood along the deck watching the island slowly but surely fade from sight, Harley was suddenly curious and pulled back just far enough to meet Damon's gaze.

"Where are they taking us anyway?" she asked.

Damon chuckled, finding humor where there didn't appear to be any. "Back to our original departure port," he informed her.

"My mother's island?" Harley asked, pressing against Damon with even more enthusiasm as her smile widened.

"It's the closest port," Damon replied, his smile matching hers. "Does that make you happy?"

Harley groaned softly and sank against Damon, practically burying her face in his chest. "Oh, yeah," she replied. "I'd love to spend a few days decompressing at my mother's beach house." She immediately pulled back and met his gaze. "As long as you're willing to stay. I don't want you to be uncomfortable."

Damon grinned and chuckled as he pulled her against him, practically smothering her. "You don't have to worry about me," he insisted. "I'd follow you anywhere." He snorted a laugh. "Besides, mothers love me."

"They do?" Harley asked, stunned.

"I'm good at fixing things, I cook, and I do yard work," Damon informed her. "Of course, mothers love me." He then hesitated. "The accent doesn't hurt either."

Harley chuckled while nuzzling his chest. "It certainly doesn't."

They held each other close as the cutter carried them away, watching the island slowly fade until it vanished into the horizon.

The End

Other books by Holly Copella!
Reviews left on Amazon are appreciated!

"The Battle for Andrea Maria"

A cruise ship attack turns six survivors into overnight celebrities after they take credit for the heroic act of a stowaway who died saving them.

The cruise is just what Jess needed--a bit of harmless fun far from her daily grind. But what begins as a relaxing vacation turns into a desperate fight for her life when terrorists take over the ship and start piling up bodies. Teaming up with a mysterious stowaway, Jess attempts to send out a distress call but knows they cannot wait for help to come. If she or the few remaining passengers have any hope for survival, Jess must act now. The papers dub it "The Battle for *Andrea Maria*," but to Jess it is the moment she fought side-by-side with her enigmatic Romeo, saving the ship--and losing him. She thinks the story ends there, but really, the nightmare is just beginning...

"Insanely Deadly"

When the dead return to life, it's up to an admiral's daughter and a mildly insane, former war hero to save their small town.

Jetta Cross, a Navy Admiral's daughter, is tasked with keeping her father's comrade, a former war hero turned town crazy, grounded in the real world. Capt. John Hunter is still fighting the war in his head, where imaginary dead people are part of his world. When a viral outbreak brings about a zombie uprising, Hunter is left to his own devices. He must resume his role as a one-man commando unit in order to destroy the ravenous undead. With Hunter still fighting his own inner demons as well as the undead, the townspeople fear their zombie neighbors may not be the only threat. Stranded at the island's luxurious resort with a handful of workers, Jetta is forced to live up to her father's reputation and take charge of the deteriorating situation at the hotel. She must wage her own war against the infected before the government declares her hometown a total loss.

"Deadly Institution"

A town recluse suspected of killing his wife teams up with a young woman in order to stop a killer.

After being accused of murdering his wife, Konrad Churchill turns his back on the town that once adored him. Ten years later, he still holds his grudge and the title of the most feared man in town. With the reopening of the burned mental institution, where his wife had died, former employees are now murdered one by one, throwing suspicion back on Churchill. A young local reporter, Jacey, is forced to reveal her long-time friendship with the infamous recluse in order to clear his name not only in the recent murders but to exonerate him in the death of his wife as well. Will Jacey's relationship with Churchill invite the killer closer to her? Or is the killer already in her life?

"Death Displacement"

A grief-stricken man travels back in time to seek revenge on the woman who murdered his girlfriend, but inadvertently falls in love with her.

Kane is about to marry the woman he loves. His life is perfect. A few weeks before the wedding, a vindictive woman from his girlfriend's past mysteriously arrives and kills her. He learns of a traumatic accident that happened five years earlier, which triggers Riley's hatred for his girlfriend. Distraught over his girlfriend's death, Kane uses an antique time machine to travel into the past in order to find and destroy the woman responsible. When he runs into Riley's younger self, he realizes she's not the monster she later becomes, and he can't bring himself to destroy her. With a little help from his oddball friend from the past, they formulate a plan to prevent the accident that sends Riley down her destructive path. Kane's plan backfires when he falls for the younger Riley. His new tortured existence is further complicated when future Riley, his girlfriend's killer, shows up with her own devious agenda that doesn't include him. Will he be able to stop the time ripple, which ultimately ends with his girlfriend's death? Or will future Riley take him out of the timeline forever--

"Dead Village"

After strange happenings isolate a small resort town from the rest of the world, nearly one hundred residents seek refuge at the closed hotel. Only eight survive the night. And that's just the beginning...

One day after the entire population of Fox Ridge Village disappears, a car wreck forces several unsuspecting crash victims to seek help at the closed summer hotel. Within the hotel, they discover the grisly aftermath of a brutal slaughter. Crash victims Vander and Devon, a reluctant clairvoyant, team up to solve the riddle of the "haunted hotel" and the mass hysteria plaguing the remaining survivors. By the time they discover the hotel's secret, they're already drawn into the hysteria. As the body count continues to climb, it's a race to isolate the source and bring everyone back to reality before they kill one another. Will Devon be able to communicate with the traumatized spirits before their fate becomes her own?

"Town Darling"

After surviving a brutal attack that claims the lives of those she loves, a young woman seeks revenge on a corrupt town.

Going back home is never easy, but for Casey, it means returning to her corrupt hometown, where she barely survived a brutal attack. Accompanied by two family friends, she seeks justice for the night that destroyed her life. Her physical scars are nothing compared to her emotional ones, forcing the local sheriff to believe that the town darling is back for revenge. As the conspiracy for her revenge appears to be leading up to the coveted town fair, the sheriff is determined to stop her from fulfilling her vengeful scheme...but guilt over his role on that fateful night continues to haunt him. Will his desperate need for Casey's forgiveness be his undoing? Or will Casey's desire for revenge destroy them both?

"Basement Dwellers"

A viral outbreak at a hospital leaves a mortician, sheriff, and coroner fighting for their lives against a horde of undead and the CDC.

After a massive car wreck leaves several survivors in critical condition at the local hospital, a surgeon uses experimental drugs on his critical patients and accidentally causes a zombie outbreak. When local mortician, Lexx, receives an infected corpse as her client, she becomes stranded in the hospital basement during CDC quarantine along with the local sheriff and the coroner. The infamous surgeon struggles to find a cure for his infectious blunder by using the other survivors as test subjects. Meanwhile, Lexx and the sheriff attempt to locate his missing sister, who's stranded somewhere in the battle zone that once was the emergency room. It's a race against time and the ravenous undead. Can they survive the undead before the CDC sanitizes the hospital of all infection?

"Misfits, Inc."

A seemingly ordinary young woman meets four misfits who claim she has given them supernatural powers.

While on a business trip to a remote island paradise, a bored secretary, Hailey, has her world turned upside down when her path collides with a psychic freak, Skyler. He attempts to convince her that they had met in his dreams, and she had chosen him as one of her four mystic warriors. After Skyler foresees a woman's death, they discover an unidentified creature has killed one of the guests. They are joined by a lounge pianist and a rich playboy, who also claim they had met her in their dreams. If Skyler's prophecies are genuine, the evil entity controlling the ravenous creatures needs to destroy Hailey to ensure its survival. Reluctantly accepting her fate, Hailey has to locate the last and most powerful of her chosen warriors, The Guardian. Their fate is in doubt when The Guardian turns out to be a self-absorbed, former cat burglar with a bad attitude. Can Hailey turn her company of misfits into an elite team of mystic warriors? Or will The Guardian's secret agenda destroy them all?

"Deadly Institution 2"

When blackmail turns into murder, a young woman finds herself caught in the killer's crosshairs.

The small town of Stony Ridge is no stranger to scandal and persecution of the innocent. When a brutal killing shakes the town's prestigious country club, Jacey McMurray seeks help from a self-proclaimed vigilante, Konrad Churchill. As her professional and personal worlds collide, Jacey fears the stress of the country club killings have finally taken their toll on Churchill. Can a stressed-out vigilante stop the killer before he strikes again?

"Witness Protection"
Also available in audiobook!

After witnessing an execution, a resourceful young woman attempts to disappear while being pursued by a hitman and a handsome federal agent.

A helicopter pilot, Jackie Remus, reluctantly agrees to go on a date with one of her clients, but her date is unexpectedly cut short when she witnesses a man being murdered. After narrowly escaping with her life, she is placed into protective custody. When the safe house is breached, Jackie makes a daring escape from both the hired killers and the handsome FBI agent, who wants to return her to protective custody. With a little help from her sly and crafty friend, Monroe, Jackie is convinced she can disappear until the trial. While on her journey to meet with her friend, she solicits help from a few shady but lovable characters along the way. Although she manages to stay one step ahead of the hired killers, the federal agent remains in hot pursuit. Will Jackie reach Monroe before she's captured by the FBI and returned to protective custody? Or will the hired killers silence her first?

"Unconditional"

A young woman puts her life on hold to care for an unstable, highly skilled combat soldier, who believes someone is trying to kill him.

A botched military coup leaves a team of elite fighters injured, with one clinging to life in a coma. When Harlan wakes from his coma, he's left with no memory of his past life. His commander's daughter, Indy, takes it upon herself to care for the fallen war hero. She's challenged with more than just his physical care as she combats with not only his memory loss but also his newly found desire for her. His infatuation with her becomes the least of her worries when he sinks back into his role of a combat soldier. Believing his life is in danger, his fighting skills emerge, transforming him into an unpredictable and dangerous man. Will his memory return to him before Indy is forced to commit him? Or will he finally find his nemesis, "the coyote", and possibly claim the life of an innocent person?

"The Pen Pal"

In order to save her friend, she must enter the mind of a serial killer.

When her best friend is abducted, no one believes Jolynn saw it in a psychic vision. With nowhere to turn, Jolynn reluctantly joins Agent Harris Slade and his team on their hunt for a sadistic serial killer known only as "The Pen Pal". Finally confronted with the killer, Jolynn realizes she must enter the mind of the psychopath in order to stop the brutal killings. But when her vision reveals a particularly disturbing death, can Jolynn sacrifice her lover for her friend?

"Witness Protection 2"
The Return of Whiskey Tango Foxtrot

Believing she holds the clue to millions in missing laundered money, a young woman is placed into the protective care of a former Navy SEAL team.

Feeling sorry for her recently separated co-worker, Leeann invites Wiley to join her and her friends on their night out. Little does she know that finding her co-worker murdered is just the beginning of her nightmare. Leeann unknowingly holds the key to fifty million dollars in potentially laundered mob money. With hired killers pursuing her, the FBI places her into a different kind of protective custody. Former Navy SEAL team Whiskey Tango Foxtrot reunites to keep Leeann alive at their secret hideaway. What should be an easy assignment takes an unscheduled turn when secrets, lies, and betrayal threaten to derail their mission. Is the team prepared for a war on their own doorstep? Will Leeann's misguided trust endanger the lives of those sent to protect her?

"Witness Protection 3"
Alpha Mike Foxtrot

A helicopter pilot risks her life to help a team of retired Navy SEALs rescue two girls from a killer.

When former Navy SEAL team Whiskey Tango Foxtrot asks for a simple favor, Jackie reluctantly offers her air-taxi services. What could go wrong? What begins as a search and rescue for two girls turns into a fight for survival against a heavily armed drug cartel. Wanted by the law with the cartel in hot pursuit and their home base breached, the team is forced to call in a favor from a questionable ally. Unfortunately, their new safe house isn't what it seems. Without knowing who the real enemy is, can Jackie and the team save their young witnesses from the hands of a killer?

"Already Dead"
Supernatural Collection

From the already dead to the undead. Three supernatural tales of "things that go bump in the night".

"Bloodletting" - A vampire-themed resort allows guests to *participate* in their Bloodletting Ritual to celebrate the island's legendary vampires.

"Reaper of Souls" - A young woman must outwit an evil sorcerer in order to save her brother or become one of his minions forever.

"Already Dead" - When Flight 220 crashes, ten passengers make it to an isolated island, but only one man lives to tell the lie.

"Witness Protection 4"
O-Dark-Hundred

A simple assignment turns deadly when a retired Navy SEAL team uncovers a plot to kill a notorious mob boss.

When Whiskey Tango Foxtrot embarks on a simple stalking case, they're not prepared for a trip to a private island paradise owned by an infamous mobster. With one of their own suffering from traumatic head injuries, the team is left scrambling to decide what is real or imagined. The situation escalates even further when they uncover an assassination plot where everyone is a suspect. Now targets themselves, can the team survive their trip to paradise?

"Witness Protection 5"
Outside the Wire

After suffering several casualties on their last assignment, a retired Navy SEAL team discovers their misery is just beginning.

When Whiskey Tango Foxtrot returns home after suffering a devastating loss, they're hit with even more bad news regarding the rest of their team. Their grief is cut short when they discover their names are all on the same hit list. Hunted by relentless assassins, the scattered team must decide whether to remain safely hidden or find the man who put the price on their heads. Against the wishes of her teammates, Jackie strikes out on her own in order to save a friend who wants her dead. In a kill-or-be-killed situation, will Jackie's emotions finally betray her?

"The Murder of Emily Fisher"

After finding their favorite teacher murdered, the lives of two teenage girls are forever changed.

Everyone loved Emily Fisher. While walking home one afternoon, two teenage girls, Sidney and Trisha, stumble upon a gruesome murder scene. The brutal murder of Emily Fisher, a young, attractive schoolteacher, shocks the small town of Marilina. After graduation, Sidney moves far away from the memories of the small town, while Trisha retreats deeper into denial. Eight years after the murder, Sidney receives a desperate call from her childhood friend, forcing her to return home. Trisha believes Emily's killer was falsely accused, and she manages to turn the entire town against her while attempting to prove it. When Trisha receives a death threat, Sidney realizes there may be some credibility to her friend's wild accusations. Is Trisha's mental breakdown a result of childhood trauma? Or is the real killer actually attempting to silence her? In order to save her friend, Sidney must answer the eight-year-old question. Who murdered Emily Fisher?

"Once Upon a Disaster"

A young homicide detective finds herself at the mercy of a hitman in the aftermath of an earthquake.

While investigating the murder of a hitman, Detective Jade Wesson pursues a lead connecting the dead man to a break-in at a computer programming company. She's drawn into the world of a nightclub owner and front man for the mob, Cody Riley. Her investigation continues to point to Cody's right-hand man and possible hitman, Vahn Lott. Despite her efforts to keep her investigation on track, Vahn has plans of his own for the attractive detective. When an unprecedented earthquake rocks their east coast town, Jade must put her life in Vahn's hands if she wants to survive. Can she trust a man who might be the killer she's hunting?

"Awaken the Dead"

A grieving innkeeper struggles to keep her haunted hotel out of foreclosure.

After losing her parents in a suspicious boating accident, Harley Brandon is determined to keep the family hotel out of foreclosure. Unfortunately, the hotel ghosts have other plans. Built with tainted money, the century-old Horizon Hotel thrives on a tradition of murder, scandal, and suicide. As the paranormal activity increases to alarming levels, Harley discovers the truth about the hotel and its residents. Can Harley save her friends from the hotel's frightening hidden secrets?

"Castle Bloodshed"
Murder Collection

From a deadly island paradise to haunted castles. Three novella-length tales of murder, mystery, and malicious intent.

"Castle Bloodshed" – A tour of Wesley Castle turns into a fight for survival as six stranded tourists discover the haunting secrets within the castle walls. A mystery writer teams up with an uptight butler in order to stop a killer who may already be dead. Novella-length paranormal murder mystery.

"Fleshies" – Is Uncle Rutger crazy? Five years ago, four business partners died within their newly purchased, fixer-upper castle. Their bodies were never found. The surviving partner, Rutger, claims a demon keeps him as its slave. Rutger's nephew schemes to save his uncle by sacrificing the lives of a group of stranded motorists and a high-profile novelist. Novella-length supernatural murder mystery.

"Demon Island" – A group of strangers are invited to a remote island for the reading of a will. The guests soon discover they were brought to the island to be executed one by one. It's up to a private detective and a tenacious young woman to solve the murders and find a way to escape paradise. Novella-length murder mystery.

"Brighton Island"

When a psychic visits a haunted island mansion, he inadvertently awakens the ghosts' tortured souls.

Something's not right with Simon. When Jacklyn brings her eccentric friend to her uncle's island mansion, she doesn't expect him to slip into psychic overload. As Simon attempts to solve a decade-old double homicide, Jacklyn is confronted with the possibility that she could be next to join the mansion ghosts. When they find themselves stranded on the secluded island, her Uncle Hyland wages his own war to save them from a flesh-and-blood killer. Will her uncle's "shock and awe" military tactics save them or get them killed? Can Simon bring peace to the tortured souls or unexpectedly join them?

"A.L.F. Resort"

A fantasy vacation turns into a nightmare when the resort's artificial life forms are compromised.

Welcome to A.L.F. Resort, where you can live out your fantasies with safe, state-of-the-art artificial life form robots! When a young journalist and a photographer are sent to A.L.F. Resort to do a story for their magazine, Shay and Becka believe they've hit the jackpot of all work-cations. The engineers pull out all the stops to make their fantasies a memorable experience. Unfortunately, the newly designed A.L.F., the Gen X, is smarter than his programming and creates havoc within Shay's fantasy. A computer malfunction removes their safety inhibitors, and the A.L.F.s play out their own hostile fantasies. Zombies, bikers, and mobsters run amok, turning fantasies into nightmares. Shay gets more of a story than she anticipates, but will she survive long enough to write it?

"Jungle Princess"

While stranded on a prison island, a young woman discovers a creature of "unknown" origin.

After their cruise ship sinks, Alex and two of her shipmates are stranded on a deserted, tropical island. Unfortunately, the castaways soon realize they're not alone. They discover an abandoned prison with over two dozen inmates living on the island's south side. While avoiding the prison on the far side of the island, Alex discovers a strange but loveable creature of unknown origin. When one of her fellow castaways is in trouble, Alex reluctantly seeks help from the prisoners. After the brutal murder of several inmates, their questions surrounding the abandoned prison are about to be answered. What really killed over one hundred prisoners? And is it still out there?

"Murder in Wax"

A series of brutal murders plagues a quiet farming community when beautiful women audition for the same acting job.

While all the young women in town are fighting over a once-in-a-lifetime acting opportunity, Devon Vincent is excited about her new job at the local wax museum. Although supportive of her friend's acting aspirations, Devon has a hard time understanding the rivalry among the women in town. When the aspiring actresses are brutally murdered one by one, Devon fears her friend may be the next victim. Devon finds herself in the middle of a murderous revenge plot that leads back to the wax museum's doorstep and possibly implicates her boss as the killer. Will Devon's newly found feelings for her boss bring a killer closer to her? Or is the killer already in her circle?

"Witness Protection 6"
Alpha Dogs

An easy rescue turns into a wild ride for retired Navy SEAL team Whiskey Tango Foxtrot when everyone wants to kill their client.

It was a simple task. Rescue a young woman from her mob boss father-in-law. Little did Jackie and company realize that rescuing the young woman was the easy part. Keeping her alive would be a massive undertaking, especially when everyone wants a piece of the mafia heiress. The team fights for survival against their toughest adversaries yet. How many innocent people must die in order to save one woman? Can the team survive the ultimate battle between mercenaries and assassins?

"Midnight Requisition"

A series of brutal murders leaves a traumatized young woman on a hunt to find a killer.

When they were just babies, Scorpio and her twin brother, Kane, tragically lost their parents under mysterious circumstances. Refusing to accept his father was dead, Kane set off on a mission to find a man he'd never met. A home invasion gone wrong leaves Scorpio grieving the loss of those she loves. Out of the tragedy of her loss, two fallen heroes are thrust upon her. Scorpio soon realizes someone wants her dead, and the killer may already be in her circle. As her entire life unravels in a web of betrayal and lies, can Scorpio trust her new, slightly questionable friends?

"Until Death"

Liars, cheaters, blackmail, and murder. It would be a wedding no one would forget.

Despite knowing he's making the biggest mistake of his life, Raina Steele reluctantly attends her father's third wedding. What should have been a boring reception turns into a web of lies, betrayal, and murder. With no one above suspicion, Raina must put aside her feud with the arrogant yet insanely handsome butler in order to catch the killer before he finds his next victim. With a murderer waiting to strike and lives hanging in the balance, the real question remains...the bride is wearing white? Seriously?

"Tainted"

What happens at the Dark Forest Hotel, stays at the Dark Forest Hotel...for all eternity.

What secrets surround Dark Forest Hotel? After her parents die under mysterious circumstances, sixteen-year-old Jeri escapes foster care and seeks refuge at a "closed for the season" hotel. Over the next six years, Jeri graduates from teenage runaway to the hotel's assistant general manager. When she learns a convention is secretly held every year in her absence, she demands answers from her boss, friends, and co-workers. After getting conflicting stories, Jeri sets out to discover the truth. She's suddenly thrown into a horrifying new world where vampires and vicious creatures are craving her virgin blood. After six years of being lied to, is there anyone she can trust?

"Witness Protection 7"
Bravo Foxtrot

An Army deserter on the run brings mayhem to a retired Navy SEAL team when his teenage daughter is caught in a mercenary's cross-hairs.

A weekend of fun turns into a race for survival as Monique and Colleen's surrogate big brother, Bogart, rescues the girls from mercenaries hunting Colleen's Army deserter father. With the girls safely stashed at their Colorado hideaway, trouble brews when the team discovers Colleen's father was framed by his former commander over a stolen, high-tech weapon. In order to clear Colleen's father and bring him home, the team must fight one of their toughest adversaries yet...a high-ranking military officer with countless mercenaries and the U.S. military behind him.

"Midnight Requisition 2"
Amateur Night

A brother and sister duo team up to catch a potential kidnapper.

After finally reuniting with her not-so-dead brother, Scorpio and her friends are taunted into helping him with his new case. A wealthy cattle rancher believes someone wants to abduct his daughter, but the team suspects her ex-boyfriend is pulling off an elaborate scheme to win her back. What appears to be a slice of paradise in the Colorado Mountains turns out to be a venomous snake pit filled with lies, lust, betrayal, and murder. Surviving the depraved family becomes the least of the team's worries when a botched kidnapping turns into murder.

"Cemetery Stalkers" Horror Collection

Four tales of horror from flesh-eating alien monsters to blood-sucking vampires.

"Night Creatures" – When a rescue party becomes stranded on an abandoned cruise ship, they discover the terrifying secret unleashed from the cargo hold. What starts out as a rescue mission rapidly deteriorates into survival as a frightening creature with a taste for human flesh hunts the small group. Novella-length horror book.

"Ravenous" – After escaping a carjacking in the back woods, a young woman seeks refuge in a mysterious mansion with a terrifying secret. Despite promises of a ride to town in the morning, she's convinced she's being held prisoner by a cult leader. Short paranormal story.

"The Feast" – Five years ago, a killer went on a murderous rampage at the church picnic. Despite eyewitness accounts of a non-human killer, the local law refused to believe the town's citizens. When a group of teenagers stumble upon the contained remains of the killer, they unwittingly set him free to continue his terror upon the small town. Novella-length paranormal book.

"Cemetery Stalkers" – When 'The Reaper' stalks a cemetery, death follows. Following a series of bizarre incidents within the cemetery, a young woman fears for the safety of her friend, who lives in the middle of spook central. Short horror story.

"Jumpers"

When a cruise ship is exposed to a deadly virus, the fate of the world rests in the hands of a lounge dancer and a conman.

An infectious outbreak threatens the passengers and crew of the "Queen Anita" and the entire world if the virus escapes back into civilization. Lounge dancer, Maxine, must find a way to prevent the destruction of the world, but in order to do that, she needs to trust a conman with unique insight into the virus.

"Witness Protection 8"
Midnight Requisition

A brother and sister duo find themselves on an explosive collision course with a team of retired Navy SEALs.

Obsessed with the belief that his father is still alive, Kane Wayland embarks on a foolhardy mission to confront the elusive former Navy SEAL, Zack Kinsley. Despite heavy protests, Kane's sister, Scorpio, joins him on his quest. The disastrous "reunion" comes with a steep price that none are prepared to pay. With the haunting reality of the botched mission, Midnight Requisition, still looming over each of them, can the two teams pull together in time to prevent another tragedy?

"Midnight Requisition 3"
Circular Run

A brother and sister reopen a hotel with a tainted history, only to discover its past refuses to stay dead and buried.

Scorpio and Kane Wayland finally realize their dream of reopening their grandfather's old, cliffside hotel in Maine. With the hotel's checkered past behind it, the relaunch is a dream come true. Unfortunately, history has a tendency to repeat itself. When guests mysteriously vanish, the hotel's somewhat seedy clientele are all now suspects. In order to save their hotel, Scorpio and Kane must stop a killer. When your guests are mercenaries, bounty hunters, and mobsters, who can you trust?

"Raven Force"

An innkeeper becomes involved in a game of espionage after picking up a mysterious hitchhiker.

After surviving a nightmare of a date, Maxine Croft didn't think her evening could get any worse...until she nearly hits a stranger on a dark back road. This unprecedented meeting would turn Max's world upside down as she's thrust into a world of murder, corruption, and deception within her own backyard. As she gets in deeper with an elite, special task force, Max inadvertently puts her sisters' lives in danger. Will Max and her sisters become just more "collateral damage" to facilitate the team's mission?

"Midnight Requisition 4"
Charlie Foxtrot

A mob convention at a remote cliffside hotel has murderous consequences.

Hotel owner, Scorpio Wayland, reluctantly books a "mob" convention at her quiet, cliffside resort. What could go wrong? When former mob boss Salvatore Romano invites friends for a "family" reunion, disaster swiftly follows.

"Witness Protection 9"

S.N.A.F.U.

A notorious mob boss turns to a retired Navy SEAL team to keep his son alive.

They were made an offer they couldn't refuse. When his son is accused of murdering known mobsters throughout Colorado, Giovanni turns to the retired Navy SEAL team of Whiskey Tango Foxtrot to keep his boy alive and prevent a war between the "families". With the mobster's son in the crosshairs of every hitman and bounty hunter on the West Coast, Jackie and the boys need to find Marco and go completely off-grid. But is the team risking their lives to protect a serial killer?

"Witness Protection 10"

Bravo Zulu

It's all hands on deck when the mob declares war on the team and those they love.

Whiskey Tango Foxtrot reunites with Midnight Requisition when war is declared by a notorious mobster and his army of highly trained soldiers. After several deadly attacks shake both teams, their skills, loyalties, and limitations are tested in an explosive and bloody rampage that will scar and change their lives forever.

"Pretty Little Dead Things"

Romance, scandal, and an unsolved murder. Welcome to snob central!

After a disastrous evening at the exclusive country club gala, Marley Temple doesn't think her life can get any worse. When someone close to her is murdered, Marley is left devastated. Although everyone else seems to move on after the unsolved homicide, Marley can't let it go. She's suddenly thrust into the inner circle of a wealthy playwright recluse, whose stage actress wife was brutally butchered just two years earlier. Although Marley fears falling for the infamous Devlin Ryker, forming a strange alliance with him brings her closer to solving the perplexing murder. But as she gets closer to learning the truth, the killer gets closer to her. Will Marley discover the killer's identity before she becomes his next victim?

"Dead Again"

After barely surviving a murderous attack, a young woman believes a cold-hearted cattle rancher holds clues to that night.

After the murder of her mother in an attack that nearly claimed her life as well, Sage Remington believes moving to the country with her sister will heal her emotional scars. Sage's near-death experience leaves her with memory loss surrounding that fateful night. A bizarre encounter with an infamous cattle rancher, Jackson Morgan, brings back fragments of Sage's lost memory. If she wants to piece together what happened to her mother, Sage needs to get closer to Jackson, who somehow holds the clues. Unfortunately, discovering Jackson's secrets opens the door to a whole other world where nothing is what it seems.

"Dead Woods"

Two magazine reporters get more of a story than they want while investigating strange happenings in a cursed forest.

While interviewing a small-town hero, two adventure-seeking magazine reporters, Kara and Lenox, hike into the infamous Dead Woods in search of a story. Their simple outing takes a chilling turn, and they soon find themselves involved in the town's haunted history filled with curses, witch burnings, and zombified minions. Narrowly escaping with her life, Kara runs into local legend Daemon Archer, a distant relative of a man accused of witchcraft and burned in Town Square in the 1800s. In order to survive a panic-stricken village prophesizing 'evil will take a mate', Kara has to trust the town's most feared citizen.

"Cinderella of Yardley Manor"

Never believing in love at first sight, a young woman finally thinks she's met the man of her dreams, only to discover he's the wrong man.

After graduating college, Ramsey O'Connell reluctantly agrees to travel with her uncle on his business trip to England. However, when she discovers her uncle's true intention--to fix her up with his wealthy colleague, William Yardley —she has some reservations. Falling in love was the last thing she expected, but falling in love with an emotionally unavailable man turns her fairytale into a nightmare.

"Protect and Serve"

Celebrating her birthday with friends on a luxury cruise ship, a young heiress is looking for a little romance on the high seas. Instead, she's confronted by kidnappers and assassins.

Kasey's birthday celebration cruise was supposed to be ten days of sun, sea, and fun with her friends. That is, until her uncle insists she take her bodyguard along. Although her bodyguard, Hunter, is undeniably handsome, he's a little rough around the edges. When her uncle's enemies exact their revenge on Kasey, the cruise turns into a nightmare. If they want to survive, they have to trust Hunter. But sometimes, the enemy is not who you think.

"Crime Scene"

The cast of a popular television crime show finds themselves stranded in a small town after a real-life murder mystery intrudes on their world of make-believe.

After weeks of filming on location, the cast of a highly acclaimed crime show becomes stranded when their luxury bus breaks down in the middle of nowhere. An inconvenient overnight in a small town turns into the beginning of a murder investigation with the cast of "Crime Scene" high on the suspect list. To save the cast's reputation, the show's writer assists the handsome but guarded sheriff and his K-9 deputy in the murder investigation. As alibis unravel, lies pile up, and the suspect list grows, can they catch the killer before he strikes again?

"Midnight Requisition 5"
Sierra Hotel

A Christmas wedding, mistletoe, and murder.

Only a few days before Christmas, a very pregnant Scorpio and her friends are planning Mac and Maverick's wedding. Little did they know that Santa would be delivering a few early presents. What was supposed to be a merry Christmas turns into an epic whodunit when a helicopter crashes on the hotel grounds, leaving eight stranded passengers and a dead man. Their once silent night is filled with accusations, alibis, and mayhem. With the assistance of former Special Agent Holden Falcone, can they solve the murders before the next body drops?

"The Rancher's Daughter"

When her town, ranch, and life are threatened, a young woman teams up with the enemy's top enforcer to reclaim what is hers.

Skyler Winchester's small hometown has become more corrupt in the five years since her parents' car accident. Little by little, wealthy business tycoon Marcus has been buying buildings, property, and people. As one of the largest ranch owners and the object of Marcus's lust, Sky has always been immune to the corruption and dirty dealings, but her friends aren't so lucky. After forming an unholy alliance with one of Marcus's top enforcers, it appears that Sky's immunity has been revoked. When her life is threatened, will the man she trusts most be the one sent to eliminate her?

"Beyond the Fence Line"

In the dust of a modern cattle ranch, a girl with wrangler dreams and her childhood protector build a bond that falters under unvoiced desires.

On a sprawling modern cattle ranch, two kids bound by loss forge an unbreakable bond. After losing his mother when he was only ten years old, Brandt wants nothing to do with the fatherless five-year-old ragamuffin, Mazie, whose mother runs the ranch house. But as years of dust and dreams shape them, he becomes her protector, and she his constant shadow, chasing her goal to wrangle cattle alongside him. Their friendship is unshakable until one reckless night sparks a truth Brandt has always known: he loves her. Mazie can't see past their childhood bond, and the rift tears them apart. Several years later, with the ranch as the only home they've known, they must confront their past, their pain, and the love that's waited years to claim its truth. A story of resilience, loyalty, and a romance forged in the grit of the open range, spanning years of heartache and hope.

"Nature of the Beast"

She claimed her father's cursed mansion...where the ghosts within the walls have long been waiting for her.

When Brandy Holloway inherits a sprawling country mansion from the father she never knew, she expects secrets, not literal skeletons in the closets. The gothic estate has all the comforts of the "Psycho" house and all the charm of "The Addams Family" home. The young maid swears it's haunted, and the handsome, mysterious butler hides secrets of his own. After Brandy invites her friends for a weekend escape, the fun turns deadly when, one by one, they vanish into the house's endless depths. Trapped in a ghostly home that hungers for souls, Brandy must team up with her eccentric butler to uncover the mansion's bloodstained secrets before she becomes its prisoner...forever.

"Hell's Paradise"

A tropical paradise where the most dangerous thing is the company.

When a luxury yacht wrecks on a beautiful but deadly tropical island, what begins as inconvenience for the wealthy and privileged quickly spirals into violence, betrayal, and depravity. As the masks slip, heiress Harley McBride learns the jungle isn't the greatest threat; the people she's trapped with are. Harley's only protection is her devoted butler and Damon, the silent but lethal bodyguard she once feared and despised. But the more the group unravels, the more she realizes the man she was warned to avoid might be the only one worth trusting. On an island where civilization dies fast and primal instincts take over, desire might be the most lethal force of all. Harley must decide how far she'll go to survive...and whether falling for the dangerous man beside her is the biggest risk of all.

"Past Lies"

Some inheritances are handed down in love. Some are guarded in silence. Some are protected at any cost.

When Sidney Bristol inherits her great-grandfather's lake house and workshop, she also inherits a single photograph that stirs questions about her family's past long held in silence. Her grandmother's careful reserve. Her mother's childhood never fully shared. Then there's Jackson Ford. The reclusive man her best friend, Amber, calls "uncle", the one who has always watched from the shadows, who has kept Amber close, who seems to carry more than he will ever say. Sidney has known him for years. Enough to fear him, enough to trust him, enough to wonder why her heart races every time he looks her way. But the deeper she looks into the past her family and friends have kept hidden, the more she realizes some things were never meant to be uncovered. Some family stories end with love. Some end with a locked door...and someone waiting on the other side.

ABOUT THE AUTHOR

Holly Copella has been writing since the age of twelve when her frustration at a book's poor plot drove her to author her own story. Over the last decade, she's written a number of screenplays, some of which she's now adapting into novels. Her fascination with zombies and other darker material lends an edge to her writing, which tends to lean toward horror. As a fan of Agatha Christie, she appreciates the craft of a good plot and the importance of creating significant characters.

Hailing from Pennsylvania, Copella lives in the Endless Mountains on a farm with her new horse, Maverick, and other animals. In addition to writing and reading fiction, she enjoys riding horses and traveling to Las Vegas.

www.ingramcontent.com/pod-product-compliance
Lightning Source LLC
LaVergne TN
LVHW010052110826
845155LV00028B/298

* 9 7 8 1 9 4 7 6 9 4 3 8 5 *